Oolong, Farewell

BOOK THREE IN THE TEA AND TAROT COZY MYSTERY SERIES

KIRSTEN WEISS

Cover artist: Dar Albert

Visit the author website: www.kirstenweiss.com

Misterio Press mass market paperback edition / September, 2020
http://Misteriopress.com

ISBN-13: 978-1-944767-61-7

CHAPTER 1

When you run a tearoom, even a tea and Tarot room, an elegant and genteel atmosphere shouldn't be too much to ask.

I hovered beside Mrs. Bicklesworth's table, a white tea towel folded over my arm, a tiered tray of scones and finger sandwiches dangling from my hand. Mrs. B. was good people—gracious, elegant, and connected. I was determined to treat her right.

"I've always felt tea is more than a beverage." The elderly woman's eyes twinkled as she raised the teacup to her lips. "It's a meditation."

Brrrrrrrt! A mechanical, grinding noise roared through the tearoom.

Mrs. Bicklesworth spat tea. Cards shot from a Tarot reader's hands and fluttered to the faux-wood floor. Watercolors of herbs rattled on the white walls, their wooden frames tilting slowly leftish.

Brrrrrrrt!

A waitress squeaked, splashing the tea she was pouring across a white tablecloth.

Brrrrrrrt!

I set the tray on the table and stretched my lips into a smile. "Apologies for the disturbance. I'll be right back."

So much for elegant and genteel. Whipping my tea towel over one shoulder, I stormed down the hallway. Twinkle lights blinked around my target—my partner's doorway.

I shoved open the door and strode into Hyperion's office, a gypsy caravan of incense, red carpeting, and New Age knickknacks. "What's going on?"

My neighbor, Brik, stood on a ladder. His upper body was obscured by the swags of white gauze that hid the ceiling pipes. His denim-clad lower body was... impressively muscular.

Not that I was looking or anything.

Hyperion craned his neck up at the contractor. "But can you do it?" Even ordering contractors around, my partner managed to look like a male model. His near-black hair fell just so across his forehead. His button-up linen shirt lay open at the collar.

My muscles tensed. "Do what?" I adjusted the snood that kept my long, blond hair from falling into someone's scone. "And unless something's leaking or on fire, don't do anymore of it now. You're rocking the tearoom, and not in a good way."

The contractor ducked his blond head beneath the fabric. "Yep, I can do it."

"Do what?" I managed not to stomp my feet, but just barely.

"Why are you wearing a towel?" Hyperion asked me.

"What? This?" I yanked it from my shoulder and held it out to him. "I wanted your opinion. Does this smell like chloroform to you?"

"Ha, ha," my partner said. "I'm not falling for that again."

"Again?"

Hyperion rolled his eyes. "You wouldn't *believe* my Thursday night."

I could believe it had been more exciting than mine. Hyperion had an active romantic life. I'd spent my free time online, killing zombie Nazis. "What are you doing?"

"Installing a fake ceiling to hide these pipes once and for all," Hyperion said.

"What's wrong with the fabric?" I asked and motioned toward the gauze draping the ceiling.

"I'm bored with it. Also, it's against the fire code."

I swallowed, acid scorching my stomach. *Fire code?* "Did an inspector come by and no one told me?" *Yikes.* Were we in violation? What else had happened I didn't know about?

"I'm being proactive," Hyperion said.

I relaxed slightly. "Can we afford a new ceiling?" Beanblossom's was less than a year old—still officially in the start-up stage. This also happened to be the barely-breaking-even stage. Most restaurants didn't survive their first year, and when I wasn't fighting zombie Nazi's, I was sweating over our finances.

"Don't worry," he said, "this won't affect the tearoom finances. My online Tarot courses have been doing well. I'd like to invest in my office, especially since I meet private clients here."

We mostly kept our tea and tarot finances separate. I was the tearoom, he was the Tarot side. It kept things simpler. And if he wanted to upgrade his office, it was his business. But he could have scheduled this for Monday, when we were closed.

Something shifted in the corner, and I took a quick step backward.

Demonic, amber eyes glowed from the low shadows of a 60s-era media cabinet. Hyperion's enormous tabby, Bastet, emerged from beneath it. The cat sneered at me and hopped onto the driftwood and crystal filled altar.

"Why didn't you tell me about this before?" I already knew the answer—because I would have griped about the noise.

His brown eyes widened with innocence. "I didn't think it would be an issue. My private reading room is a critical part of Beanblossom's Tea and Tarot." Hyperion wafted his hands as if fluffing the air around me.

I reared backward, nonplussed.

"There's something off with your aura," he said.

"You read auras now too?" I asked.

He cocked his head and squinted at me. "Forsooth, I see mother issues. Er, have you seen her yet?"

The tabby swished his striped tail.

I grimaced. "No." My mother—both my parents—had spent most of my life *out* of my life on various New Age, spiritual quests. I'd been such a drag on their groove, they'd left my grandparents to raise me.

I swallowed the ache in my throat. In hindsight, it had been a blessing. But as a kid, all I'd understood was how badly the rejection had hurt.

And now, after more than a decade away, my mother had returned to San Borromeo. She was currently camped out in my old bedroom at my grandfather's house.

"The sooner you get it over with," my partner said, "the happier you'll be. And you'll get all this nasty brown and red out of your aura."

"My aura's fine," I snapped. "And can the new ceiling wait until Monday, when we're closed?"

"Well, of course," Hyperion said loftily. "I wouldn't want to disturb the tearoom."

My eyes narrowed. That had been way too easy.

"Like I told him," Brik said, "I'm not available until August anyway. But I can schedule the work for a Monday." He climbed down the ladder and carefully did not look at me. "Hi, Abigail."

"Hi." It's almost impossible to scowl at someone who looks like a well-groomed Viking—the kind you see on TV, not in those creepy museum exhibits. His mane of blond hair was tied back in a neat ponytail. And his white t-shirt was pristine.

Almost impossible.

A month ago, Brik and I had shared a knee-shaking kiss. He'd been pretending it hadn't happened ever since.

I stared at my hands. It didn't make any difference to *me*. I mean, it wasn't like I'd kissed *him*. I'd been the kissee, not the kisser. But it was the principle of the thing.

"The new ceiling will be elegant and professional," Hyperion said.

"And more importantly," Brik said, "not a fire hazard."

"Um, what *is* this about fire hazards?" I asked nervously.

"The fire department's started cracking down on violations." My neighbor studied the filmy gauze above him and shook his head. "All that fabric... I don't think it'll fly."

"The only way that fabric would catch fire is if there was already a fire in the building. I use flameless candles." Hyperion motioned to Bastet. "These regulations are an inhuman, fiendish malignancy."

Brik shot me a look, his sea-blue eyes questioning.

"Lovecraft word of the day calendar," I said. December 31st couldn't come soon enough.

"Right." Brik nodded. "You mentioned something about that before."

My gaze flicked to the chandelier. At least Brik had remembered *that* even if our kiss had slipped his mind.

"What's wrong with my calendar?" Hyperion asked. "When you stop learning new things, brain rot sets in."

Bastet scratched behind his ear and yawned.

"Okay," my neighbor said. "I'll get you an estimate tomorrow."

"That's it?" I asked, indignant. That was all he had to say to me? True, I wasn't sure what I wanted that kiss to mean either, if anything. In fact, I'd thought I was okay with letting the whole thing lie. But his Viking nonchalance was getting a little demoralizing.

Brik's brow furrowed. "I'll be sure to include the cost of rewiring the chandelier too?"

Chandelier? Was he kidding me?

"Hyperion!" A man's voice echoed down the concrete hallway outside. "You've got to help me. Hyperion!"

The office door burst open, and Bastet bolted beneath the round table.

Archer Simmons sagged against the blinking doorframe, his ascot askew. The little man raked a hand through his thinning, silvery hair. "Thank God, you're here. It's been a nightmare. An absolute nightmare."

"Don't tell me they've shortened your newspaper column again?" Hyperion's black brows drew downward in concern.

"Worse." Archer straightened off the door and smoothed the front of his elegant gray suit, then nodded. "Much worse."

"What's happened?" I asked.

Archer groaned theatrically. "My neighbor's dead. He's been murdered, the creep."

CHAPTER 2

"Murdered?" I asked.

"And now they're going to arrest me." Archer clutched his thinning hair. "Me! And I have the most-read society column in Northern California."

"Newspapers still have society columns?" Brik asked.

"He's in shock." Hyperion led the older man to one of his throne-like, red velvet chairs.

"There are still newspapers?" Brik asked.

Archer glared.

Bastet edged from beneath the table and prowled toward the newcomer.

"What exactly happened?" I asked. "Who's dead?"

"Tom Henderson," Archer said.

Brik, Hyperion, and I shared a glance. Hyperion shook his head. I shrugged. I hadn't heard of Henderson either.

Archer lurched forward in the chair. "Tom Henderson. Tom Henderson! He has the biggest party rental house in San Borromeo, for the simple reason he's not supposed to have a party house in San Borromeo. It's completely illegal. But he's making so much money at it, he can just laugh off the paltry fines the city imposes."

"And he's dead?" Brik's brows pulled together.

"Well, of course he's dead. Why wouldn't he be dead?"

Bastet leapt into Archer's lap. Absently, the elderly man petted him.

"Why would the police arrest you?" I asked.

"It's irrational and frankly lazy," Archer said. "Just because I'm his neighbor... I mean, what was I supposed to do? Of course I called the police to complain about the scoundrel. There were helicopters! At night! And all that music. His constant parties were a nightmare."

I carefully avoided looking at Brik. My neighbor's house was party central. We'd met when I'd first complained about the near-nightly racket. "So you made noise complaints," I said.

"Me and a half dozen other neighbors." Archer adjusted his cravat. "And I might have threatened to kill him in print. But it was satire."

"I think Archer needs a cup of tea," Hyperion said, patting the older man's shoulder.

"Oh, I do." He leaned forward in the chair. "And maybe a Tarot reading."

"How do you feel about herbal tea?" I asked.

"I'll drink anything if it will take the edge off."

Empress Tea it was then—a relaxing blend of chamomile, lemon thyme, and lavender. I hurried to the front room and at the counter, I added the herbal blend to a glass teapot.

As I filled the pot with boiling water, I studied the tearoom. The noise level had returned to a mannerly murmur. The wait staff seemed to have everything well in hand. I was supposed to help serve, not gossip with Archer. But he was an occasional customer and a good friend of my grandfather's.

I set the teapot, cup and saucer, and sugar bowls on a tray, and returned to Hyperion's office.

Brik packed his drill into a large, paint-spattered toolbox.

"It's so thoughtless," Archer said. "It's cruel, having loud parties, with all sorts of cars lining the street, and the strobe lights. And did I mention the helicopters? Those celebrities who have the nerve to lecture us about global warming all fly in on helicopters. But I suppose in fairness, what else is a multi-millionaire to do? There's no parking on those narrow streets, thanks to the parties."

Hyperion made a sympathetic noise.

"But I didn't kill him," Archer said. "I only wanted him dead. Is that so wrong?"

Brik shook his head. "Nope. I can't blame you. That sort of thing will drive down home values."

I goggled at my neighbor. Brik had loud parties practically every night. True, he was good about shutting things down at a reasonable hour. But he got away with the parties because two of his immediate neighbors were elderly and hard of hearing. His other immediate neighbor was me, and I was a pushover.

I just don't like narcing on people to cops. Not unless they're doing something really wrong, like robbing a store or putting someone in danger. Also, complaining to the cops would seem pretty petty after that kiss.

My neck stiffened. Dammit, was that why he'd kissed me? To shut me up? He knew I hated those parties.

"What?" Brik asked me. "Why are you looking at me like that?"

"Like what?" I asked.

"Like he's transformed into a tubular, withered foulness," Hyperion said.

Archer eyed my partner and leaned slightly away.

I took a deep breath and held it in, released it. "You have parties every week." I set the tray on the round table in front of Archer and turned to Brik. "Several times a week in fact. Every week."

"But I don't charge for them."

"Are there helicopters?" Archer folded his arms across his navy blazer. "Because I don't think we can be friends if there are helicopters."

"No choppers," Brik assured him.

"There's no parking left on the street because of all the guests at your parties," I said slowly.

"Fortunately," Archer said, "I have a driveway where I can park. When it's not being blocked by partygoers." He thumped his fist on the table, rattling the teacup in its saucer. "And it's the principle of the thing."

Brik's brow creased. "You never complained about my parties before," he said to me.

"I complained about a million times," I said.

He blinked. "You did?"

"No one listens to me," I grumbled.

"I listen to you," Hyperion said.

"No one's listening to me," Archer said. "Wrongfully accused murder suspect. Right here."

Hastily, I poured Archer's tea. The scent of lavender and lemon thyme wafted through Hyperion's small office. "Okay," I said, "tell us what happened."

"How should I know?" Archer asked. "I didn't kill the man. It has to be one of the other neighbors. But I like them all. I don't want them to be killers, even if the man deserved to die horribly. Maybe his wife, Vanella, did it. They say the spouse is always the most likely suspect, and what sort of a name is Vanella?" He sipped his tea. "Delicious, Abigail. Well, are you going to come with me or not?"

"Come with you where?" Hyperion asked.

"To the scene of the crime, of course. How can you investigate if you don't examine the scene of the crime?"

"Investigate?" I felt my concerned smile waver. "I can't leave

Beanblossom's. It's Friday afternoon. We've got a full tearoom."

"Let one of your waitresses manage things," Archer said. "This is murder. Havoc. War. And money is no object."

Hyperion straightened.

"I don't think you're giving the police enough credit," I said. "Realistically, what can we do—?"

The phone rang in my apron pocket, and I pulled it out. Gramps. Thank God. A reason to escape this loony conversation. "Excuse me, I have to take this."

I edged into the hallway and gently shut the door behind me. The twinkle lights blinked balefully. "Hi, Gramps. How are you doing?" My chin dipped, my chest squeezing, because I knew my mother was driving him crazy. I just didn't know what I could do about it.

"You've got to get out of the tearoom," he said. "Now."

I stiffened. "What? Why?"

"She's on her way. I'm sorry, Abigail. I couldn't stop her."

My blood ran cold. I didn't need to be told who she was. My mother.

"I don't know what's gotten into her," he continued. "I think... I think you may be her new spiritual quest."

"What?" I yelped.

"I know it sounds nutty," he said, "but she had an odd look in her eye over breakfast when she was talking about you."

My heart gave an odd lurch. "Oh?"

"And she threw out all the milk and replaced it with that soy stuff. And she replaced my favorite peanut butter cereal with nuts and twigs. It's supposed to be healthy, but it tastes like sawdust."

"When'd she leave?"

"She took my Lincoln without asking. I just saw it exit my drive."

"But why do you think she's coming here?"

"She may have said something about getting a Tarot reading."

My hand tightened on the phone. Of course. My mother wasn't coming to see me. She was coming for the Tarot.

The beginnings of a headache pricked at the front of my skull. "Thanks for the heads-up." If she had the Lincoln, I had time. Good luck finding parking for that boat in tiny San Borromeo.

I leaned against the cool, concrete wall. "Aside from the milk and cereal, how are things going? With her in the house, I mean."

"The incense burns Peking's eyes. She knows we hate incense."

Peking was his pet duck. I wasn't sure if ducks could smell, but I knew Gramps hated incense.

I shut my eyes. "Look. If you need a break. She can stay at my place." Because the only thing worse than the thought of spending time with my mother was the thought of my mother breaking my grandfather.

"No," he said manfully. "It's okay. The weather's been good, so I keep the windows open. Peking spends more time in the backyard, looking for bugs. I have to keep an eye on him, in case the neighbor's cat decides to get fresh, but like I said, the weather's good. Tomas is having a barbecue tonight. I'll go there."

"You don't think she'll invite herself along?" I asked, aghast at the idea of her crashing one of his friend's family dinners.

"It's a barbecue, Abigail. Meat. Your mother won't go anywhere near it. Not after her time with that militant vegetarian group."

Right. Rumor had it she was still persona non grata in Mongolia.

"Can you get out of there?" Gramps asked. "Go home sick or something. She doesn't know where you live."

I glanced at the twinkle lights. "I've got an idea that will keep me out of the tearoom." I hesitated. Should I tell him about Archer? I shook my head. They were friends, but Archer would kill me if I ruined a good story by blabbing it first.

"Good." He paused. "I'm sorry about this."

"Why? Corralling her isn't your job."

"She's…"

"What?"

"Nothing," he said. "I'll see you soon."

We said our goodbyes, and I returned to the office.

"Abigail and I are a team," Hyperion was saying. "If she can't go—"

"I'm in," I said. "Let's go." Because when life hands you lemons, it's time to start lobbing them at some murder suspects.

Bastet perched in my lap, we followed Archer's Jaguar up the winding hillside road. The cat kneaded his paws, his claws sheathing and unsheathing. They dug into my linen skirt.

I scowled at the tabby.

"Spill." Hyperion whipped his Jeep around a tight bend, and I leaned into the door. "What really changed your mind about helping Archer?" he asked. "Was it the money is no object line?"

"No, I wouldn't even know how much to charge."

"Then what?"

"My mother's on her way to the tearoom."

"Seriously? That takes some brass. No offense," he added quickly.

"It's bad form to criticize other people's relatives. But... what are you going to do? I know I said you should rip the proverbial bandage off, but I also know it's not that easy."

"No, it isn't." I slumped in the seat. I'd have to face her someday. Just… not today.

"Do you think it's possible she wants to make amends?"

"For abandoning me at the airport when I was a toddler?" I rapped out. How do you make up for that? "No, I don't. I don't care how much self-actualization she's gone through. There's no coming back from that." My panicked grandparents had raced to collect me while my parents flew to India. I hoped my parents had at least hit turbulence.

Hyperion was quiet for a long moment. "But what if there was a way? What if she could come back from it?"

"There isn't, and she can't." But my heart pinched. A tiny part of me wanted to believe it was possible. I mentally gave that part of me a swift kick in the butt.

This happened every time my parents came back. I'd get my hopes up that they'd changed, that things would be different, that they wanted me. And every damn time I'd been disappointed.

I wasn't going through all that again.

"Do you think Archer is in any real trouble?" Hyperion asked. "He's a teensy bit of a drama queen."

That was the pot calling the kettle black, but I bit down hard on a half-dozen comebacks. Hyperion had earned a free pass for changing the subject away from my family.

"I'd like to see that satire piece he wrote about this Henderson guy," I said. "I have a hard time believing it's too awful. Archer does have an editor, and the newspaper has got to be careful about libel."

"But he said they're neighbors. If they were both at home, then Archer had opportunity. He wouldn't have done it, but it might not look good."

"If they were both at home. We need to find out when Henderson was killed and where Archer was at the time."

"All right, but you do realize Archer couldn't kill anyone?"

"Of course he couldn't." I refused to believe any of my grandfather's friends were murderers. "But like you said, it still might not look good to the cops."

"Hm." Hyperion pursed his lips. "Tony's got to be involved, don't you think?"

"Yeah." San Borromeo was too small to have more than one police detective. And Hyperion had a massive crush on Detective Tony Chase. "Is that going to be a problem?"

We slowed, lurching over a speed bump.

"No," he said. "I can't pretend to be someone else for a guy. I'm a brilliant amateur detective, and Tony's going to just have to take me for who I am."

"Are you two dating?"

He winked. "Not yet."

I sighed and settled back in my seat. It was a little depressing that Hyperion had a more active love life than I did. Of course, that wasn't exactly difficult. My love life was DOA.

We followed the Jaguar into a circular driveway. The Jeep slowed to a stop in front of Archer's sleek, mid-century modern house, white and L-shaped.

Handing Hyperion his cat, I stepped from the Jeep. I let my gaze rove from the ornamental grasses dotting the yard, the swimming pool cutting through the lush lawn, the orange umbrellas and lounge chairs. Archer lived well.

Hyperion snapped on Bastet's leash.

"This way," Archer whispered.

"Why are you whispering?" Hyperion asked.

Archer's white brows drew together. "Shh!"

Cat in the lead, we trotted across the sloping lawn. A trail appeared at the edge of the grass. It wended beneath eucalyptus trees and more clumps of tall, ornamental grasses.

Archer made a shushing motion and tiptoed to a wooden gate in a high, redwood fence. The gate was arched, with a circle cut in the top.

The older man pointed to the circle. "I had this installed years ago when a producer bought the place next door. He had all sorts of movie stars visiting—Cary Grant, Paul Newman, Sidney Poitier. Take a look."

Hyperion stepped up to the gate and peered through the hole, about the size of my fist. "Whoa. That's a lot of cops." He stepped away from the gate. "You didn't tell us the police were still here."

"Didn't I? Well, I don't like to let the grass grow under my feet. The sooner you get started clearing my name the better."

"Let me see," I said. Fortunately, Archer was roughly my height, so the peep hole was Abigail-level. I edged up to the gate and looked through.

A pair of steel-gray eyes stared back.

CHAPTER 3

"Gagh." I leapt away from the gate.

Bastet hissed.

The wooden gate creaked open, and Detective Tony Chase stepped through. "It figures I'd find you here," he drawled.

The tall, handsome detective pushed up the brim of his cowboy hat with a gloved hand. And not a cool leather glove, a latex glove. Chase was a committed germophobe.

He nodded at Archer. "Mr. Simmons. I thought I told you I'd take your statement later?"

"You did. Is later now?" Archer got busy examining his nails. "It's such a vague term."

The detective turned to Hyperion and me. "What are you two doing here?"

Hyperion and I stammered out something incoherent about old friends and modern landscaping.

"Mr. Simmons?" the detective asked.

The elderly man motioned toward us with a sweeping gesture. "Hyperion and Abigail are my private investigators," he said loftily.

"Really?" Detective Chase edged back his navy suit jacket, exposing the badge on his belt. It was almost as big as his buckle. "Neither of you mentioned getting your private investigator's license."

Gulp.

"You do know that practicing without a license is punishable by law?" he continued.

Crud. Near my sandals, which was approximately where my stomach had fallen, Bastet meowed in agreement.

Archer blinked rapidly. "Did I say investigators?" He motioned grandly toward us a second time. "Hyperion and Abigail are my private consultants."

"Mm." Detective Chase raised a skeptical brow. "And what exactly are you consulting on?"

"This and that," Hyperion said, dismissive.

"Nothing much," I said.

"They are private consultants," Archer said.

"And you're paying them, because if you're paying them to consult on a murder—"

Archer shot me a worried look.

"No money's changed hands," I said quickly. "And it won't."

The detective lowered his head and gave me the sort of scrutiny one would generally reserve for a particularly interesting bug. "Mr. Simmons, I'll speak with you later." Detective Chase stepped backward through the gate and shut it.

"Perhaps we should take our conversation elsewhere," Archer suggested.

"Let's," Hyperion said.

We scurried across the lawn toward Archer's house.

"I don't think Chase bought it," I muttered to Hyperion.

"No kidding," Hyperion said. "But all we were doing was standing by a gate, gawking at a horrific crime scene like any other red-blooded American. What could he do?"

"We don't know it was horrific," I said.

"Of course it was horrific," Hyperion said. "Did you see the expressions on the crime scene techs' faces. They looked positively ghoulish with glee."

Ugh. "More Lovecraft?" I asked.

"Alliteration, partner. Alliteration."

"One of my favorite writing techniques," Archer said. "Not that those Visigoths at my paper would recognize good prose if it bit them in the posterior. What's this about Lovecraft?"

Hyperion explained about his calendar, and we strolled into Archer's massive home.

Archer led us into a marble-floored living area with wood-paneled walls. Our host dropped onto a sleek, gray couch.

We sat more gingerly on matching chairs opposite.

Bastet made himself comfortable on a gray velvet ottoman.

"All right," Archer said. "Let's talk compensation. I've been wracking my brain on the walk over. If I can't pay you money… I can get you Mrs. Worthington-Smythe."

Hyperion's mouth parted. "You… What?"

"Who?" I said.

"She's practically royalty," Hyperion said. "She makes the people in this neighborhood look like peasants. No offense, Archer."

"None taken. But if she gives your tearoom her blessing—"

"We'd never go hungry again," Hyperion breathed.

"We're not hungry now," I said. Though word-of-mouth could be powerful.

"I hear she's into psychics," Hyperion said.

"It's true," Archer said. "She makes Sarah Winchester look like a piker."

"This could be big," my partner said to me.

"And I'll get my paper's restaurant reviewer to stop by," Archer said. "But only because when I'm under stress, I can be difficult. Consider it a bonus."

"Deal." I stuck out my hand. The local reporters had turned up their noses at Beanblossom's after we'd declined to comment in a past murder investigation.

"I'll round up the troops." Archer pulled a phone from the inside pocket of his gray suit jacket and made a call.

"Darling, have you heard...? I know, it's ghastly. I've brought in two private— consultants to help us out. They're here now... Yes... Yes... Excellent."

He pocketed his phone. "Pepper's bringing Cosmo."

"Who are Pepper and Cosmo?" I asked.

"My nearest two neighbors, and the other two members of the noise committee. Cosmo lives on the other side of the Henderson's hell house, and Pepper lives behind it."

"The homeowners association got involved?" I asked.

He looked out the floor-to-ceiling windows, at the swimming pool and lawn beyond. "Yes, but our committee isn't exactly a part of the HOA."

"Why not?" I asked. Noise complaints seemed like exactly the sort of thing a homeowner's association was made for.

"Legal reasons," Archer said.

Hyperion's brown eyes narrowed. "What sorts of legal reasons?"

"The president felt that some of our tactics might leave the HOA open to liability."

"What tactics?" I tilted my head and studied Archer. His cherubic face didn't look guilty, but he sure sounded guilty.

He examined his manicure. "Nothing illegal, I assure you."

"What tactics?" I repeated.

"Did you know the Maasai dislike having their picture taken without permission so much, they'll hurl spears right through the windows of offending safari trucks?" Archer asked.

"I get the feeling you're stalling on the tactics question," I said.

"Fine," Archer said. "If you must know, it was really no big deal. The usual things. When the wind was in the right direction, I'd have a little bonfire by the fence so the smoke blew into their party."

"Is that all?" Hyperion asked shrewdly.

"I might have made sure to add plastics to the fire to get a real chemical smell."

"And?" Hyperion asked.

"And someone may have put that extra strong glue in the locks so the renters couldn't get their keys to work. That sort of thing."

"Someone?" I asked sharply.

"Cosmo and Pepper denied it, but it wasn't me."

"Remind me never to get on your bad side," Hyperion said.

Tell me about it.

Bastet's claws unsheathed on the velvet ottoman. Hastily, I scooped up the cat and set him in my lap before he could damage Archer's furniture. He dug his claws into my thigh, and I winced.

"Normally," Archer said, "I'm a very considerate neighbor. But you have no idea what I've been dealing with. This has been going on for nearly six months." He pointed toward the window. "Once, the police came to their gates with a cease and desist notice and a fine attached. Henderson just stood on the other side of the gate and laughed at them. He told them his watch cost more than their fine, and he refused to open the gate. The city tried cutting off his water supply, since he hasn't paid the bills in months. He hired a crooked plumber to tap into my water main. Mine. You would not believe the bill. I'm still battling the water company. And did I mention the helicopters?"

"You might have," Hyperion said. "Once or twice."

"After all that, can you begrudge a person a bit of glue in the locks? It only took the bastard an hour to get a locksmith to his party mansion anyway. I'm sure the cost was trivial compared to all the money they made that night. And then they hosted that play that shall not be named."

"Macbeth?" I asked.

"No, the one about the singing Austrians escaping Nazis."

"I like that musical," Hyperion said.

"So do I," Archer said, "except they'd modernized it."

"How do you modernize a play about the second World War?" I

asked.

Archer's mouth pinched. "Rap music—which I have the greatest respect for. Sex—ditto. And a murderous conclusion involving high-kicking ninja nuns and window-rattling explosions. Why do you think I won't name it? They changed the name. It was a travesty. Henderson should have been killed just for allowing it on his property."

"You probably shouldn't say that to the police," I said.

"I have to ask," Hyperion said. "What did they call the musical?"

"So Long, Farewell."

And, moving on. "What was this satire piece you wrote?" I asked.

"Oh, it's nothing, I'm sure." He tapped his phone's screen and handed it to me.

I enlarged the article and read, my alarm growing. "Archer, this is—"

"What? What is it?" Hyperion snatched the phone from me and read. "Good grief. It's practically a help wanted ad for a hitman. I can't believe your paper published it."

"My paper is run by children. All they care about is scaring readers for clicks. Modern media's a virtual haunted house."

Hyperion angled his head, his brows drawing downward. "So…"

"Of course they let me run the article," Archer continued. "And it was accurate, and I was very careful not to name names." His shoulders sagged. "But I shouldn't have written it. I was just so frustrated."

"Constant noise can make anyone crazy," I said, sympathetic.

"I meant frustrated with my profession. I've sold my soul—" A doorbell rang, and Archer bounced from the sofa. "That will be Pepper and Cosmo." He hurried from the room.

"He seems really down about his paper," Hyperion said.

"He's got bigger problems than the state of modern media," I said, worried. "Archer might be a real suspect. This article could easily be construed as a threat."

"Tell me about it."

"He needs professional help."

Hyperion's expression turned knowing. "He isn't the only one who could benefit from a psychiatrist. Have you considered the impact of your mother's—?"

"I meant legal help. We're amateurs. And I don't need a psychiatrist. I need my mother to go back to whatever spiritual retreat she came from."

"Parental challenges aside, you were the one who agreed to

investigate."

"I know, but—"

Archer returned with a tall, voluptuous, middle-aged blonde and a tanned man who looked like he'd stepped from the pages of an over-50 bodybuilder magazine.

We rose and shook hands with the newcomers.

"Pepper, Cosmo," Archer said, "I'd like to introduce you to Abigail and Hyperion. They've solved more homicides than the San Borromeo PD."

"I wouldn't go that far," Hyperion said modestly.

"You certainly have lately," Archer said. "These two are brilliant. But of course, Hyperion has something of a leg up with his psychic powers."

"I'm a Tarot reader," Hyperion said, "not a psychic. There's a difference."

"Yes, yes," Archer said, "a distinction without a difference."

Hyperion shook his head. "Actually—"

"And Abigail. What can I say about Abigail?" He tapped his finger on his chin. "Well, I guess there's nothing much to say, is there?"

I folded my arms. "Hey, there's a lot you can say about me."

They turned to look at me.

"I run Beanblossom's Tea and Tarot."

Hyperion coughed gently.

"Well," I amended, "I run the tearoom part. Plus, I've killed ten thousand, three hundred and eighty-two zombie Nazis."

Pepper blinked.

"I killed them online," I said.

Archer's brows rose. "How... fascinating."

"I'm in the top twenty," I said defensively. "The game is very competitive. Oh, and my grandfather has a duck." Which made Gramps interesting, not me.

I had to have some cool hobbies aside from sitting in my garden and eating burritos. Oh, my garden! "And I like to garden."

They stared.

"Herbs mainly. I grow them in containers..." I deflated. Maybe there wasn't much to say about me.

I needed better hobbies.

Archer cleared his throat. "All right then. What were we talking about?" He dropped onto the sleek sofa.

"Next steps," Hyperion said.

The others sat around the low, 50s-era coffee table. Face hot, I shuffled to a chair and joined them.

"What can you tell us about the victim?" I asked the newcomers in my most professional tone.

Cosmo snorted. "You won't lack for suspects."

"The poor high school," Pepper said.

"High school?" I asked.

"The ticket sales for their play were abysmal because of you know what," Pepper said.

"So Long, Farewell?" Hyperion asked.

She nodded. "Their shows were on the same night. It was too late for the high school to switch gears. Not that it would have mattered. After So Long, everyone had lost their taste for singing nuns."

I cleared my throat. "Look, we want to help—"

"Good," Archer said.

"But this seems serious," I said. "All of you could be suspects. Hyperion and I are amateurs. Have you considered hiring a professional?"

"Professionals are hardened and cynical," Archer said. "I need someone who'll believe us no matter how many fake snakes are in the garden."

"I'm not sure—" I began, bemused.

"What else can you tell us?" Hyperion asked.

Pepper smoothed her slim, pink skirt. "Tom Henderson and his wife come and go. But they're here at least one week or so out of the month."

"Do you know when they returned this month?" I asked.

"Too soon," Cosmo growled.

"I think I saw his Mercedes in the neighborhood about a week ago?" Pepper looked to Cosmo, and he nodded.

"What about his wife?" Hyperion asked.

"Vanella? We don't see much of her anymore," Pepper said. "She knows the entire neighborhood is furious with her. Besides, this isn't exactly a community where people pop over to their neighbors to borrow a cup of sugar."

No, it wasn't. It was one of those places without sidewalks, to discourage the perambulating proletariat, like myself. Ha, take that Hyperion. I could alliterate too.

"But she doesn't seem the type to kill anyone," Cosmo said.

"Where were you last night when Tom Henderson was killed?" I asked. "I mean, you may have seen someone if you were nearby."

"I was at home," Cosmo said. "Pepper was helping me film a video for my VR firm."

"Oh, you're a videographer?" I asked her.

"Everyone's a videographer today," Pepper said. "I suggested it would look more professional if I managed the camera. That way Cosmo wouldn't have to stare at a tripod."

"How long were you together?" I asked.

They looked at each other.

"From eight until eleven?" Cosmo asked.

"That seems about right," Pepper said. "When was Tom Henderson killed?"

Whoops. We didn't know the answer to that yet.

"We couldn't say," Hyperion said quickly.

"Look," Cosmo said, "I guess the killer could have been a neighbor. You can only take so much. But personally, I blame that promoter."

"Promoter?" Hyperion asked.

The phone rang in my skirt pocket. I checked the number and my stomach rolled. It was an international number, so it had to be my mother. How had she gotten mine?

I pocketed it without answering. "Sorry. You were saying?"

"It's disgusting," Cosmo rumbled. "She lives right here in San Borromeo. She knows what an impact her parties have on this community. But she was the number one promoter booking that house."

That proverbial sinking feeling bottomed in my stomach. "Which promoter, exactly?"

"She's a PR consultant," Archer said, "not a promoter. I believe you two know her? Beatrice Carson."

Hyperion made a low whistle.

"You know her?" Pepper asked.

I swallowed. Weakly, I said, "We may have once accused her of, um, murder."

CHAPTER 4

"We have to take this case," Hyperion said after Archer closed the front door behind us. "We need to stay on Archer's good side. Can you imagine if he gave Beanblossom's a bad review?"

"He's a society reporter, not a restaurant reviewer." I skirted a banana plant.

"And a good word from him could put us both on the map. So no arguing. We're taking this case."

The headache that had been threatening sprouted behind my right eyeball. "All right, we're taking the case. But my point about professionals stands since we're not actually private investigators."

"Wait. You're agreeing?"

I shrugged. "I want to talk this over with Gramps and Tomas first. But it'll keep me busy while my mother's haunting San Borromeo. Also, let's face it. We're nosy."

He stepped into the driveway. "Thank you for finally admitting that."

We turned toward his car and stopped short.

A tall authority figure leaned casually against Hyperion's yellow Jeep.

Hyperion whistled. "That detective is so into me."

We walked to the car, Bastet in the lead.

"Hello, Detective," Hyperion said.

"Good afternoon, Mr. Night. Ms. Beanblossom." Detective Chase tipped his cowboy hat. "I was just coming to interview Mr. Simmons, when I noticed your Jeep was still here. Why is your Jeep still here?"

"He's a fascinating man," Hyperion said. "They don't make witty raconteurs like that anymore."

Bastet rubbed against the detective's ankle.

Chase's nose twitched. "Mm. And I suppose the murder came up."

"How could it not?" Hyperion asked. "A murder? Next door? How could we *not* talk about it?"

"What exactly happened to Mr. Henderson?" I asked.

The detective straightened off the car. "I can't divulge that information."

I looked away to stare at a banana plant. *Rats.* I'd expected the detective to be cagy with his intel, but I'd had to try.

"Stay out of my case, Mr. Night," he said. "Interfering in an investigation is a serious charge."

"I wouldn't dream of interfering," my partner said.

We got into Hyperion's Jeep. The detective watched us cruise down the circular driveway and onto the treelined street.

I shifted in my seat, earning an irate look from Bastet in my lap. "Chase looked serious about us staying out of this case."

"Don't be ridiculous," Hyperion scoffed, whipping around a bend. "You could tell he wants us on the case."

"He was pretty specific about us not getting involved."

"But it was the *way* he said it."

"The way?"

"He had a tone. So, back to the tearoom?"

I hesitated. My mother might still be there. "Maybe we should stop by Beatrice's PR firm, before it closes for the weekend?"

"Good idea. Strike while the iron is hot. Do we call ahead?"

"Definitely not." She'd never let us through the door. You make one little murder accusation, and you're persona non grata.

Go figure.

Beatrice Carson's PR firm was in the tallest building in San Borromeo. The six-story, brutalist-style monstrosity squatted at the edge of town, in what the powers-that-be had once hoped would become a financial district. It hadn't.

Hyperion, Bastet, and I rode the elevator to the third floor. It opened on a cheerfully modern reception area. No one sat behind the glass reception desk.

Hyperion motioned toward two seafoam-green chairs. "Do we wait?" he whispered.

"Why are you whispering?" I said in a low voice.

"I don't know. Why are you whispering?"

"Because it's so quiet."

"Too quiet," he intoned, then sobered. "Oh no. You don't think

Beatrice is dead, do you?"

"Why would she be dead?" Uneasy, I crossed my arms. "That's just silly."

"Then, where is everybody?"

"Maybe they're in a meeting."

"Or dead. They could be dead."

"No one's dead." I strode to the double doors to Beatrice's office and opened the left one.

There was a blur of motion beside my head. I gasped and leapt backward. Something shattered. Bastet yowled.

I dropped into a crouch and flung up one hand. This turned out to be a pretty good instinct. Glass and water droplets pelted the top of my head.

I opened my eyes.

Beatrice stood behind her desk, her mouth in an *O*, the blue Pacific framed in the wide window behind her. She dropped her hand to the side of her vintage red suit. Scarlet suffused the hollows of her cheeks. "Are you okay?"

A bead of water trickled down one temple. I looked around. A sort of high-tech spear quivered in the wall, just above a small shelf. A shattered vase lay on the carpet. "Wha...?"

She smoothed the front of her vintage suit. "I see you are."

Hyperion stepped into the office behind me. He hauled a reluctant Bastet behind him on his leash. "Of all the things I expected you might throw," he said, "a spear was nowhere on my list."

"It's a javelin. Sorry, I—" Beatrice straightened, absinthe eyes flashing. "What are you doing here? Where's my secretary?"

"And why are you hurling spears at innocent potential clients?" My partner bent to ponder the wreckage. Water dripped down the wall. Bits of ceramic littered the plush carpet.

Her eyes narrowed. "You're a potential client?"

"No." I picked myself off the floor.

"But we could have been," Hyperion said.

"It's not my fault," she said. "You startled me, barging in here like that."

Bull. I hadn't startled her. She'd launched that javelin *before* I'd opened the door. She hadn't been throwing it at me—at least, not intentionally. She'd been mad about something.

"Is that a cat?" she asked.

Bastet sniffed at the broken pottery. He looked up, and his nose twitched.

"Yes," I said. "It is indeed a cat. Now, what's going on?"

She lifted a shoulder, dropped it. "If you must know, I used to throw the javelin in college. I was track and field, but I was miserable at shotput, so—"

"So, you thought you'd work in some practice?" Hyperion asked. "In your office?"

She braced her fists on the smoked glass desktop. "You have a lot of nerve, barging in here. It's because of you one of my biggest clients went under."

"Tom Henderson?" Hyperion asked.

"Tom—?" She blinked. "What happened to Tom? And he's not my client. I'm *his* client."

"He's dead," I said. "Murdered."

Her mouth went slack. She dropped into her executive chair. "Oh, my."

"You can say that again." Hyperion and Bastet strolled to the desk. My partner took a seat across from her. The cat took the other.

Her nostrils whitened. "And I suppose you think I did it."

"We were hoping you could tell us about your relationship with him." I shifted Bastet off the chair and sat. The tabby scowled up at me.

"I didn't have a relationship," she snapped. "I was a client. And why should I tell you anything?"

"I suppose I could ask Razzzor..." I left that hanging. Razzzor was a tech gazillionaire, and my online gaming partner and best friend. He was also a client of Beatrice's.

She scowled. "Blackmail?"

"Never." Hyperion propped his elbows on the desk, his chin on his hands, the leash wrapped around one fist. "Now tell us everything."

"Fine. But don't even think about accusing me of murder again."

"We never went public with that," Hyperion wheedled.

"Or I would have sued and won," she said.

I shifted in the leather chair. Wow, it was soft. "You're a client?"

"I rented Tom Henderson's house on behalf of several of my clients for events."

"Were you aware the neighbors were unhappy with these parties?" I asked.

"Someone left rubber snakes in the flower beds," she said dryly. "Yes. I was aware."

That explained Archer's comments about the fake snakes.

"Do you know of anyone in particular who might have wanted Mr. Henderson dead?" Hyperion asked.

"Let's see. His wife—never marry a musician. All his neighbors. The head of the HOA. That private high school's senior class plus their drama coach—"

"Wait," Hyperion said. "How did you know about *So Long, Farewell?*"

"I booked the show. They're local players. Well, from San Francisco, which is close enough. Then there's that bridal expo woman, Maylene... Soon?" Beatrice said. "Yes, that's her name. Maylene Soon."

"Let's assume he wasn't murdered by the cast of a high school musical," I said. "Who's Maylene?"

"I told you, she runs bridal expos."

"And she wanted Henderson dead because...?" My partner prompted.

"I have no idea, but I saw them arguing last month."

"Where?" I asked. "I thought Henderson wasn't around much."

"Well, he was at the French restaurant on Pacific Street last month, and he and Maylene really got into it."

"About what?" I asked.

"How should I know?" she asked. "It was none of my business. And why is this any of *your* business?"

"Abigail's avoiding her mother," Hyperion said. "And I'm a people person."

She arched a dark brow at me. "*S-mother* issues?"

"The exact opposite." My jaw set. My mother hadn't been around enough to smother me. My grandmother had tried to make up for it, but she'd died when I was ten.

"Really?" Beatrice shook her head. "Never mind. I don't actually care."

"Neither do I," I said. "Now, where can we find Maylene?"

CHAPTER 5

Beatrice was not able to tell us where to find Maylene. The PR consultant claimed she didn't know. I didn't quite believe her, but we had a name, and this was the internet era. If Maylene was local, we'd find her.

I shut Beatrice's office door behind us. Hyperion and I wandered through the reception area toward the elevator.

"I'm loving your enthusiasm, Abs, really I am. But don't you think it's time you get back to your real job? Because I'm teaching a class this evening, and *I* should get back."

I *had* left the tearoom for a shamefully long amount of time. We were near to closing. My mother had to be gone by now.

"Sure," I said, "I—"

The elevator doors glided open. "Yes, Chief," Detective Chase's voice drifted from the elevator.

We looked at each other. Looked wildly around the reception area.

"Yes, sir," the detective said from the elevator. "I'm looking into that."

Hyperion grabbed up the cat, leapt sideways, and yanked open a door. He thrust me inside a supply closet, then eased the door shut behind us.

I edged backward. My elbow nudged a shelf. *Great.* I couldn't see a thing, but I was pretty sure there was a bucket and mop by my foot.

"So," he whispered, "your mother. Have you seen her yet?"

"No."

"Oh."

We were silent a long moment.

"I just don't know what to say," I said in a quiet rush. "She wasn't around when I was a kid. She hasn't been around for a long time."

Hyperion didn't respond.

"When I was a kid..." I swallowed. "My grandparents were wonderful, but they were older than the other parents. They came to all my school events, and I was ashamed. It just made me more different. And don't get me started on my mother's hand-me-down clothes I got stuck wearing." I shifted my weight and brushed against a shelf. "Now, I'm ashamed of being ashamed," I muttered.

"You were a kid."

"My grandparents really *were* great. I was lucky to have them. I was lucky..." I grimaced. Note to self: in future, avoid dark closets. Apparently, they made me want to spill my guts.

"I know you were lucky," he said. "Your grandfather's the best. Look, whatever happened in the past, you came through it, because you're strong. Your grandparents raised a good person. Whatever happens with your mother, you've got this."

I needed to change the subject before I started blubbering. "Do you think Chase saw us?"

Bastet sneezed.

"If he saw us, he'd be here by now," Hyperion said in a low voice. "And he'd be laughing. Right before he put us in handcuffs."

"I thought you said Chase didn't mean it about interfering. Do we really need to hide?"

"He needs to keep up appearances. And he *might* have meant it. Why do I smell bleach?"

"We're in a supply closet."

He fell silent again.

"On the positive side," Hyperion finally said, "this means we really are good detectives. We're on the same trail as Tony. In fact, we're ahead on the trail."

"Except he knows how and when Tom Henderson was killed, and we don't."

"And yet, he's here, and so are we."

My breathing accelerated. "And what do you bet Beatrice will tell him he just missed us?"

"Oh. Damn." He gulped.

Bastet growled.

"He must be in her office by now. Let's get out of here."

"Let's give it another minute. Besides, I do my best thinking in the dark."

"Why doesn't that surprise me?"

"If there's an insult in there, I'm ignoring—"

The closet door opened, and I winced, raising my hand against the light.

A pudgy, balding man in a pale-blue uniform gaped. "What are you two doing in here? Thinking you're going to make out in my supply closet? And is that a cat?"

"Ew." Hyperion pulled his arms in to his chest. "Is this a supply closet?"

The man puffed out his chest. "There's nothing wrong with my supply closet."

"I wasn't talking about—never mind." Hyperion brushed past him.

Sheepishly, I followed. The janitor clunked around, removing supplies from the closet. He shot suspicious looks at us as we waited for the elevator.

My gaze darted toward Beatrice's office door.

It swung open. "Thank you again, Ms. Carson," the detective's voice floated from the office.

The elevator creaked open. We sprinted inside.

"Hold the elevator, please," the detective called.

Hyperion jabbed at the first-floor and close-doors buttons in quick succession. I looked around wildly for an exit. The door closed, and the elevator began its descent.

Clutching the tabby to his chest, my partner collapsed against a mirrored wall. "That was close."

"Let's hope Chase doesn't decide to take the stairs."

Hyperion's eyes widened. He lurched forward and pressed the first-floor button again.

"That's not going to make it go any faster," I said.

"It can't hurt. Did you hear how he said *please?* Tony's got manners. You'd never catch him being rude to a waiter."

"Unless he caught him interfering in an investigation."

The door opened, and we sprinted from the elevator. Booted feet clunked on the stairs above us. We raced through the hallway and outside to Hyperion's Jeep.

"Hurry, hurry, hurry." I snapped my seatbelt on.

Hyperion handed me the cat, reversed the Jeep, and we roared from the lot.

I glanced over my shoulder. I didn't see the detective emerge from the building, and I blew out my breath. "We're clear."

"What a Friday. I need a drink."

"I really do need to get back to the tearoom."

"Then I shall drink alone." He winked. "But probably not for long."

We drove back to Beanblossom's, and I checked my watch. We'd close in thirty minutes. I had to be safe from a maternal visit by now.

I watched Hyperion stride through the rear parking lot to the wine bar. Shaking my head, I walked through the tearoom's rear entrance and to the kitchen. A waitress, Maricel, was artistically arranging finger sandwiches on a tiered plate.

"How did it go while I was gone?" I tied on an apron.

"No problems. Though we sold out of Empress Tea."

"I'll mix a new batch tonight. Thanks. And thanks for holding down the fort while I was away." I strolled into the dining area. A trio of elderly ladies sat at a table, and I smiled. They were regulars, and they'd linger.

A slim woman in a brightly colored caftan sat with her back to me. Long gray hair cascaded down her back. Her voice rang out across the tearoom. "I prefer to think of the Three of Swords as that irritant that drives one toward creativity." The scent of patchouli penetrated the smells of baked goods and herbal teas.

I stiffened. *My mother.*

I looked around wildly. Footsteps sounded in the hallway behind me. There was only one escape.

I dove behind the counter and crouched beside rows of brushed nickel tea cannisters.

A Tarot reader, Sierra, leaned over the counter and gave me a puzzled frown.

I pretended to check the cannisters, and Sierra left for a table.

This was stupid. This was more than stupid. So someone had been in the hallway. I still could have gone that way instead of behind the counter. Now I'd have to stay down here until my mother left.

I clutched a tea cannister to my chest so it looked like I had a reason to be down here. But how was I going to get out?

A man cleared his throat above me, and I looked up.

Brik, one elbow braced on the white stone counter, stared down at me. "Lose something?" His muscles bulged beneath his white tee.

I pointed in the direction of my mother and made a strangling motion with my free hand.

"You've lost your voice?"

"Cause a distraction by the front door," I whispered.

"You've got to be kidding."

I shot him a pleading look. "Please."

He rolled his eyes and stomped away. The bell over the front door jingled. "Hey, Sierra," he said loudly to the Tarot reader with my mother. "I'm having a party at my place tonight. You should come."

I duck-walked to the end of the counter and bolted for the hallway. Racing into the kitchen, I shut the door.

My head waitress stopped positioning pots of herbal spread on the tray. Her brow wrinkled.

"Okay," I said. "This is going to sound really immature, and I'm not proud of this, but that woman in the caftan by the window is my mother, and—"

"You're avoiding her?"

I nodded.

She raised a beringed hand, palm out. "Say no more."

"Look, I'll manage the kitchen. Would you close up the front, and, um, if anyone asks, say I called and won't be returning today? I'll manage the clean-up. You can go home early. And I'll pay you as if you'd stayed for the cleaning."

Her round face brightened. "You don't have to do that, but thanks." She exited carrying a tray of avocado, egg and cress sandwiches.

I got busy cleaning the kitchen. When Maricel returned, she confirmed the coast was clear and the tearoom closed. I sent her home and strode to the dining area.

Hyperion would be holding a Tarot class here tonight, so I decided to clean this room first for his students.

An hour later, I was back in the kitchen.

Hyperion appeared in the doorway. "Thanks for rearranging the tables out front. I could have done it."

I made a dismissive motion. "After all the waitresses I took advantage of today, it was the least I could do to reduce my Karmic debt."

"*You* believe in Karma?"

I lowered my brows, and he took a hasty step backward. "Just kidding. I take it your mother was gone?"

"She was not. I had to hide behind the counter while Brik created a diversion so I could escape into the kitchen."

"What was Brik doing here?"

"He—" I closed my mouth, canted my head. What *had* he been doing here? "He didn't say."

Hyperion shrugged. "He was probably dropping by the estimate for that new ceiling. No biggie. I'll just—" His phone rang, and he pulled it from the pocket of his blazer. "It's Archer."

He pressed the phone to his ear. "Archer, how are you?"

"Terrible!" His voice squawked faintly from the phone.

"I'm putting you on speaker," Hyperion said. "Abigail's here."

"I've been asked to come to the station tomorrow. The station!"

"Why?" I asked.

"To answer questions, of course. At the station! This is all my fault."

"How is it your fault?" I asked, gripping the metal countertop.

"Have you solved this murder yet?" Archer said.

"Um, no," Hyperion said.

"Well, why not?" he asked.

Hyperion cleared his throat. "It's early days, but we're making amazing progress—"

A dial tone sounded.

"He hung up," Hyperion said. "Archer sounds a little stressed."

"More than a little." And how was the murder his fault?

"It's not like they're arresting him," Hyperion said. "I mean, he's not being taken to the station in handcuffs."

"No, but Chase already spoke to Archer once at his house."

"So why *does* he need to make a repeat appearance at the station?"

"Exactly," I said. "Chase must have learned something since he last spoke to Archer, something Archer needs to clear up." And if I was Archer, I'd be worried too. I just hoped he wouldn't make comments about things being his fault at the police station.

"But what could it possibly be?" Hyperion said. "We've talked to everyone Tony's spoken with. I didn't get any brainstorms, did you?"

"Nope."

Tony Chase was a good cop. He wouldn't have pulled in Archer without good reason. We stared at each other.

What had we missed?

CHAPTER 6

Hyperion suggested a change of scene might improve our mental accuity, so we walked to the wine bar on the other side of the parking lot. There, we conducted an online investigation over drinks and paninis.

Hyperion found Maylene on a professional networking site. We agreed to track her down on Monday, when the tearoom was closed, and she was more likely to be in the office.

Then he abandoned me for his Tarot class, and I drove home. Feeling at loose ends, I decided to test a new recipe for turtle scones.

I pretty much love all things chocolate, and adding caramel made the recipe even more decadent. I chopped pecans and mixed them with chocolate chips into the dough. I cut the dough into triangles and slid them into the oven. As the scones baked, I cooked a caramel-based turtle sauce over the stove and wiped down the counters.

If only relationship messes could be cleaned up that easily.

The sauce was ready just as I pulled the scones from the oven. I spread it over the scones. Then, for good measure, I drizzled some extra pecans on top, counted to ten, and took a bite.

"Oh, yeah." They were comfort scones on steroids. I let them cool then packed them up to test out on friends and family.

The next day, I called Archer from the tearoom, thinking he might like to try one. He didn't answer.

Concerned, I left a voicemail. Okay, I might have left three voicemails. I liked Archer, and I really hoped he was alright, and we hadn't screwed things up.

At lunch, I took a quick break in Hyperion's office to scan the local newspaper online. I found only a brief article about the murder:

Police in San Borromeo have launched an investigation into the death of a man who fell from his balcony.

```
The body of Thomas Henderson, 42, was found
outside his house on Saturday morning by a
wedding manager.
  Police said his death is being treated as
suspicious.
  Mr. Henderson is survived by his wife,
Vanella Henderson.
```

Found by a wedding manager? Could that mean Maylene Soon? I sighed and leaned my head against the high-backed red chair.

At least now I knew how Thomas Henderson had died. I stood and brushed cat hair off my linen slacks then returned to the Saturday bustle of pouring tea.

Sunday was also predictably busy. I kept checking my phone for a message from Archer and watching the door for my mother. The latter didn't show up. But why would she? My mother had already gotten what she'd come for: a Tarot reading.

I called Archer again that evening, after we'd closed.

"Yes?" he asked. "Did you find anything?"

"We may have found a lead," I said cautiously from my perch on the kitchen's long, metal table. "How did it go at the police station?"

A glass clinked. "Any meeting at a police station that involves one leaving a free man is a success. I'm at home recovering with an excellent bottle of Pinot."

I stopped swinging my legs. "Was it that bad?"

"Bad? It was ghastly. Have you been in that police station? I've been trying to think of a word to describe the wall color. Ichor isn't quite right."

"I call them ick-colored." I slid off the table.

"Hm. A little low-brow," he said, "but at least it's original. I'll accept the description."

"Did they tell you how Tom Henderson died?" Maybe there was more to this balcony story.

"Shoved over a balcony on Thursday night."

Or maybe there wasn't. "And he wasn't discovered until Friday?" I glanced toward the open kitchen door.

"It's a very big house."

That was for sure. "But you'd think his wife would have noticed he never came to bed."

"You haven't met his wife."

"Are you saying they didn't share a room?" I asked.

"How would I know? It's not like I'm a peeping Tom."

Considering the peep hole in his gate, I suspected he sort of was. But I said nothing.

"I simply meant their marriage appeared—from a casual outsider's perspective—to be fraught," he said. "But what do I know? I've never been married. Ghastly institution. And who wants to live in an institution?"

"And the police are certain Tom didn't just fall from the balcony?" I asked.

"They were certain enough to drag me in for questioning and warn me not to leave the state."

I shifted, uneasy. "How big was Henderson?"

"Oh, maybe five-ten, five-eleven."

"And his build?"

"Fairly solid, I'd say. You're wondering how much strength it would take to shove him over?"

"Something like that," I admitted. Archer wasn't a big man, and he wasn't one of those Mr. Senior America muscle-builders, either. So why were the cops suspicious of him? Tony Chase was no dummy. He must have a reason.

"*Could* you have done it?" I blurted. "Not that I think you did, but in a parallel universe, if you wanted to throw him over, could you?"

"I don't see how."

A door closed in the hallway outside.

"What if he was knocked unconscious first?" I asked.

"Coshed on the back of the head and then tipped over? Oh, I could definitely do that. But only if he happened to fall on top of the railing. I can't imagine having to dead lift him."

I rubbed the back of my neck. "Is there any way you can learn more about how he died?"

"I can, and I will." He chuckled darkly. "I have sources everywhere."

"Great. Let me know what you find out."

"Naturally. And now, I must leave. I'm expecting a guest."

"Okay, have a good night."

"Oh, I *will*." He hung up.

"Abigail? There you are." Tomas ambled into the kitchen.

"What are you doing here?" I hopped off the table. Tomas is my grandfather's best friend and my honorary uncle. He's also my landlord and a retired lawyer. His jacket—an orange and black windbreaker for his favorite baseball team—rustled as I hugged him.

He grinned, his face wrinkled as a raisin. "I'm just checking in. How do you like the new answering machine?"

He'd surprised me by installing one in my bungalow last week. I hadn't had the heart to tell him only he and my grandfather still used answering machines. Or landlines. "It goes great with the gray countertop," I said, truthfully.

"I heard your mother stopped by Beanblossom's."

"I just missed her."

He chuckled. "I'm sure you were heartbroken. But seriously, how are you doing?"

"I'm okay. Feeling guilty."

"Guilty about what?"

"About dumping her on Gramps." I grimaced. And now I was trying to absolve myself by confessing to Tomas. *Pathetic.*

"You didn't dump her on him," he said. "She asked your grandfather if she could stay with him, and he told her she could. You had nothing to do with it."

I leaned against the metal table. "I know she's driving him crazy with her incense and morning yoga chants, but… Has he said anything to you? How bad is it, really?"

Tomas shook his head. "She's his daughter."

And one way or another, she'd always be a part of our lives.

"This is his penance, Abigail," he said in a low voice.

"Penance? For what?"

"He thinks he failed her, and she in turn failed you." He shook his head. "I don't know what happened. He says he made mistakes with her, and maybe he did. Let him do this. You wouldn't be doing him any favors by taking her off his hands."

Which fit so well with my desires, it didn't seem right. And I couldn't imagine how Gramps might have failed my mother. He'd been a wonderful parent for me. My throat tightened. Change of subject. "Have you heard about Archer?"

"What's that old rascal up to?"

"One of his neighbors was murdered, and he was brought in for police questioning."

Tomas winced. "I'm not a practicing attorney anymore."

"I know. The thing is, he asked Hyperion and me to look into the murder. But I wonder if we'll do more harm than good."

Tomas folded his arms, his brow wrinkling. "We have some very good police in San Borromeo."

I nodded.

"I don't trust a single one of them."

"You don't?" I gaped. "Why not?"

"It's not the individuals. It's the system." He shook his head. "What's more important is Archer trusts you, and he's… Let's just say he's a unique individual and leave it at that. He's a genius in his own way. But he's got some blind spots. I'd feel better with you looking out for our old friend."

"So you think we should help him?"

"Did you seriously want me to stop you?"

"No," I said, surprised. "I didn't."

I sent Tomas home with a plastic container packed with scones and tiny sandwiches. Then I called Hyperion and filled him in on my call with Archer, drove home, and plotted our Monday off.

"This place doesn't look like it produces the premier bridal shows on the West Coast." Hyperion stepped from his Jeep, checked his phone, and squinted at the squat, one-story building. We'd parked at the bottom of the steep street in the only spot we could find.

Uneasily, I glanced up the hill. I hoped everyone had curbed their wheels, and the dumpster at the top had good brakes. Hills meant lots of ocean views, but parking could be tough.

"We're never going to get away with this." I jammed my hands in the pockets of my loose, linen slacks. I'd wanted to stop by without an appointment and use the element of surprise on Maylene. Hyperion, however, had had other ideas.

"It beats her telling Tony that she was interrogated by two amateur detectives."

"Does it though?" I asked. "What if—?"

He slapped me on the shoulder. "Now put on your chipper wedding planner face, and let's go undercover."

He opened the door and strode inside. "Helloooo!"

Pasting on a smile, I followed. Photos of bridal expos lined the walls of the low-ceilinged room.

Hyperion leaned one elbow on a high reception desk. He smiled at the bored-looking receptionist, a young man in a faded cardigan. "Logan Fellman and Vertuna Salid to see Maylene Soon," Hyperion said.

"I'll tell her you're here." The young man rose, his chair squeaking, and left the linoleum-themed reception area.

"Vertuna Salid?" I hissed. "No one's going to believe that name."

"Your other option was Trixie Normous."

"Vertuna it is." It was too late to change my fake name anyway. "*Logan.*"

"I wanted something simple," he said.

The receptionist trudged into the room. A tall, slim woman about my age—early thirties—followed him. She brushed back a length of blue-black hair and extended her hand. "Mr. Fellman? Ms. Salid? I'm Maylene."

"Please," Hyperion said, "call me Logan."

"Vertuna," I muttered, shaking her hand.

She tilted her head. "Come into my office."

We followed her into a simple office stacked with boxes, partially obscuring a bookshelf. The tops of trophies edged from behind the cardboard boxes.

"Sorry," she said. "We don't get many visitors." She sat behind a plain, wooden desk and motioned us into chairs. "You said you're wedding planners?"

"We're local," Hyperion said, "and we heard you were putting on an expo right here in San Borromeo."

She picked up a pen and clicked it. "The status of that event is... uncertain."

"What happened?" I asked.

"The owner of the property passed away. I haven't had a chance to talk to his wife yet. Right now, we're assuming we're going forward. But it would be irresponsible to invite other businesses until I get some clarity."

"Oh, no," I said. "What happened?"

She clicked the pen again. "It's unclear. He, um, died on Friday."

"Wait," Hyperion said. "Wait, wait, wait." He snapped his fingers. "That big house didn't belong to Tom Henderson, did it?"

She nodded.

"I read about his death in the papers," he said. "And Maylene Soon… You were the one who found the body. That's where I knew your name from."

She stiffened. "Is that why you're here?"

"Of course not," he said. "But finding a body… How awful for you."

Her lips trembled. "It was. I had a meeting with him that morning. The gate was open, so I just went in, like I always—" She swallowed. "I was walking to the door, and noticed all these crows. I thought maybe they'd found a dead animal."

"But it was Tom Henderson," Hyperion breathed.

"He was beneath the wedding balcony," she whispered.

"Wedding balcony?" I asked.

"Where we have our bridal photo shoots," she said.

"Did you do much business with him?" I swiveled my chair and my elbow hit a stacked box.

She shook her head. "We used the house on several occasions. But as I guess you read in the papers, he was murdered. We're not sure if his home is still the appropriate place for a wedding expo."

"More appropriate than ever," Hyperion said. "Brides are utter ghouls. Haven't you noticed?"

A flicker of a smile crossed her face. "If you give me your contact info, I'll let you know the status of the event."

"Did you know Tom well?" I asked.

She blinked. The pen clicked. "No. Not at all. I mean, I met him once or twice. You know how it is."

Right. Sure.

"I heard some of the neighbors weren't too happy with that house being used as a venue." Hyperion leaned forward conspiratorially. "Do you think one of them could have killed him?"

Her face tightened. "Since one threatened me the last time I was there—to show the space to one of our contractors—it wouldn't surprise me at all."

"Someone threatened you?" I asked. "Do you know who it was?"

Maylene nodded. "We'd hoped to invite her to the event. She's a fairly big-name influencer online, though she caters to the over-thirty crowd. But women are getting married later in life, and we'd hoped to lure her in."

Not Pepper?

"What happened?" Hyperion asked breathlessly.

I shot him a look.

"She threatened to run me over with her car and set my office on fire."

I blinked. "What?" I said. "That's a…"

"Dazzlingly fearful, Eldrich horror?" Hyperion asked.

I glared at him. Not his Lovecraft word-of-the-day calendar *again*?

"Did you tell the police?" I asked.

"Not at the time. I wasn't worried about her." She cocked her head.

"I suppose I should be now."

"She sounds a little unbalanced," I said. "Maybe her not coming to the expo is a good thing." I edged my chair slightly backward. "Sorry, but you're not talking about Pepper Schripsema, are you?"

"How did you know?"

"I've been looking at wedding influencers too, and I noticed she lived near that house."

"Vertuna is nothing if not thorough," Hyperion said.

"Well," Maylene said, "I don't know what her problem was, but we all have our triggers. So, have you got a card? I can call you once I know anything."

"Of course." Hyperion stood and whipped a card from the inside pocket of his blazer. He extended it to her.

She took the card. Her dark brows drew downward. "Hyperion Night?"

My partner blanched.

I smothered a groan. He'd given her his actual card? "That's the name of our company," I said quickly. "Hyperion, god of the..." Oh, heck. What was he the god of?

"Heavenly light," Hyperion said. "We liked the juxtaposition of light and dark. But heavenly light and dark," he babbled.

"Right." I pushed back my chair. "It was great meeting you, Maylene."

"And you too, Vertuna."

We shook hands, and Hyperion and I left.

I crossed the narrow road toward Hyperion's Jeep. "I can't believe you gave her your card. Your *real* card. What were you thinking?"

"I was thinking it only had my name on it and nothing about our business. I'd forgotten it was my real name. Did you see those trophies?"

I nodded. "For martial arts. She might have been able to throw a grown man over a balcony."

"What a story. Crows? Do you think his eyes were pecked out like in that Hitchcock movie with all the birds?"

"You mean, *The Birds*?"

"Rod Taylor, Tippi Hedren… Think Archer spied on any of them through that hole in the fence back in the day?"

"I'm afraid to ask."

"And what do you think about that business about not knowing Henderson? It didn't quite ring true."

"No. It didn't." I squinted up the hill. The dumpster at the top was now right in the middle of the street. What idiot had moved it there? We'd barely be able to get past it, and I knew who'd be pushing that dumpster out of the way if we couldn't: me.

"Interesting about Pepper though. We knew she had issues with that house, but threats?" he asked.

"I wonder if Archer knows Pepper threatened violence?"

Hyperion pulled his keys from his pocket. "Let's hope not. I can't believe he'd partner up with a lunatic—assuming Maylene's story is true. And is Maylene a suspect or not?"

"It looks like she had the means. She might have had motive, though we don't know what it was."

"A fatal flaw in our investigation. We'll need to do more sleuthing, check her social media accounts, stalking—"

"You know how I feel about stalking."

"It's just another word for a stakeout."

"Or we could talk to Henderson's wife," I said.

He grimaced. "I hate to bother a freshly made widow."

"Cheer up. She could be a murderer."

He brightened. "There is that."

Something rumbled above us. I looked up. But the sky was blue, with nary a thundercloud in sight. A typical summer day in sunny San Borromeo.

Hyperion opened his door. "Let's see if Archer can get us in to see the black widow."

The rumble grew louder.

"What *is* that?" Hyperion asked.

We turned toward the noise.

The dumpster barreled down the hill.

Hyperion flung himself from the Jeep. "Run!"

I bolted toward a purple stucco building.

There was a tremendous crash. Car alarms blared. Heads popped out of offices and nearby homes.

Hyperion wailed. "My Jeep!"

I opened my eyes.

The dumpster had hit his car dead on, crumpling it in the middle like an aluminum can.

Shaken, I stepped into the street. "Are you okay?" I asked.

"Of course I'm not okay." He gestured toward the wrecked car. "Look at my Jeep!"

I looked up the street. People peered from doorsteps. If someone had pushed that dumpster—and of course someone had—they were long gone. Or well hidden.

And watching.

CHAPTER 7

"Near death by dumpster?" Hyperion paced the street and raked both hands threw his thick hair. "Are you kidding me?"

A tentacle of smoke emerged from the dumpster.

"Um…" I swallowed. "Hyperion..."

My partner shook his fist at the dumpster, pressed into the side of his Jeep. "This shall not stand."

A caustic scent wafted through the air.

I cleared my throat. "Maybe we should—"

A blossom of flame exploded upward, heat washing over us.

We yelped and leapt away. Doors slammed on the street, bystanders retreating inside their buildings.

I pressed a hand to my chest, my heart thumping beneath it. We could have been killed. Anger quickly followed on the heels of my fear. We could have been killed.

"Exploding dumpsters?" Hyperion shouted. "A *literal* dumpster fire? What fresh hell is next?"

The fire crackled merrily inside the dumpster. Acrid black smoke rose into the blue sky.

My eyes stung. I pressed my sleeve to my nose. "On the plus side," I said shakily, "technically it didn't explode. It ignited."

"Explode, ignite..." His eyes widened. "My Jeep. It's going to set my car on fire."

He raced around the side of the dumpster and pushed, straining against its blue metal sides. "Help me move it into the street."

I didn't think it would really set the Jeep on fire. But on the off chance it might, moving the dumpster into the center of the cul-de-sac made some sense.

I squeezed between the dumpster and the car. Grime coated the dumpster, and its sides were unpleasantly warm. I made a face and pressed my back against it. Pushing and heaving, the two of us rolled the thing into the middle of the road.

I studied my grimy hands. "Yuck." I was starting to have some sympathy for Detective Chase. Disposable gloves weren't all bad.

Gingerly, I dug through my purse and found a bottle of hand sanitizer. But it only seemed to spread the muck around. "I need water."

"I need a tow truck," Hyperion said. "And revenge. Whoever did this is going to pay."

Whoever did this had probably killed Tom Henderson. And now he or she had targeted us. "We need to figure this out," I said. "But first, we should call the cops."

He brightened. "Tony? I'll make the call so you can clean up."

Hyperion walked away to phone. I returned to the Jeep and found an unopened water bottle in the back seat, which I used to wash my hands.

The police arrived, and the fire department. An hour later, warning alarm beeping, a tow truck backed toward the crushed Jeep.

"That dumpster was obviously pushed," Hyperion said hotly. "This was attempted murder. Look at my Jeep."

Chase adjusted his medical mask and ran a finger inside the wrist of his latex glove. "I'll get a uniform down here to try to get prints. But the odds are low. That thing's filthy."

I nodded fervently and wiped my hands on my capris again. It really was disgusting.

"Why is it always my Jeep that gets attacked?" Hyperion turned to me. "It's not fair. Why don't your cars ever get assaulted?"

"That Tesla I was driving last month was wrecked," I reminded him.

"But it wasn't *your* Tesla," Hyperion said.

Like I could afford to buy one. "The point is, this was a warning. That dumpster wasn't at the top of the street when we got here. Someone moved it to the middle of the road and got it rolling downhill."

"Did you see anyone?" the detective asked.

"No," I admitted.

"What were you doing here?" Detective Chase asked.

"Doing here?" I asked

The detective's eyes narrowed. "Yes, what were you doing here?"

"Why wouldn't we be here?" I hedged.

"Don't bother prevaricating," Hyperion said wearily, staring at his Jeep. "We have to tell him the truth."

Darn it. "Fine. We were talking to Maylene Soon." I motioned toward her building. "She runs wedding expos, and she rented out Henderson's mansion. We heard she got into it with Henderson."

"I believe I told you both that playing detective constituted interfering in an investigation."

"Well," I said, "yes, but—"

"It seems you're not taking me seriously," Detective Chase said. "You're under arrest."

My mouth dropped open in an unladylike fashion. "What?"

He motioned to two uniformed men. "Officers? Please take these two to the station. Book them for interfering with an investigation."

Arrested.

I pressed my hands against the concrete bench and jiggled my heels. I'd never been arrested before. And I really didn't like the feeling of being in other people's power.

"Shove over." A large woman in thigh-high boots and—judging by its stratospheric height—what could only be a blond wig, jostled me.

I scooted closer to the wall of my prison. How was this going to look on loan applications? Would I ever be able to get a mortgage? Or lease a car? Not that I believed in leasing. Gramps had drummed that idea out of me. No loans for consumer goods. Period.

"I said, move over." She pushed me again.

I've seen enough women-in-prison movies—okay, one—to know not to show weakness. So I tried to play it cool, though my heart was banging against my ribs. "You've got plenty of room. What's your problem?"

"You're my problem, *elf*."

Why did people call me that? True, she was roughly three times my size. And come to think of it, cage fighting had never been my forte. Prudence was called for. I moved over, one shoulder nearly touching the swamp-green wall.

Her mouth stretched into a snarl. "Move *over*, sailor girl."

"I *can't* move over anymore." I tugged down the hem of my blue-and-white striped top. Okay, it looked a little Russian-sailory, but not like I'd just gotten off my yacht.

"Then just move," she said.

"What is this? We're not in prison, this is the town jail. You don't need to jockey for position. You win. I concede. You're queen of all you survey."

"You think you're funny? You think all strippers have a heart of gold or something? Well, I don't."

Stripper? "Since I can't crawl onto the ceiling, I'm not moving any further. You'll have to learn to share." My hands fisted. Given the difference in our weight classes, she was no doubt going to kill me, but it was the principle of the thing.

I hate bullies.

To my surprise, she relaxed, leaning away from me. "What are you in for?"

"A dumpster fire," I muttered.

"Arson? Cool. Trying to burn your old man's stuff, huh?"

"It wasn't exactly my fault."

"That's what they all say." She patted her massive hair. "They got me for borrowing my ex's car."

"Borrowing?"

She shrugged. "The jimmy messed up the door. I never was very good with those things. But I can hotwire like nobody's business." She winked.

"That… seems like a useful talent." Briefly, I wondered if she'd teach me, but this wasn't the time to learn new skills.

"You have no idea. What do you do?"

"I run a tea and Tarot room." I winced. I probably shouldn't blab about that to felons.

"Beanblossom's?" she asked, and I shrank lower. "That place looks great. I've always wanted a Tarot reading."

"I've always wanted to know how to hotwire a car," I said absently. If my jailtime got out, how would that affect sales?

"Yeah, I get you. And I get the fire, too. You were trying to make a statement. It's not fair. Society has no room for people who color outside the lines, people with flare. They just shut us down. Drag us to jail. It isn't right."

"You can say that again."

I let her ramble and went back to worrying about my blighted future. At least I was self-employed. I couldn't be fired because of my criminal record.

But what was Gramps going to think? I'd used the most humiliating phone call of my life asking Tomas for a legal referral. I hadn't asked him not to say anything, because of course he'd tell Gramps. They were best friends.

"I'm Wanda, by the way."

"Abigail."

"I mean," she said, "the fire was contained, right? What harm was it going to cause? They were just going to dump it all in a landfill anyway."

"Uh, huh."

"Landfills create greenhouse gases. And a lot of the stuff that goes in them is toxic. All of that leeches into the ground or worse, into the groundwater. And have you heard of leachate?"

I felt my eyes start to glaze. "Um, no."

"It's terrible," Wanda said. "It's a liquid that forms when the waste breaks down. It goes right into the soil and the groundwater too. And then there's methane..." She shook her head. "Of course, setting a garbage fire is polluting too. You should have thought about that."

"I really should have."

"But the worst, the absolute worst, is what we're doing to our oceans. Do you cut the plastic rings that come on six-packs of bottles and cans?"

I straightened on the concrete bench. "Of course I do. I don't want some poor bird or otter to get stuck in one of those rings."

She nodded. "Good. Now let me tell you about chlorinated solvents..."

I slumped back and studied the bars of my cell. Just my luck I'd get stuck with a socially conscious stripper. Words like *gasoline oxygenate* floated past, and I nodded and said "uh, huh" at random moments.

This was terrible. I clawed my hand through my hair. I'd never make it in the big house. I had to get out of here.

A policewoman walked to the cell and unlocked it. "Beanblossom. You're out."

I leapt to my feet. "I am? How?" I hadn't been arraigned or anything.

The policewoman raised a brow. "You want to stick around?"

"No." I turned to the stripper. "I mean, no offense."

Wanda motioned toward the bars. "None taken. Go."

I speed walked out of the cell. The policewoman locked it behind me.

"And don't forget to compost," Wanda hollered.

"Sure thing," I said.

I followed the policewoman through a concrete maze and past a warren of desks. "What about Hyperion Night?" I asked. "Is he free too?"

She shrugged. "They told me to come get you. I got you." She handed me a plastic bag filled with my watch, jewelry, and purse. "Here."

"Thanks, but—"

She opened a door. "Enjoy your freedom."

Dazed, I walked into a waiting area.

Gramps and Tomas turned creakily toward me. Tomas smiled. Gramps did not, and my stomach squeezed.

"Abs, we're free." Hyperion leapt from a plastic chair. "You wouldn't *believe* my cell mate."

"*You* got us out?" Guilt stricken, I hugged Tomas. "I thought you were going to call another lawyer. But thank you."

He patted my back. "Of course I got you out," he said gruffly. "What kind of a lawyer would I be, if I couldn't get you out? I killed a man with a bottlecap. You think I can't handle a simple jail break?"

I stepped away and glanced at Gramps. "But how did you manage it?"

Gramps adjusted his checked, cabbie-style hat and stared at the linoleum. My heart pinched. I'd disappointed the one person who mattered. Badly.

"Apparently," Hyperion said, "we're too small to prosecute."

"What?"

"I had a talk with the DA," Tomas said. "The system's so overcrowded, they'll let anyone out."

"And the DA's your friend," I guessed.

Tomas pressed a finger to his nose. "You bet he is." He glanced at my grandfather. "There is, um, one thing."

"We don't have to wear one of those ankle bracelets," Hyperion said, "do we?"

"No," Tomas said. "As far as San Borromeo is concerned, you were never arrested."

"You're a genius," Hyperion said. "A true master of your craft. Thank God Abigail called you."

"Who did *you* call?" I asked my partner.

"My date for tonight, of course. I didn't want to stand him up. That would be rude."

"Seriously?"

"I knew you'd be calling Tomas," he said. "Who else would you call?"

"Abigail," Gramps said, "there's something I need to tell you."

"This looks serious," my partner said. "I'll give you three some alone time." Hyperion flung open the door, and a Pacific breeze wafted into the waiting room. "Free at last!" He strode outside.

"Gramps, I'm so sorry. I didn't mean for you both to come down here."

Gramps shook his head. "I knew it would come to this."

I felt the blood drain from my face. He thought I was a disaster, like my mother. "You did?" I asked in a small voice.

"It's your mother again."

"No," I whispered.

My grandfather's head dropped lower. "I failed you."

"No," I said. "You've been wonderful. I'm the one who failed. This is on me, not you. And I'm so sorry I dragged you both into my mess. I shouldn't have—"

"Frank, shut it," Tomas said. "She thinks you're accusing her of having bad genes." He turned to me. "We don't care you were arrested. You wouldn't believe the trouble Frank and I got into when we were young. And that flatfoot was throwing his weight around. We're happy to get you out."

I winced. Detective Chase had always treated me fairly in the past. "Well, that's not exactly—"

"Frank," Tomas said, "just tell her."

My grandfather's expression turned pained.

"Tell me what?" I asked.

"It's about your mother," Tomas said.

I folded my arms. Of course it was. "Let me guess. She left for Katmandu?"

"Not exactly—"

A familiar feminine voice floated through the open door. "Where's Abigail?"

My shoulders hunched to my ears.

"She's outside," Tomas said.

CHAPTER 8

"Abigail!"

I stood stiffly one concrete step beneath my mother. She enfolded me in a hug.

Behind her, Gramps shuffled his feet. "When your mother heard you were in jail, she insisted on coming."

On the police station's forecourt, my mother took a step away from me. She gripped my shoulders, her filmy caftan clinging to my clothing, static crackling. The fabric slowly peeled free. "It's so good to see you again. How long has it been?"

"Over ten years, I think." Suddenly, my heart squeezed until I felt it crack under its own pressure, a heaving that lunged up my throat. I looked away. It had been more than twenty.

Tourists wandered past in board shorts and tank tops. One threw me a curious look.

I pretended not to notice and studied the candy shop across the street. Built in the storybook style with a wavy thatched roof, it was worth looking at. My grandfather had taken me there the first Friday of every month when I was a child. I'd loved those Fridays and red licorice ropes. And now my mother was here, and the only things I wanted to say were hard and bitter.

"And who is this?" My mother motioned grandly toward Hyperion, on the sidewalk below.

"My business partner," I said, "Hyperion Night."

"And partner in crime, apparently," she said. "I had no idea you'd become the sort of person who got arrested. You really should sage yourself after being in prison."

Hyperion brushed off his sleeve. "Sage, shower, and decontaminate from the inside with a shot of tequila."

"I don't think it works that way, dear," my mother said.

"I'm pretty sure it does," Tomas said.

"But what was it like?" my mother asked. "I've endured solitary quests, but those were all voluntary. I'm fascinated by the idea of having no way out, of being completely at the mercy of the experience."

I lowered my head and smiled cynically. So *that* was why she'd come. Not to see me, but to learn about life in the big house. "You meet all sorts of interesting people," I said. But suddenly my tale of the stripper environmentalist didn't seem so interesting. I had to get out of here. "I…"

My grandfather rescued me. "Abigail has a business to run," he said. "She probably needs to go."

"Right," I said. "Thanks again, both of you." I hugged Gramps. "Is everything all right?" I whispered.

"It's fine," he said and stepped away. "And never forget I'm proud of you. And if that cop gives you any more guff, you call me. Now go."

"But..." I darted a sideways glance at my mother.

Gramps smiled wanly. "I'll manage."

"Go?" my mother asked. "But I just got here."

"Gramps is right," I said. "I have a business to run, and we're burning daylight."

"Nonsense," my mother said. "Time is an illusion. We have infinity in the present moment."

"Besides, we're closed today," Hyperion said.

I scowled at my partner. "But there are *other* things I need to do."

"How?" Hyperion asked. "My car was totaled, and where's yours?"

"Do you need a ride?" Tomas asked.

"Yes," my mother said, "we'd be happy to drop you both."

An uneasy look crossed Tomas's gnarled face.

"No thanks," I said. "My car's at the tearoom. And Gramps, Tomas, I'll see you both soon."

"I'm coming with you. Thanks, Tomas," Hyperion said.

"I'll see you at home," my mother called.

The two of us hurried down the sloping sidewalk toward Beanblossom's.

"Have I mentioned lately how amazing Tomas is?" Hyperion said. "I can't believe he got us out like that. We should get him a cake."

"I know." Though I wish he hadn't blurted that old bottlecap story out at the police station. And what did my mother mean about seeing me at home? Did she think I was going to Gramps' house tonight?

"I mean," he said, "that was above and beyond."

"Right." *Good Lord.* She wasn't planning on going to my house, was she?

"And then there was your mother." He hesitated. "At least she came."

"Only because she thought jail might be a cool spiritual experience."

He shuddered. "It's not. It was awful. I was all alone, no one to talk to. I tried to meditate, but all I could think of was the disgusting toilet in the corner. Did you have one?"

"Yeah."

"Did you use it?" He shrugged into his blazer.

"No. And that's a little personal."

"We went to jail, Abigail. There's no such thing as personal in the big house." He paused. "What do you think it means that Tony arrested us?"

"I think he doesn't want us interfering in his investigation."

"Okay, that, yes. But *besides* that."

"What else could there be?"

He stopped beside a brick planter box overflowing with multi-colored impatiens. "You know we've been doing this will-we-won't-we get together dance for ages. This is either his way of saying he can be with me and be a detective, or..."

"Or what?"

"I don't know. That's why I asked your opinion."

"We need more intel." Did my mother even know where I lived? She could have just asked Gramps or Tomas, but—

The phone rang in his pocket, and he pulled it out. "It's Archer." He pressed the phone to his ear. "Archer, you wouldn't believe... Oh. Let me put you on speaker. Abigail's here." He extended the phone to me.

"Hi, Archer."

"Vanella is expecting you in an hour," he said.

"Expecting us for what?" I asked.

"A condolence call. I told her you were business acquaintances of her husband."

"What sort of business acquaintances?" I asked.

"You'll have to make something up. Don't be late." He hung up.

Hyperion winced. "Okay, I know you must be feeling red-hot humiliation over your arrest—"

"You were arrested too."

"—plus a sidecar of guilt over dragging Tomas and your grandfather to the police—"

"Next time I'll use a public defender."

He opened his mouth, closed it. "Next time?"

"Yeah," I said. "Let's go."

"Hold on. We just got out of jail for interfering in an investigation. And while I'm loving your enthusiasm, a minute ago you were pink and sweating, and now—"

"My mother said she'd see me at home."

"And?"

"At my *home*."

"Oh. Are you sure avoiding your mother is worth risking jail for?"

"Oh, it is. It is."

The Henderson's house was even more gobsmackingly impressive through the front gate. And that's how we viewed it, since the iron gate refused to open for my Mazda. The red light on a nearby security camera blinked balefully, but no one answered the call box when we buzzed.

"Archer did say an hour?" I asked.

"Yes," Hyperion said. "He did. Do you think Vanella's dead too?"

"Will you please stop predicting murders? It's starting to creep me out."

I backed from the drive and looked for a parking spot. New NO PARKING signs sprouted along the tree-lined street.

"I'll call Archer," Hyperion said.

He called and got us permission to park in Archer's driveway. I pulled into the curving drive and stopped beside a banana tree. Then Hyperion and I walked down the road to the three-story mansion. We entered through the open, pedestrian gate.

"She's making us take the servants' entrance," Hyperion sniffed.

"Wouldn't that be in the back?"

"Potato, potahto. This is obviously a power play. I don't see why she couldn't just answer our buzz and let us in." He lowered his voice. "Unless she's dead."

"She's not dead." My stomach butterflied. I hoped she wasn't dead. She probably hadn't let us in because she didn't want my low-rent hatchback bringing down the tone of her driveway.

The house was styled like a French chateau with a blue tile roof, turrets, and a gravel path meandering through a topiary garden.

Gawking, Hyperion and I wandered to the double front doors. I rang the bell. A gong echoed through the house.

"Do you think they have a butler?" Hyperion asked.

"They only live here a week or two out of the month," I said. A butler for a week a month seemed weird. But who knows? Maybe you can rent them by the hour?

The door opened, and a supermodel of modern, waif proportions smiled wanly out at us. She dabbed one eye with a tissue and brushed her blond hair off one shoulder. "Yes?"

"Hi," I said. "We're Abigail and Hyperion. Archer said—"

"Oh, yes. Come in." She turned and walked deeper inside.

Hyperion and I looked at each other.

"Not dead," I mouthed.

He shrugged, and we followed her into a high-ceilinged foyer.

Vanella walked up a winding, marble staircase. "I'm sorry, I have to get ready for an event tonight. Do you mind?"

"No problem," I called up from behind her.

"This place gives me the creeps," Hyperion hissed in my ear. "Did you see that giant penguin topiary? It looked like something out of *The Shining*."

We followed Vanella into a bedroom the size of most normal people's houses, and into a closet bigger than my bedroom. A chandelier glittered above a long, high table.

She motioned us toward a pink couch and lifted a remote control from the marble table. A section of the wall glided forward, displaying racks of dresses. Inset, overhead lights illuminated the gowns.

"Whoa," Hyperion said.

"Darn it," she said. "That wasn't the section I wanted." Vanella pressed another button, and the closet wall withdrew. "It's new, and I'm terrible with technology."

"I've never had to learn a closet before." Hyperion's voice had a jealous tinge.

"I thought you only lived here a week or two out of the month," I said.

"Oh, I do. But I need clothing."

Hyperion nodded mutely.

"You were friends of Tommy's?" she asked.

Hyperion blinked. "What? Oh. Right. Tom. No. We were business acquaintances."

On the drive here, we'd prepared a simple yet hopefully believable story on how we'd met. I opened my mouth to deliver the tale.

"That's nice," she said. "He had so many friends, especially from his days as a musician."

"We just wanted to give you our condolences." I grimaced. Her husband had been horribly murdered. Lying to her made me a terrible person. "We're so sorry," I said, with feeling.

"You heard then?" she asked.

"Ah..." Wasn't that obvious? I'd just said *condolences.*

"I've been, like, in shock all day."

"All day?" Hyperion asked and looked to me.

I shook my head, puzzled. Her husband had been discovered dead three days ago, on Friday.

"I'd no idea he was having an affair," she said. "It's so nice of you to come and comfort me."

I blinked. If I'd found out my dead husband had been having an affair, I'd be throwing things right now. "You're... welcome?"

"I'm sure she's the one who killed him." Vanella pushed another button. The first section of wall retreated. A second glided outward, displaying racks of high-heeled shoes.

"She who?" Hyperion asked.

"Pepper, of course. I could, like, kill her," she said serenely. The wall retracted.

"You seem very calm," I said.

"It's the Valium. And the Botox. And the Chardonnay." She pressed a button, and a section of wall unfolded itself, displaying more shoes.

"How did you find out about the affair?" I asked.

"They were on video, sneaking out to the pool house together. I never watch those videos, but last week, something told me I should. It was like a voice in my head. A psychic intuition."

Last week? She'd said she'd been in shock all day. Was this the valium and booze talking?

"Hold on," Hyperion said. "There are security videos?"

"Of course."

"Did you show the video of Pepper and your husband to the police?" I asked her.

"I couldn't. I accidentally deleted it. Like I said, technology. The detective wasn't happy, but it was *my* video."

I'll bet Chase wasn't happy. "So you found out a week ago?"

She nodded.

"And you've been in shock all *day*," I clarified.

"I didn't understand what I was seeing at first. Now I do."

"Why now?" Hyperion asked.

"It just hit me. Like a... a..."

"Gory perversion?" Hyperion asked. "Teeming fire? Bellowing anomaly?"

She snapped her fingers. "Thunder bolt."

"Did the security system catch anyone coming to the house the night your husband, er, died?" I asked.

Her lips compressed. "No, it was off that night."

"Why was it turned off?" I asked.

She pinked. "Because I was home. I didn't mean to be home. I wasn't supposed to be home. But I got bored at the party, and came home early, and there was no sense running the video camera when we were both home. It's for security."

Closet sections folded and unfolded like something out of a sci-fi movie. Vanella stomped her foot. "Where *is* that dress?"

"But you said you had video of your husband and Pepper at the pool house," I said. "He was home then."

"Walking into the pool house," she corrected. "*I* wasn't home that night. And that's why I couldn't have killed him."

"Because you weren't home?" I asked, confused. "But that wasn't the night he was killed."

"Because we had an infidelity clause in our pre-nup," she said. "If I wanted to get rid of him, like, all I had to do was divorce him."

Except she'd deleted the video of Pepper and her husband. She had no proof of infidelity.

The phone in Hyperion's blazer pocket buzzed. He checked the screen. "Would you excuse me for a moment?"

"Whatever." Vanella picked up a pair of shoes, discarded them, and grabbed another, identical pair.

Hyperion hurried from the room.

"Are those the same shoes?" I rose and walked closer.

"When I see something I like, I get at least a dozen pairs. The others are in our Paris apartment." She glided away and fiddled with the remote. More walls swung forward and back.

I stared, fascinated by the shoes. Even I, who never spent money on expensive shoes or purses, knew what red soles meant. She must have had a hundred-thousand dollars in shoes in this closet alone. How much money had her husband made on this house?

"So, what did you and Tom do, aside from renting the house?" I asked.

"Do?"

I picked up a shoe and squinted at the label. It looked legit. "You know. For work."

A wall quietly whirred behind me.

"Work?" she asked. "I thought you were, like, business associates?"

Rats. She wasn't as dimwitted as she looked. "I always got the feeling there was more to Tom than met the—"

Something nudged me from behind. I turned. A closet wall hummed toward me. I stepped left to avoid it and another wall blocked me, bumped my shoulder. My chest tightened. "Vanella?"

"Darn it," she said, hidden behind the folding walls. "It's not working."

Walls accordioned in on me like an Escher drawing, forcing me backward.

"Vanella?" my voice rose, panicky. Walls of shoes and dresses squeezed me closer. I'd be crushed. I leapt into a rack of gently swaying dresses, assuming I'd come out the other side, and I crashed into a wall. "Hyperio—"

Everything went black.

CHAPTER 9

The closet was dark and silent, the only sound my own quick breathing. So I was alive, which was nice.

I raised my fist, and my elbow slammed into something hard. I winced, reaching to rub my elbow, and bashed my knuckles on another wall.

Sweat stung my eye. I was being smothered by folds of fabric. My pulse thrashed in my ears. My breathing grew labored. I'm not technically claustrophobic, but my body didn't seem to know that.

I kicked a wall. Fabric whispered past me, hangers rattling. "Vanella! Hyperion!"

"Abigail?" Vanella's voice was muffled. "Where are you?"

"I'm in your closet."

"What are you doing in there?"

"Just get me out!"

Silence fell.

Something whirred. My prison didn't open.

"Vanella?" I shouted.

No one responded. Had she left me? How long would the oxygen last? The air felt close, stuffy.

"Hyperion?" I shouted. "Hyperion, I'm trapped." My breath stilled. Or had this been a trap all along? Could Vanella really have been that ignorant about how her closet worked? Granted, it was a complicated closet.

But why wasn't she responding?

I dizzied, my knees shaking. She'd separated Hyperion and I. While I was locked in here, out of the way, she could attack Hyperion.

I banged on a wall with my elbow. "Hyperion! Look out. It's a trap. I'm trapped. Don't trust Vanella. Don't—"

The floor beneath me jerked. I staggered and grabbed a handful of fabric for balance. Hangers tore free, and I fell on my butt. My section of the closet glided forward, and I blinked in the glare of the chandelier.

Brik peered down at me.

I stared up at him. Heat washed from my chest to the top of my skull.

"Huh," he said. "I never figured you'd be the partner coming out of the closet."

"Very funny," I snarled, and rolled onto the carpeted floor. "Where's Vanella?"

"In her bedroom. She was too scared to come back in here."

Good. Maybe my time in jail had given me a tougher presence. I staggered to my feet. "Of me?"

"Of the closet."

"What are you doing here?"

"Vanella hired me to knock down her pool house." He plucked a filmy scarf off my shoulder.

"What? Why?" And how suspicious was new construction after a murder?

He shrugged, his muscles bulging. "Didn't ask."

Of course he hadn't. And why hire Brik for a simple tear down? How well did he know Vanella? I scowled. "What is it with you and party houses?"

Brik's face reddened. "What's that supposed to mean?"

Dammit. I shouldn't have said that. "Nothing. Never mind. I'm still recovering from being attacked by a closet." Or by Vanella.

A sheen of sweat glistened on his brow. He rubbed the back of his muscular neck. "Look, I don't have a party house. I'm not anything like Henderson was."

"How can you—?" I snapped my mouth shut. I'd been about to ask how he could think that, much less say it. How could anyone have parties four or five times a week and *not* expect his neighbors to be furious? Even without helicopters.

But Brik was looking a little sick. And though I didn't understand why, I felt a sudden surge of sympathy for him. Now wasn't the time to bust his chops about the parties.

"You're right," I said. "You're not."

His shoulders dropped, obvious relief relaxing the lines of his face.

Oh, heck no. What was I doing? Now was my opportunity to shut down his parties once and for all, and I was backing off?

But there was something weird about his reaction... "Why *do* you have so many parties?" I asked.

His gaze slid sideways, avoiding mine. "Oh, you know. They're good for networking. And I like people."

Brik didn't network. A shock of realization chilled my gut. He was lying. But why lie about something so trivial?

Unless it wasn't trivial.

"Abigail, you won't believe—" Hyperion strode into the closet and stopped short. "Why is there an evening gown stuck to your heel?"

"Another one?" I shook the garment free. "Because that closet tried to kill me. If I hadn't jumped into the evening gown section, I could have been crushed."

Brik shook his head. "That's unlikely. There are safety features. If something's blocking a sensor, the closet won't close."

"It closed on me."

"Maybe you shouldn't have jumped inside it," my neighbor said. "From the inside, you weren't blocking anything."

I scowled. "Where's Vanella?"

"Curled in a fetal position on her bed," Hyperion said.

"Oh, brother." I took a step, stumbled over a tumble of sequined fabric, and kicked the dress wrapped around my ankle free. It arced into the air and landed on the marble table. I stalked into the bedroom. "Vanella..."

She bolted upright on the four-poster bed. Tears streaked her face, smearing her makeup. "Are you all right?"

"I'm fine," I grumbled. It's hard to yell at someone who's been crying, even though I really wanted to.

"Thank God." She clawed her blond hair from her face. "I kept, like, pushing buttons and none of them worked. I went for help, but I couldn't find Hyperion, and then Brik came, and—"

"It's fine," I said.

"You need a simpler closet," Hyperion said.

"I really do," she said fervently.

"Vanella!" A woman's voice echoed through the house.

Vanella's shoulders hunched.

"Is that Pepper?" Hyperion asked. He turned to me. "Abigail, you won't believe—"

Pepper stormed into the bedroom, blond hair flying. She pointed at the woman on the bed. "You killed him."

Vanella straightened, doe-eyes blinking rapidly. "What? I—I didn't."

"Did too."

"No." Vanella looked around wildly. "I didn't. Pepper, what are—?"

"Liar!" Pepper lunged toward the bed and took a wide and

incompetent swing at Vanella.

Vanella made a squeaking noise. She scampered off the bed and ran behind me. "If anyone killed him..." Her voice grew louder. "If anyone killed him you did. You were sleeping with him in the pool house."

I stretched out my hands. "Hold on, let's calm—"

Pepper plowed into me.

I staggered backward to escape. Something caught the back of my heel. I crashed into an end table with an exotic flower arrangement and sat hard on the carpet. Water dowsed my head.

Hyperion's eyes bulged. He lunged toward me. "Abigail, look—"

A crash. Pain jolted through my skull, and I swayed. "Ow." I pitched sideways and clutched my head, clenched my jaw. *OW.* That hurt.

"You and Tommy in that pool house," Vanella said.

"You're one to talk," Pepper spat. "You're a murderess."

"I'm tearing it down," Vanella said. "I can't stand to look at it."

Brik cleared his throat. "Um, ladies..."

Someone touched my shoulder, and I opened my eyes.

"Still conscious?" Hyperion asked.

"Ow."

"You were hit by a vase."

"A Ming vase," Vanella said. "And you broke it."

"Cheer up," Hyperion said. "It's got to be the most expensive thing you've ever broken with your head."

My head throbbed. "*I* didn't break it." I sat up. "It fell on me."

"Well," my partner said, "technically—"

I growled low in my throat, and Hyperion scooted away from me.

The air conditioning kicked in. I shivered, wet hair plastered to my head.

"I'll help you clean up." Brik extended a hand and helped me to my feet. "Hyperion, why don't you deal with..." He looked around. Pepper had vanished. "Help Vanella."

Brik led me, wobbling, into a vast bathroom and handed me a towel. Even in my dazed state, I could tell this was the best towel that had ever touched my skin. I sighed and rested my head on it.

"No falling asleep. You're not concussed, are you?" Brik grabbed my head and gently parted my hair.

I jerked away. "Stop it."

"I need to see how bad a lump you got."

Beneath us, the doorbell gonged through the house.

"I'm not concussed," I said. "The vase didn't fall that far."

"Far enough to break. How much do Ming vases go for, do you think?"

"I don't care, because I'm not paying for it."

"You're really cranky when you get hit with vases."

"I'm cranky because none of this makes sense," I hissed. "Vanella's acting all Zen about her husband's murder, but she wants to tear down the pool house where he was having an affair. It doesn't track."

"I'm sure she's going through a lot."

"What about Pepper? She just made herself a suspect in front of the three of us. And Pepper didn't strike me as a completely stupid woman. Why'd she do it?"

"Because she's stressed?"

"And why the hell did Vanella run behind me, the smallest person in the room, to stand behind to block an attack? And why did I jump away? Pepper weighs approximately ninety pounds." She hadn't pushed me into the table with the vase. I'd barely felt her. Was I responsible for a Ming vase? Because I didn't think my insurance would cover it.

Brik lowered his head toward mine. "I don't think Vanella's the sharpest knife in the drawer," he said quietly.

Face pale, Hyperion burst through the open doorway. "Out of the frying pan and into the fire. We need to go."

Reluctantly, I set the luxury towel on the marble counter. "What? Why?"

"Tony Chase is here."

I felt the blood drain from my face. "Chase...? Run."

CHAPTER 10

It wasn't hard losing Detective Chase in the mansion, because the place was a maze. We raced around corners and down wide hallways.

Hyperion yanked open a door. "This way!"

I followed him down a narrow staircase leading to a cramped foyer. Hyperion and I stumbled out a back door and into a formal garden.

We sidled around the corner of the chateau.

"*That* was the servant's entrance," I said.

Hyperion stepped backward, onto my foot.

"You don't need to get shirty about it," I said.

He spun and clapped a hand across my mouth. "He brought more cops," he hissed.

"Mrph?"

"Look."

Hyperion released me, and I peeked around a potted topiary. A black and white police car was parked beside Tony's Jeep Commander. A uniformed officer leaned against the car and studied his cell phone.

Anxiety spiraled in my gut. How were we going to get out of here? In spite of what I'd said about public attorneys, I didn't want to go to jail again. I couldn't handle another lecture on composting.

"Aren't you glad now we parked at Archer's?" my partner whispered. "Tony would have recognized your car in the driveway." He paused. "How *are* we going to get around that guy?"

I rubbed the back of my neck. "We're not," I said. "We'll just have to wait until they all leave."

"Wait? That's not a plan."

"Would you rather chance get arrested again?"

"I'd rather get out of here." He sighed. "Why don't you? But what should I expect from someone who let herself be locked in a closet and beaten by a couple of bottled blondes?"

"That's not fair."

"You just took it all like a lump on a log."

"They caught me by surprise," I said.

"Excuses, excuses."

"Why are you so hot to get out of here? Have you got somewhere to be?"

He stuck his nose in the air. "Just because I have a social life and you don't, is no reason to get snippy. Today's our day off."

In other words, he had a date. "Is your social life worth getting arrested over?"

"Yes. Yes it is." Hyperion pointed at the cop, still staring at his phone. "Look, he's not even paying attention."

I shivered in my damp shirt. "I think he'll notice if we stroll down the driveway."

"We can use Archer's gate."

That wasn't a half-bad idea. I scanned the rolling hill, and the thicket of trees at its crest, where I thought the gate might be. "We'd have to cross the topiary garden. If we stay off its gravel paths, he might not notice us."

"That's good enough for me." Hyperion darted onto a strip of lawn and ducked behind the topiary penguin.

The cop didn't look up.

Hyperion motioned for me.

I rolled my shoulders and took a breath. Bent nearly double, I skittered across the lawn and joined Hyperion.

"See," he whispered. "It's easy."

I gazed uneasily at a long stretch of topiaries impossible to hide behind—a giraffe, a flamingo, a turtle. "It's a long way to that giant cone," I said in a low voice, motioning toward the bush.

"I'm telling you, he's too absorbed in his phone to even notice. Let's go." Hyperion raced away, past the giraffe. He looked over his shoulder, toward the cop, and didn't notice the strip of gravel path. He bolted across it, the gray stones grinding loudly beneath his shoes.

The cop straightened off the car and whirled.

Hyperion dove for the turtle.

I closed my eyes. When I didn't hear any shouts, I opened one.

Hyperion still crouched behind the turtle topiary.

Footsteps crunched on gravel. The cop. He was looking for us. The footsteps grew louder. The cop was coming toward *me*.

The only place to hide was back behind the house again, and I had no idea which way the cop was looking. I couldn't take the chance of running.

The footsteps stopped on the other side of the penguin.

I swallowed. *Go away.* But magical thinking had never worked for me.

There was another crunch, and then a softer footstep. The policeman had stepped onto the lawn.

I bit back a curse. He'd round the penguin's fluffy green butt any second and see me. I edged around the penguin, trying to keep it between me and the cop.

Tiptoeing past a wing, I stopped, teetering on the edge of a gravel path. If I stepped onto the gravel, he'd hear me.

I swayed, dizzy. I was trapped.

I looked toward the turtle and felt the blood drain from my face.

Hyperion was gone. I pressed a hand to my mouth and tried not to be sick.

A familiar dark head popped from behind a cone-shaped bush. Hyperion made a frantic motion, as if waving me back. But that direction would send me into the arms of the cop.

Hyperion made a hair-on-fire gesture. What was *that* supposed to mean?

I stooped, grabbed a piece of gravel, and pitched it toward the cars. It pinged off the Jeep's fender, and I winced. Chase would jail me for sure if I scratched his ride.

But the trick worked. The cop strode toward the cars.

I ran for it. Past the giraffe. Past the flamingo and the turtle.

Hyperion loped ahead of me, chugging up the hill.

I kept going, not daring to look back, until I plunged into the line of flowering plants and eucalyptus trees.

Hyperion clung to Archer's gate, panting. I did a double take. Not panting, *laughing.*

"Whoop! Another successful madcap adventure," he said.

I pressed my hand to the stitch in my side and nodded toward the gate. "Let's get out of here."

"Your wish is my command." He tugged on the gate.

It rattled and didn't budge.

Hands clammy, I glanced over my shoulder. Had the cop heard the noise?

Hyperion rolled his eyes. "Duh. It's a push, not a pull." He gave the handle a shove.

Something metallic clanked, and I flinched.

"Are you kidding me?" he whispered. "Archer locked it?"

"Is someone there?" a masculine voice called from behind us.

Adrenaline spiked through my veins. "The heck with this." I took three steps back and took a running jump at the gate. I grasped the top, scrambled over the clattering gate, and fell awkwardly to the damp ground.

"Hurry," Hyperion whispered.

I unbolted the gate, and Hyperion lunged through. We shut and locked it behind us. Giggling hysterically, we raced up the slope of Archer's manicured lawn.

"You should have seen your face when you were stuck behind that penguin," Hyperion said.

"It's been a day. Getting eaten by a closet, attacked by a pair of crazed socialites, running from the cops—"

"And don't forget breaking a priceless vase."

"I didn't break it," I huffed testily. "It fell on me."

We circled the swimming pool and made our way around Archer's low house to the front door. Hyperion rang the bell.

Archer opened the door, looked us up and down, and raised one hand in a "stop" gesture. "Your shoes are filthy. I thought you were interviewing Vanella, not doing her gardening."

I toed off my tennis shoes. "We were trying not to get arrested again."

Hyperion leaned against a wall and pulled off a loafer.

"Well, you really should make an appointment next time instead of just dropping in like this. It's only professional if you're going to be private consultants."

"You're absolutely right," Hyperion said. "Abigail, make a note of it."

I studied the elderly man. He was usually friendly, but something had soured his mood.

"Did you learn anything useful?" he asked.

"Pepper stopped by and accused Vanella of murdering her husband," I said. "Then Vanella accused Pepper."

"It turned into a bodacious battle of the blondes, a real-live cat fight," Hyperion said. "And you should have seen it when they assaulted Abigail. *Meow.*"

"Pepper always was a hothead," the older man said. "But I'm not sure how that helps me."

"Me neither," I said, "but the whole thing seemed kind of... performative." Or had I been imagining that? Or had I been too rattled by near-death-by-closet to be seeing things clearly? I rubbed the top of my head, where the vase had landed. My hair was still damp.

"Everything's performative now," Archer said. "And I blame social media. It's so hard to find anyone *real.* Or any real reporting," he muttered. "Sometimes I wonder if I brought this on myself."

"The murder?" I asked.

"All of it," the older man said gloomily. "I used to do real reporting. Double page spreads! Now I just do what my corporate masters tell me to."

"Can't you suggest changes?" Hyperion asked.

"I tried, but it was an uphill battle. And then I realized it was a battle I was doomed to lose."

Hyperion patted him on the shoulder. "There's always a way forward. Sometimes it's just not obvious."

"When's the next HOA meeting?" I asked.

"Wednesday."

"Can you get us in?"

He smiled. "I knew you were the right professionals for the job. And yes, I can. It will be easy, since I'm not actually welcome." He brushed a speck of lint from his lapel. "You'll be my proxy. I'm still allowed that."

"Why aren't you welcome?" I asked, insides knotting.

"For some reason, I was blamed for everything that... Well, you heard about the rubber snakes incident."

"And that wasn't you?" Hyperion asked.

Archer folded her arms. "I believe in the power of the pen. My writing campaign was much more effective than any super glue in the gate locks."

"Who exactly did that?" I asked.

He raised his white brows. "I don't know. I assume it was Pepper or Cosmo. Those two are thick as thieves. Though I suppose it could have been any other number of neighbors who snapped."

"But you were blamed," I said.

"As I said, I was using the power of the pen. My name was out in front." He sighed. "And I did enjoy my little bonfires. Mind you, they weren't any good for s'mores, because of all the burning plastic. But they were quite cheerful."

"Do you know anything about a wedding expo planner named Maylene Soon?" Hyperion asked.

Archer's nose wrinkled. "I'm a society reporter. I do not report on wedding expos. I'd never do anything so tacky."

"According to the local paper," I said, "she was the one who found the body. Well, it said a wedding manager found the body, and—"

"Wedding manager?" Archer adjusted his cravat. "What on earth is that? It's shoddy reporting, is what it is. The fourth estate is an utter disaster. Take it from a reporter, don't believe a word you read, young lady."

"But Maylene did confirm she was the one who found him," I said.

"And then someone tried to kill us with a flaming dumpster," Hyperion said. "So we must be on the right track."

Archer raised a brow. "Flaming dumpsters? Cat fights? The Hendersons have no sense of style."

"In fairness, I think we have to blame their killer for the dumpster," Hyperion said'

Archer sniffed. "Like attracts like, as they say in the New Age game. And speaking of New Age—"

"Please don't," I said.

Hyperion sighed. "You want another Tarot reading."

"No, I just had one. She also suggested there was an alternate way forward."

Hyperion pressed a hand to his chest. "She who? You've found another Tarot reader? I feel cheated on."

"From me." My mother strolled into the foyer, a gauzy caftan billowing around her slender form. She stopped short and stared. "Good goddess, what happened to you?"

"Abigail tried to break up a fight," Hyperion said.

"Fighting? That's a very low vibration action, Abigail. You need to learn not to be the participant. Be the observer. Or at least try a juice cleanse."

"Only if mimosas count." I scowled. "And I was trying to break up the fight."

"The action seemed pretty high vibe to me," Hyperion said. "Until the vase landed on her head."

"A vase?" Archer motioned toward my top. "Is that why you've got this wet t-shirt look going?"

"Wet...?" I looked down. Warmth crept across my cheeks. The white parts of my t-shirt had gone a little sheer. Fortunately, the blue horizontal stripes covered the critical bits.

I forced a smile and turned to my mother. "What are you doing here?"

"Helping with the investigation, of course."

"Helping..." I grabbed my muddy shoes and headed for the door. "Thanks for letting us use your driveway, Archer. It turned out to be a real lifesaver. We'll keep you posted."

"Ta." One shoe'd, Hyperion hobbled after me.

"Oh, wait," my mother said. "I need a ride."

Fuming, I got into my Mazda. My mother fluttered past Hyperion and beat him to the front passenger seat. She smiled sweetly and slithered inside.

Hyperion smiled in a pained sort of way and wedged himself into the backseat.

My mother shook her head. "No one will believe you're successful driving around in a car like this. And if no one believes it, *you* won't believe it either. So you can't possibly *be* successful. It's a law of universal attraction."

"A car is transportation," I said, "not a fashion statement."

"True, but it also lets the universe know who you see yourself as. Who *do* you see yourself as, Abigail?"

My jaw hardened. I started the car and we glided down the driveway. "What are you doing?"

"Spending time with my daughter."

My hands clenched on the wheel. "I meant that business of telling Archer you were helping with the investigation."

"But I *am* helping."

"No, you're not," I said.

"But I have to," she said. "The challenge for spiritual people like myself, is we can become so air focused—"

"Air?" I asked.

"In their heads," Hyperion explained.

She twisted in her seat. "Exactly. In the realm of the spirits."

"Right," I said.

"We can become so air focused," she continued, "that we lose our grounding in the mundane world. I can't imagine anything more grounding than murder."

"So this is just a new spiritual quest," I said.

"In a manner of speaking."

I clamped my jaws shut.

"I accept you as you are," she continued, "but you didn't used to be so closed-minded."

"You mean, when I was two? Because we haven't seen each other a lot since then."

"And whose fault is that?"

Amazed, I stared at her, realized the car was still moving forward, and jerked my gaze back to the winding road. "You abandoned me at an airport."

She shook her head. "We didn't abandon you."

"You and my father left me in the departures lounge and took off for India."

"It was Sri Lanka, and we called your grandparents to get you. We knew they'd take care of you while we were away."

My chest tightened. "You were away for years. You told me I was going with you, you—" Heat blurred my vision. I let my foot off the gas and took deep breaths. I couldn't drive and have this conversation. Besides, it was pointless.

In the back seat, Hyperion cleared his throat. "So, how's Dad? Abigail's dad, I mean."

"We're following our own journeys now," she said serenely.

A marriage between two narcissists had been doomed from the start. "Where can I drop you?"

"The tearoom," Hyperion said.

"Wherever you're going is fine with me," my mother said. "I blow with the wind."

Pain shot through my jaw, and I forced my muscles to loosen. How low vibration, I wondered, was matricide?

CHAPTER 11

I added a reservation to the appointment book and gazed around the tearoom. Tarot readers sat across from customers, turning cards on the tables. Women clinked teacups against saucers and murmured secrets in low voices. We'd seemed to have reached peak gentility and elegance.

I must have overlooked something.

The princess phone rang on the hostess stand. I answered warily. "Beanblossom's Tea and Tarot, how can I help you?"

"I'm trying to reach Abigail Beanblossom?" a man asked.

I fiddled with my pen. "Speaking."

"This is Cosmo. Cosmo Terzian. Archer's neighbor?"

I straightened. "Oh, hi. Has something happened?"

"Aside from Henderson's murder you mean? No. I just wanted to check in and see how your, er, investigation was going."

Archer was our client, not Cosmo. Sure, he'd told Cosmo and Pepper we were investigating, but they were suspects too. "It's moving forward," I said, keeping it vague.

"Have you learned anything useful?"

"Have you got anything useful to tell us?"

Hyperion strode into the tearoom. "I have wheels!" He raised his clenched fists in a triumphant gesture.

The tearoom applauded. An elderly lady with blue-tinted hair whooped. So much for peak gentility. Had Hyperion been telling the entire tearoom about the dumpster attack?

What was I thinking? Of *course* he had.

"...like some Texan Colombo," Cosmo was saying.

"Sorry, what?" I asked.

"He said the mayor's on his back," Cosmo said. "Apparently, this is a high-profile case."

"That surprises me," I said. "Tom Henderson wasn't exactly a fixture in San Borromeo society. He spent most of his time out of town."

A woman shrieked.

I whirled.

Tarot cards shot into the air and fluttered to the floor. A redheaded customer pressed one hand to her chest and laughed. "I told you I couldn't shuffle."

Her Tarot reader, Sierra, shook her head and bent to pick up the cards.

"...what the detective said." Cosmo coughed. "It would set my mind at ease if I knew this case was in good hands."

I untangled myself from the phone cord. "Detective Chase is a diligent and dedicated officer of the law."

"I meant you and your partner," he said. "Archer raves about you both."

"That's generous of him."

Hyperion bent to speak to the old lady with blue-tinted hair.

She banged her fist on the table, rattling the teacups. "Outrageous."

"I *know*," Hyperion said.

"Never trust a clean garage," the elderly woman said loudly. "Is that silk?"

"...worried," Cosmo finished.

"That's only natural," I said. "Absolutely." What were we talking about?

There was a long silence.

"Excuse me?" Cosmo asked.

"Sorry, I must have misheard you. I thought you said you were worried, and I said that's only natural. Murder investigations are stressful. You don't know who to trust. You feel like everyone's looking at you..."

Another silence stretched on.

"Obviously, I should stop talking," I said. "The tearoom's a madhouse." And that was *not* the approved tearoom vibe. "Why don't we talk later? What's your number? I'll call you back, and we can have a more private chat."

He recited his phone number, and I noted it in the margins of the reservation book. "We'll talk soon."

I hung up and turned to glare at Hyperion. Did he always have to whip up chaos?

But the customers were smiling and laughing. The blue-haired woman fingered the cuff of his blue silk shirt. The Tarot readings went on.

I blew out my breath. Hyperion could set the tearoom on fire, and everyone would still love him. He was just that kind of guy.

I helped the waitresses bus tables. While they set up for the next seating, I knocked on Hyperion's office door. Twinkle lights blinked erratically around its frame.

He yanked open the door. "Thank God." Hyperion grabbed my elbow and hauled me inside.

"New shirt?" I asked.

"Retail therapy. You would not believe what that garage charged me. And I won't have my Jeep back for two weeks. *Two weeks.*"

"That's the pits. But I thought you said you had wheels."

Bastet yawned at me from Hyperion's makeshift altar, decorated with driftwood, crystals, and candles.

"A rental," he said. "I think my insurance will pay for it. It's not my fault a dumpster lost control and smashed my Jeep. I even have a police report and a mention in the local paper."

"It was in the paper?"

"Crime blotter." He lifted his wallet from his rear pocket and pulled out a clipping.

Monday, August 8.

At 3:40 p.m. police were called to the scene of a dumpster fire and car crash. The car owner stated the dumpster had rolled down the hill and struck his parked car. Fire extinguished.

"You're famous," I said.

"I only kept it for investigative purposes." He looked around and shut the door. "I have a crime board." He strode to a wall, where a square of gauzy fabric had been thumbtacked. He yanked it free, and there was a tearing sound.

I winced.

"Ta dah. Crime board." He pinned the clipping to the wall, beside a blurry photo of Maylene Soon. "I need a better printer."

I studied the other photos—Vanella Henderson, Beatrice Carlson, Pepper Schripsema, and Cosmo Terzian.

I tapped Cosmo's photo. "He just called me."

"Please tell me no one else has died."

"Not that I know of. I think he just wanted to know how our investigation was going."

"You didn't tell him, did you?"

"What kind of schmuck do you take me for? Don't answer that."

Hyperion pointed to index cards beneath each photo. "I figured we could fill these cards with means, motive and opportunity. Where were they at the time of the crime? What was their motive? And could they have physically thrown Tom Henderson over his balcony?" He checked his watch. "But not now. I've got an online appointment."

Hyperion bustled me out of the office.

"But—"

"We'll talk later," he said and slammed the door in my face.

"Okay..."

The bell over the front door jingled, customers for our next seating arriving. I strode down the hall toward the seating area.

"Abigail's my daughter." My mother's voice rang through the building.

I stopped short and hung my head. It was going to be a long afternoon.

Since my mother didn't have a reservation and the tables were full, she planted herself at the counter. I guess she'd gotten bored at my grandfather's house. My mother sat at the counter for the rest of the afternoon demanding scones, Tarot readings, and free tea refills, while I ran my butt off serving customers.

The sky dimmed outside. We closed the tearoom. Wait staff set chairs on top of the tables so we could clean the floors.

Teapot clutched to my chest like a shield, I approached the white stone counter.

I swallowed. "Hi. We're closing."

"Oh, that's all right," my mother said. "I thought I'd catch a ride home with you. Unless you were planning on doing anything interesting tonight?"

I pressed a hand to my apron. I'd called it again. She was bored.

"Have you considered meditating at the beach?" I asked.

"I did that this morning."

"There's a nice metaphysical store a few blocks away. I think it's open until eight."

"I bought a yoga chakra CD there yesterday."

I gave up. "Okay, I've got to clean the tearoom."

"As above, so below. We cleanse the physical space and in so doing, cleanse our souls."

"Does that mean you want to help?" I asked.

"I wouldn't dream of interfering in your spiritual cleansing." She leaned sideways and motioned toward one of the waitresses, sweeping the floor. "Oh, no, dear. You want to sweep widdershins. No, no, widdershins means counterclockwise." She straightened and shook her head, frowning. "You'd think she'd know the proper direction for banishing."

Why would she? "I have to go." I scurried to the kitchen and gave it the cleaning of its life. I even pulled out the refrigerator and scrubbed the linoleum beneath.

Hyperion came to lounge in the kitchen doorway. "You can't avoid her forever, you know."

Bastet meowed at his feet.

"I can try."

My partner arched a brow.

"And I really did need to clean beneath the fridge."

"Your staff left an hour ago," he said.

"Not an hour." I checked my watch. *Yikes.* "Oh." I looked around the sparkling kitchen. "I guess I'm done then."

"I'll walk you and your mother to your car. Consider it moral support."

I sighed. "You don't have to."

"Good. I've got a date." He sped from the kitchen. The tabby shot me a questioning glance and followed.

Demoralized, I collected my bag. And then I collected my mother.

We meandered into the dusky parking lot, my mother spouting New Age philosophies.

Teeth grinding, I wound through the still crowded lot toward the wine bar. I'd had to park a distance away—the lot had been packed even in the morning. But that's life in a beach town on a sunny summer day.

"Perhaps the two of us have past life issues to work out," she was saying. "That must have been what brought me back."

"You didn't just run out of money?"

"Oh, money. What do I care about money? It's only an exchange of energy."

"But you can use it for buying things like food and plane tickets."

"Don't come from a perspective of lack, Abigail." She pointed. "Isn't that your partner? What is he doing?"

I turned to follow her gesture.

Hyperion staggered from behind a parked Hummer. He did an awkward spin and collapsed on the pavement.

"Hyperion?" Muscles tight, I raced to him and knelt. "Are you okay?"

He raised his head and blinked. "Is he gone?"

"Who?" Frantic, I looked around. "What happened?"

He groaned. "I was mugged."

"What?" Since when did we have muggers in San Borromeo?

"It was probably that person who's been watching your tearoom all day," my mother said.

My breath caught. "Someone was watching the tearoom?"

"From across the street."

"What did he look like?" I rapped out.

She studied her nails. "Oh, I couldn't say if it was a *he*."

"It was a woman then?" I said.

"I couldn't say that either. After all, gender is only a social construct."

"But it's helpful for identifying criminals," I snarled.

"Ladies?" Hyperion said weakly. "Is this really the time?"

"Oh," I said. "Sorry. Are you bleeding? Where are you hurt?"

He sat up and rubbed the back of his head, checked his palm. "No blood. I don't think I'm concussed—just temporarily stunned and ashamed. I didn't even hear the guy until it was too late."

"Let me see." I edged behind him and gasped. The back of his shirt had been sliced from hip to shoulder. I dizzied. Someone had tried to kill my partner.

"What?" he yelped. "What is it? What's wrong?"

"Nothing." I gingerly ran my hand along his thick, black hair. "I don't feel a lump."

"Then why did you gasp?" he asked.

"I didn't gasp."

"You definitely gasped," my mother said.

"Your shirt's... torn." I didn't want to tell him the truth in front of my mother. Or maybe I just didn't want to admit the truth.

"No! I just bought this." Hyperion twisted, tugging on his shirt, and there was another ripping sound. "Is it fixable?"

"Um, no," I said.

Hyperion's fist clenched. "The fecund, dreadful slug."

At least if my partner could remember his Lovecraft, he couldn't be badly hurt. "What happened?"

"I was at my car, and I sensed a sinewy convolution behind me."

Twin lines formed between my mother's brows. "Sinewy convolution?"

"I started to turn," Hyperion said, "and he hit me on the head."

That made sense. Hyperion was a pretty good martial artist. The only way he would have been caught out is if the other guy had snuck up behind him.

"I must have fallen against something sharp if my shirt was torn," he said. "Are you sure I'm not bleeding?" He twisted.

"It wasn't exactly torn," I said.

"You said it was torn," he said.

I bit my bottom lip. "It looks like it was slashed."

"Slashed?" His voice rose. "With a knife? I didn't see a knife."

"What exactly did you see?" I asked.

"There was a sort of moldering—"

"No more Lovecraft," I warned.

"A shadow." Hyperion motioned vaguely.

"Was it tall?" I asked. "Short? Thin?"

"I don't know," he groused. "I only saw it out of the corner of my eye."

A Volvo cruised down the aisle and slowed as it approached. It honked at us and flicked its high beams.

"All right, all right already," Hyperion said irritably.

I helped my partner to his feet, and we moved aside. The Volvo jetted into a nearby parking spot.

We walked through the rows of cars.

"Where's your car?" I asked, and looked around the shadowy lot. Someone had taken the time to stalk Hyperion and had had the cojones to attack him. I didn't like the idea of any of us being alone.

His face spasmed. "It's… that."

He stopped in front of a bulbous red car, if it could be called a car. It looked like the back of an SUV had been spiced together with the front of a compact.

"What *is* that?" my mother asked.

He hung his head. "My rental."

"It's not... that bad," I said.

"Please," he said. "It makes your Mazda look like a classic. But it was the only loaner they had."

"Why is it leaning?" my mother asked.

"What do you mean, leaning?" he said.

I cocked my head. She was right. The car *was* canted at an angle, the right passenger side tilting toward the pavement. I walked around the blocky car. Both wheels on the passenger side were pancaked.

"I think we can guess what your mugger was doing with that knife,"

I said.

Hyperion hobbled to my side of the car. "Are you kidding me? What are the odds the rental agency left me *two* spare tires?"

"What are the odds you have one?" my mother asked.

"For a spiritual person," I said, "you're being very negative."

She lifted her chin. "I don't think that criticism is coming from a pure place."

"Maybe whoever did it left fingerprints?" I said to Hyperion.

"Maybe," he said doubtfully.

"This is bad," I said, and even I could hear the tension in my voice. "This isn't your usual car. The only way someone could have known it was yours was if they'd seen you drive in with it. That means some serious stalking."

Hyperion nodded, then winced and clutched the back of his head. "This has to be connected to Archer's case."

"I told you about the person across the street," my mother said.

"Can you or can't you describe that person?" I asked her.

"Of course I can. They had a very dark aura. Lots of black and red."

"And?" I asked.

"And what? I'd recognize that aura again anywhere."

I groaned and covered my eyes with one hand. *Auras. Unbelievable.* She'd had hours to study whoever it was, and that was all she could come up with?

She touched my shoulder, and I jerked my head up.

"It's all right," my mother said. "We won't have any trouble finding this person. I'm on the case."

A chill touched my core. "You're what?"

Hyperion grew paler.

"Now I understand what brought me back," she said. "To help you." She linked her arm with mine. "We'll solve this crime together."

CHAPTER 12

"Tell me the truth." My mother fixed me with a steely gaze. "When's the last time you've prioritized your personal growth?"

It is, of course, impossible that the top of my scalp lifted off, and steam blew out of my skull and ears. But it sure felt like it had.

Detective Chase and Hyperion spoke out of earshot in the parking lot. The sky above had taken on that misty, deepening blue that comes right before the sun disappears for good.

"Never." I edged closer to the two men. "I've never prioritized personal growth."

"You really should."

"Now's not the time for this conversation."

"Why not?" she asked.

"Because I'm trying to eavesdrop," I hissed.

She rolled her eyes. "That's a very low-level way to vibrate. If you want me to help you, you need to take my advice."

"I am. You were the one who said I should be the observer. I'm observing."

"You know very well that isn't what I meant."

"And you gave up your right to an opinion when you abandoned me in an airport."

"Your obsession with airports seems a little unhealthy."

There was no way to answer that politely, so I walked to the two men.

Detective Chase tipped his cowboy hat. "Ms. Beanblossom. We're not quite done here."

"Then please hurry up before I commit a homicide."

"Your mother?" Hyperion asked. "That didn't take long."

"I've spent at least twenty minutes with her. Maybe thirty. What do you people expect of me?"

"I'm going to take a look at your, er, car," the detective said, and ambled to the rental.

"That bad?" Hyperion asked.

I gulped. "You have no idea. I'm trying to be patient. I know I can't change her. But in the past, accepting her as she was meant not having to deal with her, because she was never around. Now what am I supposed to do? Even if my parents hadn't abandoned me, even if she'd spent the last twenty years lost in an amnesiac haze, I'd still have no idea how to relate to her. And frankly, I'm not sure I want to."

"Maybe you should look at this as a spiritual challenge?" he asked.

I glared. "You know how I feel about spiritual challenges."

"That they're horrible, irrational incongruities? Blasphemous, amorphous monuments to unreason?"

"I can't believe you're quoting that stupid calendar."

"But it kind of fits the mood."

I sighed. "It does. Hyperion, this is serious. You could have been killed."

"And I'm extremely offended by that. I like being alive. It pisses me off that someone tried to take that away from me."

"This was a warning to back off. Maybe we should."

"And I'm not going to." His jaw set.

And he wouldn't back off. Hyperion didn't like being thwarted. His stubborn streak was why he'd gotten as far as he had. It was why we were in business together. It was why we *had* a business.

"Okay," I said. "Then I'm in. Did you learn anything interesting from Detective Chase?"

"Vanella didn't delete that video of Pepper and her husband going into the pool house."

"The police saw it?"

"No," Hyperion said. "All videos automatically delete after seven days, to save space. She just didn't *save* the video so it wouldn't delete."

"She really doesn't get technology."

"But the front gates automatically record the times they're open. No one came in through the auto or pedestrian gates after Tom Henderson got home the night he was killed."

"Huh. He was killed at night?"

"Looks that way," he said. "And something else—that business about the security not being on when Vanella and her husband are home is bull. That system is running practically all the time."

"Practically?"

"It was off during Tom Henderson's murder."

"Convenient." I narrowed my eyes. "Detective Chase was awfully free with his information—" The skin at the base of my neck prickled. I glanced over my shoulder.

My mother wafted toward us. Abruptly, she turned and made for Detective Chase. He knelt beside Hyperion's front passenger tire and jacked up the rental.

Hyperion grasped my elbow. "Why is she going that way?"

"To talk to the detective, I'm guessing." *Better him than me.*

"We have to stop her," he said in a strained voice and launched himself toward the two.

Reluctantly, I followed.

"—no," my mother was saying. "I don't think Hyperion drove off the attacker at all."

"Mrs.— ah, Beanblossom?" Hyperion said.

"Ms. Beanblossom," she corrected. "I didn't take my husband's name. That patriarchal tradition is so retrograde. Speaking of which, Mercury will be going retrograde soon. We're in its shadow now. That's why things are going so badly, and in the short-term, they'll only get worse. So you need to solve this crime quickly."

The detective removed the hubcap. "Fascinating."

She fluttered her eyelashes. "And call me Leaf."

"Hyperion needs to help the detective with his tires," I said. "Let's give them some space."

"How sensitive of you, Abigail. I knew I raised you right."

"You didn't—" I clamped my mouth shut and exhaled through my nose. *Raised me?* "There's a wine bar on the other side of the parking lot. Why don't we take a break there?"

"Lovely idea."

She followed me to the wine bar's rear entrance, and we walked through the covered patio to the main restaurant. Oversized paintings hung from its bare wood walls. Rows of tables filled the space between the open patio door and the black granite bar.

The owner, Barry, caught my eye and hurried toward us. "Hi, Abigail. Where would you like to sit?"

"Is the patio all right?" I asked.

"Sure. Grab any free table."

We returned to the patio and found a table beneath a strand of twinkle lights. I ordered a glass of Zinfandel. My mother ordered iced tea.

"So," she said after Barry had departed. "What's our next step?"

"Our next step for what?"

"Investigating this murder, of course."

"I'm having a drink," I said.

"You shouldn't. Alcohol dulls the third eye."

"I'm counting on it."

She sniffed. "If you dislike the spiritual world so much, I don't understand why you opened a Tarot room."

"Tea and Tarot. And it's a long story."

"I adore stories."

So I told her how Hyperion and I had been conned into renting the same building. I told her how the con artist had been murdered. I told her how we'd both been suspects. Hyperion and I had solved that crime together. Since we'd never gotten our money back, we'd gone in together on the tearoom. "It only made sense," I finished. "He uses the tearoom at night to teach classes, and the Tarot readers are a big draw."

She nodded, her eyes glazed. "I hear you." It was approximately the thirteenth time she'd said that since my story had begun.

I sighed. "You weren't listening, were you?"

She pulled her phone from the pocket of her caftan. "It was a very *long* story. And I find business matters so unspiritual. We're at the end of late-stage capitalism, you know. It can't last."

I gulped down my wine and frantically scanned the patio for another waiter.

Hyperion strode through the opening in the lattice fence. "There you are." He was wearing a fresh blazer to cover his ripped shirt.

"How'd it go?" I asked.

"Tony lent me one of his spares, and I had a spare jacket in the car, so I'm ready to roll. But I thought we should, um..." He glanced sideways at my mother. "Plan next steps?"

In other words, he'd come to rescue me, and my heart flooded with warmth. Even after an assault and battery, he had my back. "Thanks. That's a great idea."

"And I think you should give me a Tarot reading," my mother said. "I've gotten readings from everyone at Beanblossom's but the part-owner."

"Sure." Hyperion pulled a deck from the pocket of his blazer. "Do you have any questions you're interested in?"

She waved a negligent hand. "Just tell me what you see."

"A three-card reading then." He shuffled, dealt three cards face down, then turned the first one over.

Death.

"The Death card rarely means death," Hyperion said.

"It refers to a significant change," my mother said. "An ending. I know. You're reading is spot on so far. Leaving the world of spirit to come to the mundane world of California has been a transition, a letting go."

And sometimes the card really *did* mean death. But I kept my mouth shut. Death couldn't have much to do with my mother's life in the world of spiritual retreats.

Hyperion flipped over the next card.

The Tower.

"Oh." My mother pressed a beringed hand to her chest. "That's not good."

Hyperion paled a little. "A dramatic upset," he said. "Disaster. Or a breakthrough."

Abruptly, my mother laughed. "Of course. Abigail's going to have a spiritual breakthrough and stop being so negative."

"I am?" I asked.

"It's possible…" He drew out the word. "But this reading is about you, not Abigail."

"Of course that's about Abigail. We're together now, what else could it be?" she asked. "What's the next card?"

He turned it over.

The Six of Swords.

"Ah." She pulled out her phone. "Passage from rough water to smooth."

"Leaving a difficult situation," Hyperion agreed. His gaze flicked to me.

"At least things are getting better for you." She patted my hand.

"And you'll be moving on," Hyperion said. He turned to me and mouthed, "*She's leaving.*"

Hallelujah. There was light at the end of the tunnel, if I believed in Tarot. Normally, I didn't, but tonight was an exception.

"So what's our next step?" she asked, gaze affixed to her phone.

"Next step?" I parroted.

"In the investigation," she said.

"I'm not sure there is one." I fiddled with my wine glass. "We don't want to be accused of interfering with an investigation again." She wasn't letting go of this idea of investigating. I had to derail her.

Hyperion tapped his long fingers on the table. "We would have to keep things on the DL. That's downlow."

She nodded. "You mean casual. Like randomly running into a suspect without it really being random."

"That doesn't seem very practical," I said.

My mother stared at her phone. "It seems obvious to me where you should go."

"You could stake out the tearoom tomorrow," I told her, "and see if our watcher returns." She'd probably be there in any case.

"What if he doesn't?" Hyperion asked.

"We should go to the pier," my mother said.

She was probably hoping there'd be a palm reader there tonight. Ignoring her, I turned to Hyperion. "Your attacker tonight has to be one of the people we talked to."

"They were good," he said. "And Maylene had those martial arts trophies."

"But I don't see how Maylene could have pushed that dumpster into your Jeep. She would have had to have snuck past us to get up that hill, and she would have had to have moved really fast."

"All right," Hyperion said. "That leaves Beatrice, Vanella, Pepper and Cosmo."

"Why don't we just go to the pier?" my mother asked.

"Why?" Exasperated, I swiveled in my chair to face her. "Why the pier?"

"Because that's where Pepper is," she said.

"How do you know that?" I asked. "Do you have an intuition?"

She extended her phone toward me. "Her social media account. She's taking pictures at the pier. Her last photo posted two minutes ago."

My jaw hardened. I shouldn't be irritated that my mother had made a good suggestion. But sometimes I'm petty. So sue me.

Hyperion shrugged. "It *is* only a few blocks away."

"Fine." I motioned for the waiter. "We'll go to the pier."

I paid, and the three of us walked down San Borromeo's crooked streets to the ocean. San Borromeo's pier is wide enough to drive two trucks down and still have space for pedestrians. It's split level, with a lower and upper deck, and a fish restaurant at the end. Gramps and Tomas sell horseradish and salsa there during the farmer's markets. In short, it's big, and it's a nice place to wander.

The sun was a slender gleam on the Pacific horizon. People rambled past speaking in low voices. Fishermen leaned against the railings and waited for a bite. I felt the tension in my neck releasing.

"There she is." Hyperion pointed.

Pepper and a tall, slender woman with equally blond hair walked down the pier, their heads close together.

I stopped. "Is that...?"

The woman turned.

"Vanella?" Hyperion finished for me.

Vanella tossed her hair and laughed in bell-like tones.

Quickly, I turned my back on them so they wouldn't recognize me. "They seem pretty friendly for two women who recently tried to claw each other's eyes out."

"*Some* people are forgiving," my mother said.

"I don't think those two are," Hyperion said. "Something's fishy." He wrinkled his nose. "Literally."

Pepper struck a pose against a rail, and Vanella snapped a picture.

"Idea." I pointed to the stairs leading down to the lower level. "Maybe if we get beneath them, we can hear what they're saying."

"Eavesdropping?" my mother asked. "That seems like an invasion of privacy."

I strode toward the stairs. *She* was the one who'd suggested this adventure.

Our footsteps sounded hollowly on the stairs, and I stepped onto the lower platform. It swayed atop the water.

"This way." Hyperion motioned down a narrow wooden walk on the left, and we followed him. He stopped beside a piling. "Here."

I looked up, but all I could see was the bottom of the pier. "Are you sure?"

"I counted pilings. They were standing by this one. Listen."

We craned our heads upward.

"—you sure?" Vanella asked.

Pepper's reply was inaudible beneath the lapping of the waves.

I shook my head. "They're still too far away."

"Get on my shoulders," Hyperion said.

I edged away from him, my heel striking the pier's edge. "Excuse me?"

"You want to get closer," he said, "don't you? Come on, you've done it before."

"You have?" my mother asked.

"Long story," I said.

"Oh," she said, "then don't bother. You're not very good at storytelling."

I braced my hand against a piling for balance. Hyperion squatted, and

I awkwardly clambered onto his shoulders.

"Oof." He straightened. "I told you to knock off those Bundt cakes."

"Stop complaining. This was your idea." I reached up and grasped a metal peg jutting from a beam in the pier's roof.

"—know it's hard," Pepper said. "But you have to stay the course."

"I'm just not sure we're—"

A motorboat put-putted up to the dock. Its captain jumped out and tied it off, leaving the engine running.

"Can you hear anything?" Hyperion shouted.

I shook my head. "Not anymore. I need to get closer." I hauled myself up and rested one foot on his shoulder.

"Are your shoes clean?" he asked.

"Of course not." I stepped the other foot onto his shoulder and pressed my ear to the crack in the dock.

"…no one will believe…" Pepper said. "…weren't involved…"

Hyperion jerked beneath me. My grasp on the peg slipped. Hyperion swayed, dragging me sideways.

And then I was airborne. I pitched into the cold shock of the Pacific.

When people think of California, they think of beaches. What most people don't know is that the Pacific Ocean along the California coast is farking cold.

I came up sputtering and embarrassed and certain a great white shark was circling beneath me.

I looked around, expecting to see Hyperion reaching over the side to haul me out.

He wasn't there.

Shivering, I grasped the edge of the pier and pulled myself closer. "Hyperion?"

No answer.

"Mother? I mean, Leaf?"

Detective Tony Chase peered over the side.

I gasped and pushed away.

He adjusted his cowboy hat. "Looks like you're all wet."

CHAPTER 13

Detective Chase hauled me onto the dock. "You never listen." He wiped his palm on his jeans. "Why don't people ever listen?"

I raked wet hair out of my eyes. "What?"

On the shore, lights twinkled on, the low hills turning purple in the twilight. Pastel buildings along the beach made impressionist blurs on the darkening Pacific.

He pulled a bottle of hand sanitizer from the inside pocket of his blazer and rubbed it onto his hands. "You were interfering in my investigation again, weren't you?"

"No. I was only… I fell in." I hugged myself and tried not to let my teeth chatter.

"Sure you did. Where's that partner of yours?"

"Hyperion? I don't know," I said truthfully. He and my mother had vanished from the pier. I was torn between relief at being rid of her and concern for Hyperion. But the worst she could do was try to convert him to veganism.

"Hear anything good from Pepper and Vanella?" the detective asked.

"No." He'd figured out we'd been spying?

"Withholding evidence is a serious crime."

"Honestly," I blurted, "I didn't hear anything. That stupid motorboat was too loud. But Vanella and Pepper nearly came to blows yesterday, accusing each other of murder. And today they're buddy-buddy. It's weird."

"So you admit you were interfering."

"Did I?" I asked weakly.

"You did."

Shivering, I hunched my shoulders. The evening was balmy, but that water had been *cold.* "Are you going to arrest me?"

He sighed. "Not this time."

"You're not?"

"What can I say? I have moods." He turned and strode away. "And you've got seaweed in your hair."

"I can't believe you ditched me." I glared at Hyperion and braced my fists on my hips.

Sunlight brightened Beanblossom's white tablecloths. Around us, waitresses bustled, Tarot readers made predictions, and teacups rattled in their saucers.

"I can't believe your mother's a part of our investigation. And she's *here*. Did you know she's trying to convert me to veganism? She's being really pushy about it."

"That's..." *Well deserved.* "You ditched me in the *ocean*."

"You can swim."

"There are sharks in the ocean."

"The odds of a shark attack are lower than getting killed by a falling coconut. And Tony was on his way. We were really saving you. If we all got arrested, who would bail you out?"

I folded my arms. "Nice."

"Listen, I know you have abandonment issues," he whispered. "But leaving was your mother's idea." He cut a sideways glance at her, sipping Oolong at a table by the front window.

"And you went along with it."

"I thought she was going to throw *me* in the Pacific when she saw Tony coming down the stairs." He rubbed his wrist. "She's creepy-strong."

"It's all the yoga. Where were you hiding anyway?"

"We hopped into that motorboat. The owner was surprised when we hopped aboard, but he turned out to be decent about it."

"You got his number, didn't you?"

"Duh."

It figures. I got dunked and nearly arrested, and Hyperion got a date. At least I hadn't had to drive my mother, a.k.a. Leaf, back to my grandfather's. I hadn't been able to find them last night.

In fairness, I hadn't been trying very hard.

"Maybe I should have stayed," he said. "I'm sorry, okay? Especially after she dragged me to that palmist."

What the…? There really *had* been a palm reader on the pier? "You got your fortune told while I was being told off by Chase?"

"Forget the palmist. You have to do something about your mother."

"Don't worry, she's not going to be a part of our investigation. I'll figure out some way to divert her."

"The investigation's not the problem."

"Then what?" I asked. "Has she sacrificed another victim on the altar of New Age platitudes?"

"She's been here three hours," he said. "And she's annoying the Tarot readers. Why is Beanblossom's her new hangout?"

"You could always give her a Tarot reading and find out."

"She's your mother. You talk to her."

And she was my responsibility. It wasn't fair, but what was I going to do? Oh, right. I was going to stall. "How is she bothering the Tarot readers?"

"You'd know, if you hadn't been hiding in the kitchen all morning. If she hears a reading she disagrees with, she'll tell the customer why."

Oh, boy. I blew out my breath. Hyperion was right. It was time to put my big girl pants on and face the dragon. I'd just tell it to her straight, since my hints hadn't had much affect. Smiling tightly, I strode to my mother.

"My tea's gone cold," she said. "I'd like a fresh cup, please."

"As much as I'm enjoying having you around," I lied, "I'm afraid you can't stay here all day. We've got to turn this table over."

She glanced up at me. "Do you talk to all your customers that way?"

"No." I shuffled my feet guiltily. "But I wasn't kidding about that table. We really do need it."

She swirled her tea. "I can't leave. I'm helping your investigation, remember?"

I narrowed my eyes. "Helping?"

"It was your idea to stake out Beanblossom's. It *is* nice having my name on a Tarot room, by the way. Anyway, I still haven't seen the person who was watching your tearoom yesterday. But if they return, I'll catch them."

My stomach sank. That *had* been my idea. "Would you even be able to recognize them? You couldn't describe them to us at all."

"I told you, the person's aura was very dark." My mother twisted in her seat to face the table behind her and tapped a card there. "I never sugar coat the Tower card," she said to a startled Tarot reader and her client. "It's a sudden, unpleasant upset. It could be big or small, but it's no fun, believe me."

She turned back to me. "Now, where were we?"

The Tarot reader snatched up the cards and reshuffled.

"You can't *do* that," I said. "You need to stop butting into other people's Tarot readings."

She sniffed. "I really don't think it's helpful when you project your sense of wrongness onto me."

I scrubbed a hand over my face. *Tell her straight.* "It's not about right or wrong. It's about my tearoom. And these are my rules."

"Yours?" she asked, arch. "I thought Hyperion was your partner. Isn't he in charge of the Tarot side of the business? I don't see him complaining."

"Because he doesn't want to be told to go vegan or go home."

"*You* should go vegan. It's much better for the planet. Or do you simply not care about mother earth?"

Stay calm. "Please stop interfering in the Tarot readings."

My mother sniffed. "I think your Tarot readers are afraid of growth."

"Yes," I said dryly, "that's exactly it."

"Sarcasm is the lowest form of humor." She sighed. "I'm very disappointed in you."

An icicle stabbed my heart. But what did I care if she approved of me or not?

"I just don't understand it," she continued, her eyelashes fluttering. "Where did I go wrong?"

"You— Seriously?" I sputtered.

"Are you even woke?"

"I'm not even sure what that means."

She smoothed the white tablecloth. "Very well," she said. "Everyone has their own path to follow. Including your Tarot readers. I won't interfere, even if they're readings are wrong. And I'll have another pot of tea."

So much for me being firm and direct. My mother wasn't leaving, and I couldn't throw her out. My grandfather would never forgive me, and she was still my mother. But at least she'd agreed not to pester the Tarot readers. "A fresh pot it is."

"And I wouldn't mind some avocado toast."

"We don't sell it," I said in a strangled voice.

"You don't? In California? How disappointing."

My mother spent the entire day in that window, drinking free refills and ordering scones and finger sandwiches.

At five o'clock, I set a bill at her elbow. She ignored it, and I knew she wouldn't pay it. But at least she'd been out of my grandfather's hair for the day.

We closed Beanblossom's, and she continued her window-side vigil.

I watched her nervously for a little while, then fled into the kitchen to clean up.

"We've got a problem." Hyperion lounged in the open doorway. "My office."

I followed him across the hall and shut the door behind me, blotting out the twinkle lights. "What's wrong? My mother stopped butting into the Tarot readings, didn't she?"

Bastet looked up from the altar and yawned. His tail flicked an oversized quartz crystal.

"We're supposed to go to an HOA meeting tonight," Hyperion said.

"I didn't forget." And though I'm not a meeting person, I was kind of looking forward to this one. Archer had told us the food was pretty good.

"Is your mother coming with us?"

"Of course not," I said uncertainly.

He lowered his head and raised his brows.

"Okay," I admitted. "She might. You didn't tell her about the meeting, did you?"

He straightened. "What do you take me for?"

"I didn't tell her either." I gnawed my bottom lip. We needed to get her out of Beanblossom's before we left, or she'd follow us. "We can send her on a quest. I mean an assignment. Something innocuous. Something that looks like real investigating but isn't."

Hyperion snapped his fingers. "Vanella's Instagram photos."

We hurried into the tearoom.

My mother looked up. "Are you finished cleaning?"

"Not quite," I said. "Since our stalker didn't return, we were wondering if you could check up on Vanella? Where is she posting from now?"

My mother nudged the phone on the white tablecloth. "She's at home."

"Oh." We couldn't send my mother there. She might try to break in.

"But that Pepper is at a French restaurant not far from here," she continued.

"Could you follow her?" I asked.

She scraped back her chair and stood. "I do love French food."

"Great," I said. "Thanks."

"However, I'm a *bit* short on funds."

Oh, for Pete's sake. I stretched my mouth into a smile. "No problem." I returned to the kitchen and fished my wallet out of my purse. I returned and laid twenties on her table.

My mother shook her head sadly. "It's a rather expensive restaurant."

I added another twenty.

My mother arched a brow.

Jaw clenching, I added another bill.

She gathered the cash from the table. "I'll let you know what I discover." My mother wafted out the door.

"Whoa," Hyperion said. "That was a lot of—"

"I don't want to hear it." I ripped off my apron. "Let's get out of here."

The HOA meeting was in a swank club house on the grounds of a private, nine-hole golf course. My Mazda felt out of place amidst the Teslas, Hummers, and Ferraris, but I was starting to get used to the feeling. The latest tech boom had changed the character of our little beach town, but change was life, even if I hated it.

We arrived early. A slim, middle-aged woman in tailored slacks and a berry-colored blazer met us at the door.

"Greetings," Hyperion said. "Hyperion Night and Abigail Beanblossom."

"Right," the woman said, "Archer's consultants. I'm afraid you can't stay for the board meeting. However, you're welcome for the venting of grievances."

Hyperion's mouth quirked. "That's what it's called?"

She sighed. "That's what I call it. I'm June, by the way. June Marcus."

"Nice to meet you," I said. "Archer told us you've been having quite a time of it with the noise complaints."

"It's been... interesting. I knew being HOA president would be work, but I'd no idea something like this would happen. I've never dealt with the police before."

"The police questioned you about the murder?" I asked.

"No. I mean, they did. But before that. I must have complained to the police about the Henderson house at least a dozen times. The police were very nice, but their hands were tied."

"We heard the Hendersons simply paid the city fines and partied on," Hyperion said.

"At first. Then they stopped paying the fines. They've been getting away with murder." She flushed. "Not literally."

"It must have been maddening," I said.

"For everyone," she agreed. "And now Tom Henderson is dead,

and…" She shrugged.

"Some cause happiness wherever they go, others whenever they die?" said Hyperion.

She shot him an uncertain look. "I… wouldn't exactly say that. But I suppose some people are taking it harder than others."

"Oh?" I asked. "Who?"

"You already know about Archer's unofficial noise committee."

I crossed my arms over my chest. "He wasn't the one who put the fake snakes in the yard."

The HOA president shifted her weight. "So he says. A part of me doesn't blame him—or Pepper or Cosmo. Cosmo's trying to sell his house. Who wants to live near a party house? But the HOA has to stay on the right side of the law."

"Were any of the other homeowners especially outraged by what was going on?" I asked.

She flushed again. "I really don't think I should say. I can't believe any of my neighbors did this. We were all furious about the noise, but none of us are killers."

"*Someone* killed Tom Henderson," Hyperion said.

"I know," she said in a low voice. "And so help me, when I heard he'd died, my first feeling was relief. After what they did to our kids…"

"What happened to the kids?" I asked.

Her mouth firmed. "The senior class was putting on *The Sound of Music*. And then…"

"They wouldn't let them use the party house?" Hyperion asked.

"We wouldn't use it if they paid us. They let *So Long, Farewell* stage their performance on the same night. The students' ticket sales were dismal. Not that it mattered. No one could hear the show over that racket."

"Where was it being staged?" I asked.

"Here, at the club house. We have a Shakespeare garden out back with the perfect stage," she explained. "But because of the *So Long* musical, cars blocked the streets. Many of the ticketholders couldn't even get to the show."

"Those poor kids," I said.

"We live in such a *nice* community," she said. "But now, now I realize there's a killer stalking our neighborhood. I feel sick."

"Stalking it?" I asked. "You think someone from outside the neighborhood killed Tom Henderson?"

"I know it's not realistic. I know the most likely suspects are right here in this club house." Her gaze roved the growing crowd. "But... I know these people." She motioned toward a cluster of chattering, well-fed, middle-aged couples.

"Where's your house?" I asked.

"At the other end of the neighborhood, fortunately. I didn't hear as much. Except for the helicopters. We could all hear the helicopters. There's wine and snacks on the table," she continued, dismissing us.

We wandered to the snack table, and I poured myself a glass of red wine.

"Is that gruyere?" Hyperion stabbed a wedge of cheese with a toothpick.

"What did you think of June?" I asked.

"I suppose Archer's HOA president could have killed Henderson for everyone else's sake. But is it likely?" He popped the cheese into his mouth.

"Not really."

There was an outraged cry behind me, and I turned.

Cosmo Terzian stood in the center of a small and growing crowd. "She's not backing off," he said.

"Her husband was murdered," a narrow-faced, gray-haired woman said. "How can she go on?"

"For the money," Cosmo said, expression grim.

The crowd muttered darkly, and Hyperion shot me an uneasy look.

I tasted something sour. If Vanella wasn't the killer, she just might be the next target.

CHAPTER 14

"What next?" I asked Hyperion.

We sat in my Mazda amidst the glory of the club house parking lot. We'd interviewed everyone at the HOA meeting. They'd all hated Tom. They were all furious at Vanella. Several worried about dropping property values. Most had mortgages, which might now be higher than the value of their homes.

But with the exception of the HOA president, everyone we'd talked to had been at an "escape party" the night Tom had been killed. They'd rented a yacht and toured the bay to escape the noise.

In short, we hadn't found a single viable new suspect.

Even the HOA president had been home taking care of her two children, while her husband was in Atlanta.

My partner pulled his phone from his pocket. "I'm calling Vanella." He listened then shook his head and hung up. "Voice mail."

"Should we go to her house and warn her? Or is that an overreaction?" None of the people we'd spoken with could have killed Tom Henderson. What were the odds they'd kill Vanella?

"She must know the neighborhood hates her by now. And even if we did, she's not answering her phone. How could we get in?"

"True."

"Let's regroup at Brik's place," he said. "I could use a drink."

I groaned. "He's having *another* party? On a Wednesday night?" How could the man be so aggravating? He'd never get away with it if he weren't good looking.

But since I was one of the people letting him get away with it, what did that say about me?

"The text went out this afternoon," Hyperion said. "Didn't you get it?"

"No."

"Interesting."

I crossed my arms. "He probably figured I don't need party alerts, since I live next door."

"But wouldn't you prefer a heads-up? You should get on the list."

"There's a list?"

"If it's anywhere worth going," he said, "there's always a list."

My neck stiffened. "Whatever." I started the ignition, and we drove off.

As the crow flies, my bungalow was probably only three miles from the HOA club house. But those miles were separated by a valley. The drive to the bottom of the hill was mazelike, the houses shrinking as we descended. Finally, we drove into San Borromeo proper and began the ascent to my more modest community.

As we neared my home, the street thickened with parked cars. My Mazda vibrated to a bass beat. I stopped in front of my driveway and unbuckled my seatbelt.

"Why are there traffic cones in front of your driveway?" Hyperion asked.

"Brik started putting them up a month ago, whenever he was having a party. He got tired of telling his guests to unblock my driveway."

"That's thinking ahead," he said, choking back a laugh.

I shot Hyperion a sideways glance.

"I mean," he said, "how thoughtful."

I got out, moved the cones, returned to my car, and pulled into my short driveway.

Hyperion drummed his fingers on the knee of his khaki slacks. "You do realize Brik might have some intel."

My heart pounded more quickly. "Oh?" I asked, trying to keep it casual.

"He was doing work for Vanella. Maybe he did work for her husband too. Maybe he saw or overheard something. Maybe he has some insights into her finances."

"Okay, okay," I said, feigning reluctance. "I'll come to Brik's stupid party with you." I'd dressed well for the HOA meeting in a linen wrap dress and low heels. Granted, Brik had once seen me in my teacup pajamas, but it's never too late to dress to impress.

"I *could* go by myself."

"No," I said quickly. "That wouldn't be fair. We're partners."

My cell phone rang, an international number. I declined the call.

"Telemarketer?" Hyperion asked.

"My mother." She didn't have a US-based number yet. I hoped that meant she didn't plan on staying long.

"You don't think she has anything important to report, do you? I mean, we did send her off on a mission."

"I'm sure we'll hear about it tomorrow." But my insides wriggled uneasily. "Besides, it was a bogus mission to a French restaurant. She's probably calling to ask for more money."

He angled his head and hesitated. "I don't know what it's like to have parents who abandoned you. But your mother's here now. It seems like she's making an effort."

"That's because you're a good person who thinks the best of people."

"I do not," he said in an outraged tone.

"Someone who gives them the benefit of the doubt," I amended.

"I see a woman who's returned to her daughter to make amends—"

"*Possibly* make amends. And that possibility is low to nonexistent. She's not here for me." But my pulse sped. *Could* that be why she'd returned?

Nah.

"Leopards don't change their spots." I opened the car door and put one leg out. "I see someone who ran out of money, or got into some sort of trouble, and ran home to live off her father. I'm just an interesting distraction because I own Beanblossom's Tea and Tarot."

"Co-own, partner."

"Right. Sorry. I haven't forgotten."

"You'd better not."

"The point is, she's not taking an interest in this murder because of me." I dropped my keys in my purse and stepped from the car. "She's taking an interest in the murder because it's interesting."

Hyperion emerged from his side of the Mazda. "Isn't that why *we* got involved?"

"Okay, but we never claimed to be dwelling on some higher spiritual plane. Plus, we're helping out Archer."

"We do have complicated lives."

"Yeah." Having parents who'd abandoned me was a complication I could have lived without. But that was history, so I might as well move on and investigate a murder.

We rounded the corner of the redwood fence and strode up the wide, square wooden steps. Brik had recently added them to his front yard. Ground-level lamps uplighted palm trees, spiky plants, and massive bushes of garden sage. Brik's place had curb appeal.

The interior he'd remodeled was even more impressive. He'd

knocked down several walls, leaving wide-open spaces. They led to sliding glass doors opening onto a back patio. The house was packed and vibrating with noise—The Gypsy Kings on the speakers and the laughter and chatter of guests.

"Abigail!" My grandfather squeezed through the crowd. "You weren't home," he bellowed at me over the noise. "So I came here." He gripped a red plastic cup in one hand. A button on his sweater vest had found its way into the wrong hole, one side hanging lopsided.

My heart squeezed at the sight, and I resisted the urge to fix the buttons.

"Where's your mother?" he asked.

"At a French restaurant."

His round face blanched. Gramps reached for his back pocket, where he kept a frayed wallet.

"She didn't take your credit card," I said. "I gave her the money."

His shoulders sagged, and he blew out his breath. "I keep worrying she'll use one of my cards to buy herself a spiritual getaway in Bali. And then I think that's not such a bad idea, except she'll come back again when the money runs out."

"That bad?" Hyperion shouted sympathetically.

"Every sunrise she bellows out mantras. Peking's started losing feathers over it."

"Why *did* she come back?" I asked. "Was she out of money?"

He shook his head. "I get the feeling there's more to it than that."

My heart gave a catch of excitement. Ruthlessly, I crushed that tiny flare of hope. She hadn't come here for me. I wouldn't believe it. I'd been let down too many times before.

Gramps hiccupped.

"How many of those have you had?" I asked.

"Not enough." Tomas joined us. He jammed up the sleeves of his orange and black baseball jacket. "I keep telling your grandfather he should come stay with me, but he refuses."

Gramps harrumphed. "Lisa—I mean Leaf—will claim squatter's rights, and I'll never get her out of the house."

"Cheer up," Hyperion said. "You're free tonight, and at the hottest party in town."

"Thanks," Brik shouted, emerging from behind two construction workers in heavy boots. "It is a good party. Hi, Abigail. Can I get you a drink?"

"Actually," I said, "have you got a minute?"

His expression turned wary. "Is there a problem?"

"No," I said, "no problem." He wouldn't be in violation of the noise ordinances for another two hours. "It's about Vanella."

"Okay." He angled his head toward the big windows at the back.

I kissed my grandfather's rough cheek. "I'll be right back. And I've got lasagna in the fridge."

He brightened. "I'll be at the bar."

"I'll keep an eye on him," Tomas said to me.

"I'm not drunk," Gramps said. "I don't need you to keep an eye on me."

Hyperion and I followed Brik onto the concrete patio, and down the steps to the lawn. A barbecue smoked beside a redwood pergola. People lounged in chairs beneath it.

"What's going on?" Brik asked.

"Probably nothing," I said, "but when did you see Vanella last?"

"This afternoon, after I finished tearing down her pool house. Why?"

Hyperion and I looked at each other.

"We're actually a little worried about her," my partner said. "Word on the street is she's planning on continuing renting her house out for big par— events."

A giggling couple stumbled past us. Brik watched them climb the concrete steps to the house.

"Did she say anything about that to you?" I asked.

"She wanted to hire me to do some minor repairs. I told her she'd be better off with a good handyman."

"Do good handymen exist?" Hyperion asked. "I thought they were myths, like unicorns or dragons."

"I thought she was planning to sell—she said she was sick of the house and the neighbors." Brik rubbed the back of his neck. "But maybe she wanted to fix things up for the next party."

"Did you notice anything odd when you were there?" Hyperion asked.

"Yeah," Brik said. "An old guy watching me from over the fence."

Hyperion rolled his eyes. "Archer."

"Did anyone else come to the house while you were there?" I asked.

"There was someone," he said. "A woman stopped by. She was wearing a sort of old-fashioned outfit, like something out of the 1940s."

"Beatrice," I said to Hyperion. "She loves vintage clothes."

"Anything else?" Hyperion asked.

Brik shrugged. "She paid me with a check? You don't think it will bounce, do you?"

"I doubt it," I said. "They were able to laugh off city fines. They've got to have money."

"It's not about ability to pay," Brik said. "It's about willingness to pay. How's your investigation going?"

"It's been full-tilt weirdness," Hyperion said. "We interviewed a dozen people this evening. They all gave us unconvincing *what-a-tragedy* statements, but they all have alibis. The entire neighborhood wanted Henderson dead over his non-stop parties."

A cheer went up from the house.

An awkward silence fell between us. I stared at the barbecue.

Hyperion's cheeks darkened. "But those were *super* crazy parties," he said quickly. "Rap star mini-concerts and helicopters... Did I mention the helicopters?"

Brik turned to me. "You told me my parties don't bother you. Is that how you really feel?"

I toed the lawn. "Well, you do have a lot of them."

"No one else has complained," Brik said.

"Your other closest neighbors are old and deaf," I said.

"Why didn't you say something earlier?" Brik asked.

"I'm pretty sure I did. Repeatedly. Then I just got earplugs."

Brik swallowed, a panicked look on his face. "If they really bother you, I can cut the parties back to weekends."

This was it. I finally had my chance for weekday peace and quiet.

Sweat beaded Brik's brow.

I opened my mouth, shut it.

Brik's shoulders hunched. He blinked rapidly. Brik was... terrified. And I was pretty sure he wasn't scared of me. "Brik—"

"You know what?" Hyperion said. "We should call Vanella and check in on her." He grasped me by the shoulders and steered me up the concrete steps. "BRB!" he called over his shoulder.

"We can't make a call inside," I shouted. "It's too noisy."

"I know. I had to get you away from Brik before you said something you'd regret."

"Like what?" I bellowed.

"Like tell him he can't have his parties."

Exasperated, I said, "I know you have a fun time at these, but his parties are making me nuts."

"Have you ever considered his parties are what's keeping him sane?"

I stopped beside a construction worker snoring on the sofa. "What?

What do you know?"

"Nothing. But I've seen this behavior before. I mean, parties nearly every night just aren't rational. Brik doesn't like being alone, and this is his way of coping."

Hyperion was right. Brik wasn't some drunken frat boy. He was having these parties for a reason. I swallowed, my chest tightening. Why hadn't I picked up on that? Was I as self-involved as my mother?

"I need to get my grandfather." I wound through the crowd to the kitchen bar.

Gramps sat on a stool swigging from his red cup. Beside him, Tomas braced his elbow on the bar. "...killed him with a bottlecap. Just like that."

I rested my hands on their shoulders. "I'm headed home. Want some lasagna?"

"I'm in," Gramps said.

"I guess I'll come too," Tomas said, "check out the place. Got any problems? No leaks?"

"That seems a little personal," Hyperion said.

I elbowed Hyperion. "Nope," I said to my landlord/honorary uncle. "Everything's running fine."

"How's the new answering machine?" Tomas asked.

"It works great," I said.

We wove through the crowd and left, walking to my house. I let them inside, flipping on the lights, and I beelined for the kitchen. I'd made the lasagna that morning to take to my grandfather's, but the investigation had gotten in the way.

I preheated the oven while the men chatted on my rear deck.

Hyperion wandered up to me. "I've been calling Vanella, and she's still not answering."

I clutched the lasagna dish. "Maybe she's left her phone in another part of the house."

"Are you kidding? Vanella? Can you see her more than two feet away from her phone?"

"No," I admitted. "You don't think something's really happened to her?"

"I only said that to get away from Brik before things got too weird, but now I am worried. I know I'm not a psychic, but I've got this feeling."

"Me too," I said. "I mean, it's probably nothing."

"But people at the HOA meeting were pretty angry," Hyperion said.

"Okay," I said. "Let me finish re-heating the lasagna. If we haven't reached Vanella by then, let's go over there."

Hyperion nodded absently and wandered from the kitchen.

Thirty minutes later, Hyperion and I had left the older men and were driving to Vanella's.

"I'm sure she's fine," Hyperion said.

"Yeah, me too."

"But better safe than sorry."

"Right. Vanella's fine."

We turned onto Vanella's street and crested a low hill. Red and blue lights flashed, strobe lighting the privacy walls and the street.

In front of Archer's house, I lifted my foot from the gas. We coasted down the hill, my dread growing.

Clusters of people huddled in driveways, peering at the activity on the street. Police cars blocked the iron gate in front of Vanella's house.

"No." Hyperion rolled down the window and stuck his head out.

A coroner's van drove to the gate, and a uniformed officer waved it through.

Acid boiled up my throat.

Hyperion turned to me, his face stricken. "Why did I have to get a psychic premonition about this? Why not love or lottery tickets?"

I swallowed, unable to speak. It didn't take a psychic to know Vanella wasn't fine.

CHAPTER 15

"Hssst. Hyperion! Hssst."

Hyperion jerked his head and banged it on my car's window frame. He scowled, blue and red lights careening across his face.

"Hyperion. Abigail." Archer motioned from his driveway.

I blinked. Archer wore a blue smoking jacket and black velvet lounge pants.

And he managed to pull off the look.

I slowly reversed, and the older man stepped aside for me to park. Hyperion and I stepped from the car.

"How did you *know*?" Archer asked. "Did someone call you?"

Hyperion shook his head. "We had a bad feeling."

"Of course you did. I knew I was right to hire you. Though your mother, Abigail…" He shook his head.

"She's highly meditated," I said, and Hyperion snorted. "What's happened?"

"Vanella's dead," Archer said. "You'd better come in. We can see what's happening over my other gate. It has the best view."

We followed the older man across the sloping lawn to the gate. The eucalyptus leaves rustled like dried paper. A waning moon cast wavering shadows through them. Archer cracked the gate open. The three of us smushed together and peered through the gap.

Police congregated around an open garage.

"The garage?" I asked.

"It was ghastly," Archer said. "She was completely blue."

"Wait." I turned to him, bumping Hyperion. "Are you telling us you found her?" This was so not good.

"Abigail..." A feminine voice fluted.

My shoulders hunched.

My mother floated across the lawn, her caftan wafting about her legs.

"I should have known you'd be here," she said.

I forced a smile. "What are you doing here?"

"Well." She motioned toward the gate and the fateful house beyond. "That."

Hyperion frowned. "But how did you know?"

"Did you follow Pepper here?" I asked.

"Of course not," she said. "I left her back at the restaurant. Dinner was delicious, by the way. It is so hard to find really good French cuisine."

"Don't you want to hear my dramatic story?" Archer asked.

"Oh," I said. "Right. Sorry. You found the body?"

He adjusted his cravat. "I did. I was relaxing by the pool, enjoying the stars—"

"They're so much brighter in the South Pacific," my mother said. "Less light pollution."

"Er, yes," Archer said. "As I said, I was relaxing, and I heard a motor running. At first I didn't think anything of it. There was something rather soothing about the sound. It was so much quieter and more regular than the usual shrieks and bass beats from that house."

"The motor was white noise," my mother said.

"Exactly," he said. "But the motor kept going on and on. It became irritating. So I walked over there to complain."

"Through this gate?" I asked.

"I had to use this gate. The front gate was locked."

"You're sure?" I asked.

"Yes. And no one answered when I rang. But her front door was wide open. I called out, and no one answered. The motor was obviously coming from the garage, so I made my way there and found her. Dead in her Mercedes, a garden hose running from the exhaust pipe to her window. Of course, I opened the garage door right away. The car doors were locked, but it was obvious she was dead."

"Fascinating," my mother said.

"Horrifying," Archer corrected.

"This never would have happened if she'd owned an electric car," she said.

I drew a breath to tell her it had nothing to do with the car, then thought better of it. "At least the security camera will be able to verify you coming and going," I said. Maybe that would make Archer less of a suspect. But finding the body… that was never good.

"Oh, the security was off," he said.

"How could you tell?" Hyperion asked.

"The red light on the gate camera wasn't flashing."

"What time was this?" Hyperion asked.

Archer checked his phone. "I called the police at nine thirty-seven."

"The HOA meeting ended at eight," I said. "And the club house is only five blocks away."

"Enough time for someone to go to her house, kill her, and escape," Hyperion said.

"One doesn't kill someone like that," my mother said. "Do you think a woman would sit in her car, watch while someone rigged a hose to her exhaust and shoved it through her window, and wait to die?"

"No," I said. "Vanella would have had to have been killed first and placed there. Or else she was somehow knocked unconscious and put there."

"You have a devious mind," my mother said, her tone disapproving.

"It's come in all sorts of handy," Hyperion agreed.

"It could have been suicide," my mother said. "Vanella likely killed her husband, and the guilt overwhelmed her."

Archer, Hyperion, and I shared a glance.

I shook my head. "That doesn't really seem like Vanella."

"One never knows what's going on in another person's mind," my mother said. "I remember in Tibet, there was a young teacher who seemed to shine with light wherever he went. He gave the most remarkable teachings. And then one day he was found hanging behind the temple. It was terribly tragic."

"How awful," Archer said.

The leaves above us rustled.

"And then in Goa," she said, "a young Australian tourist visiting my yoga retreat slashed her wrists. She bled out in the bath. Her boyfriend was utterly distraught. He had no idea she'd been so depressed."

Hyperion frowned.

"And at my shamanic retreat in Peru, a young man broke into the shaman's hut and overdosed on Ayahuasca. We were told quite clearly what the safe dose was, and only to take it under shamanic supervision. We were never sure if he was simply foolish, or had intentionally killed himself."

"That's... a lot of violent deaths at spiritual retreats," I said slowly.

"Oh," she said, "some were quite peaceful. In Song Saa—"

"Okay," I said. "It's not weird at all that death follows wherever you go..." I trailed off. Lately *I'd* gotten involved in more murders than the norm. Was it genetic? A chill prickled my spine. Or was my mother... a murderer?

Nah. Not even she was that bad. After all, she'd called my grandparents to come get me at the airport.

"It's *not* weird at all," she said. "The spiritual quest can bring up all sorts of challenging emotional issues. It's not for the faint of heart."

"That's fascinating," Archer said. "However, we have a bigger problem at present." He motioned toward the open gate. "Either my irritating neighbor committed suicide, or she was murdered. And if the latter, then there's a killer loose, and odds are it's one of my other neighbors. Also, I found the body. The police already consider me a suspect. That Texan detective actually told me not to leave town, and said he'd deal with me later. The questions he asked me were quite pointed."

"Have you called your lawyer yet?" Hyperion asked.

Archer straightened. "Good heavens, I forgot. Thanks for reminding me."

He trotted up the lawn.

"I knew hiring you was the right decision," floated back to us.

"This is terrible," I said. "We should have gone to Vanella's after the HOA meeting."

"How were we to know someone would come straight here to kill her?" Hyperion asked. "And I did call."

"And you left a message," I said. "Do you think Detective Chase has heard it yet?"

Even in the dim light from Archer's solar lamps, I could see Hyperion pale.

"Is a phone call interference?" he asked weakly.

It probably was. "Meh… It's probably not."

"Has Abigail always been such a terrible liar, Mrs...?" Hyperion looked around. "Where did she go?"

I looked over my shoulder. Archer's gate had swung wider.

My mother flitted down the hill, past the remains of the pool house and towards the gathered police. "Hello?" she called. "I have a bone to pick with you."

"No," I whispered. My leg muscles tightened. Like a malfunctioning robot, I turned left, then right. My instinct to run warred with the need to stop her, whatever she had planned.

"What is she doing?" Hyperion rasped.

"How should I know?" I asked, shrill.

I jogged through the gate after my mother. If she got arrested, my grandfather would have to bail her out, and I suspected she'd already put a sizable dent in his wallet.

A tall, lean silhouette stepped from behind a topiary and intercepted her.

Tony Chase thumbed up his cowboy hat. "Ma'am. What do you think you're doing here?"

"You've put the fear of divine retribution into that lovely little man on the hill," my mother said. "It's unkind."

"Divine retribution? Are you saying he's guilty of murder?"

"No," I panted. "No, she's not."

"Of course not," she said. "Mr. Simmons is no killer. I have a sense about these things."

His gray eyes narrowed. "Do you now?"

"No," I said. "No, she doesn't. And we were just leaving." I tried to steer her away.

"Hold on," he said. "What are you two doing here anyway?"

"Me?" I swallowed. I couldn't lie. I'd only get caught. There were too many witnesses to our investigation tonight. "Hyperion and I attended tonight's HOA meeting."

"And why would you do that?" he drawled.

"Archer needed a proxy."

"And why would he need that?" The detective brushed his jacket back and rested his gloved hands on his hips.

I eyed the holstered gun. "So, we went, and lots of people were talking about how Vanella planned to continue renting her house out for parties. They were really angry. So Hyperion called Vanella to see how she was doing and give her a heads up, but she didn't answer. Then we went to Brik's house—Hyperion wanted to go to his party—"

"Party?" my mother asked.

"And we kept trying to call Vanella, but she didn't answer. So we got worried, and drove up here, and saw the police lights. Then we saw Archer, and he invited us in."

"And where do you fit into all this?" he asked my mother.

"Oh, I was sleuthing at that divine French restaurant in downtown San Borromeo. And then I came here."

I mentally smacked my head.

"Why exactly were you sleuthing?" he asked.

"Because my daughter was at the HOA meeting, obviously, though she didn't tell me that at the time. We're *supposed* to be partners, but we couldn’t be in two places at once.”

“I want you two to leave my crime scene. Now.”

“Yes, Sir. Thank you, Sir,” I babbled and dragged my mother away. I stopped. Turned. “So it *is* a crime scene?”

His square jaw clenched. “Go.”

I scurried up the hill, half-pushing my mother before me. We reached Archer's gate. As I turned to slam it behind us, two uniformed men wheeled out a body bag on a gurney.

I glared at Hyperion. “Thanks for the assist.”

“If you got arrested,” he said, “I was totally going to work on getting you out.”

“Now,” my mother said. “Let me tell you about that marvelous French restaurant.”

“I need to talk to the neighbors.” I raced up the hill and out Archer's front gate, because there *had* to still be some neighbors gawking. Also, I didn't want to hear about all the great food my mother had eaten on my behalf.

An elderly woman strode, her cane tapping, toward Hyperion and me. I did a doubletake. “Mrs. Bicklesworth?”

She raised a brow. “Abigail? What are you doing here?”

“Um, we came to see Vanella.”

“We?” she asked.

“My partner and I.” I motioned toward Archer’s gate, across the street.

“I hope you weren’t here to rent that awful house.”

“No,” I said quickly. “Are you a neighbor?”

“To my eternal regret. I’ve been able to remove my hearing aids during the parties, but that does nothing to stop the annoyance of the crowded streets and blocked driveways. What’s happened?”

“Vanella’s dead,” I said.

“I suppose one of the neighbors finally snapped.” She sighed. “I told her to be careful.”

“You did?”

“Of course we were all upset by the parties, but her immediate neighbors caught the brunt of it.” She aimed her cane at the houses on either side of her. “I’d like to think Archer would take a more mature approach to things, but that article...” She shook her head. “The whole neighborhood enjoyed it immensely, but he never should have written the thing.”

“I’m sure he didn’t mean it,” I said.

She leaned closer and lowered her voice. "I heard he was taken to the police station for questioning. I believe someone is trying to frame him, and he's such a dear man. And that article he wrote gave them the gateway to make him appear guilty."

"Who would want to frame Archer?"

"Someone who wants to get away with murder, of course. Now I understand you have a new Tuesday special?"

"Yes, Temperance Tea Tuesdays."

Mrs. Bicklesworth patted my arm. "I'll make a reservation." She strode away.

I blew out my breath. At least I hadn't lost her as a customer after the drill incident. But framing Archer… I hoped she was wrong and feared she was right.

Across the street, a woman in comfy and expensive looking loungewear stood on tiptoes. She craned to see past the police cars.

I approached her. "What's going on?" I asked, playing innocent.

"Something awful, I hope," she said. "I heard Vanella killed herself."

"Who did you hear that from?" I asked.

"Oh, someone," she said vaguely. "Everyone's talking about it."

I looked around. She was the only person left on the treelined street. "Everyone?" I asked. "Where'd they go?"

"Home, I think. There's only so long you can stare at police cars." She smiled wanly. "I guess I have more stamina for tragedy. I'm Deedee."

"I'm Abigail."

We shook hands.

"Did you see anything strange earlier?" I asked. "Before the police arrived, I mean."

"There was a sex-on-a-stick blond here earlier."

"You mean, Pepper?"

Deedee made a face. "No, a guy. Thick, blond hair in a ponytail and muscles like… wow. Just… wow."

My stomach rolled. *Brik.* "Did he drive a blue pickup?"

She smiled wickedly. "I wasn't looking at his car."

"And he left late afternoon?"

"Yes, around five, I think. Do you know him?"

"I heard Vanella was having her pool house knocked down."

"I'd let him knock down my pool house any day." She laughed.

I tried not to roll my eyes. "What about later in the evening?" I asked briskly. "Did anyone else come by?"

"Oh, no, I didn't see anyone then."

Detective Chase would find out about this, and he'd track Brik down. My insides squeezed unpleasantly. Brik had nothing to do with Vanella's death. He had nothing to worry about. But there'd always been an odd sort of tension between the two men.

I frowned. Actually, Brik got a little tense whenever cops were around.

It couldn't mean anything. It had to be nothing. Brik wasn't a criminal, and he certainly wasn't a killer.

But his dislike of being alone, his suspicion of the cops...

Maybe there was more to Brik than met the eye.

I just wasn't sure if this was a mystery I wanted to solve.

CHAPTER 16

"I won't say you dumped your mother on me," Hyperion said, "but you dumped your mother on me last night. Was that revenge for the pier?"

I whipped out a tablecloth and let it flutter onto the table. We were between seatings at the tearoom. I usually loved this in-between time. It gave me a chance to catch my breath, plan, and recharge. But Zen escaped me this afternoon.

"And I won't say you hid behind a six-foot fence while I smoothed things over with the cops," I said. "But that's exactly what you did. Besides, I didn't abandon you. I abandoned her. And turnabout's fair play, even if it is twenty-plus years too late."

"Hm." Hyperion rubbed his chin. "I don't think your mother's going to see it that way."

"Of course she won't. Since she's returned, I've told her exactly how I feel as directly as I know how. She thinks I'm just unevolved."

"Well, you'll have to figure out something. We've got a meeting with Archer and his noise committee after closing, and she can't come."

"We do?"

"I arranged it last night."

"Oh. Thanks. And I'll deal with my mother."

He took a long step backward and out of reach. "Since you can't change her, have you thought about, maybe changing yourself?"

I flicked out a fresh cloth and let it settle atop a nearby table. "Why should *I* change?"

"I'm just saying, some calming deep breaths might make you happier. Have you tried alternate nostril breathing?"

Was he kidding me? "If you can't beat them, join them? No thanks."

He edged further away. "Then what about forgiveness? Not for her benefit, for yours," he said quickly.

I blew out a breath. "I know—"

"You're supposed to breathe through your nose."

I scowled. "I know forgiveness is the right thing to do. I know I'd be a happier, better, higher-vibe person if I forgave. But how? My mother abandoned a little girl at an airport and called my grandparents to pick me up. Then she left them to care for me for two decades. And she not only hasn't apologized, she doesn't see anything wrong with it. I've tried to let it go. I've tried to forgive her. But I honestly don't know how."

"I say fake it 'til you make it."

"I'm serious, Hyperion," I said quietly.

"It totally works. I pretended to be a professional Tarot reader for *years*, and now look at me. Here I am, not only a pro, but part-owner in Beanblossom's Tea and Tarot."

"So, *pretend* I forgive her." I laid silverware and plates on the table.

"Yep. Just pretend. It'll eventually become real."

"That sounds like magical thinking."

"Nope, it's sound human psychology. And oh, look. Now's your chance."

I glanced toward the door. My mother breezed in wearing one of her filmy caftans and big sunglasses like a gently aging movie star.

My hands bunched in a folded tablecloth.

Hyperion gave me a little shove toward her. "Pretend you're an Academy Award winning actress with nothing to worry about except all the horrid jealous people who want to take you down. And deep breaths."

I stretched my mouth into a smile and set the tablecloth on a nearby chair. "Hello, Mother. Are you here for a table?" *Fake it. I'm faking it.* I scanned the reservation book. "We have one available by the bookcase. Or if you'd prefer, you can sit at the bar."

"Abigail, I have so many ideas for our investigation."

My stomach clenched. I inhaled slowly. And yes, through my nose. "I'm afraid I'll be a little busy with customers for the rest of the afternoon—"

"*I'm* a customer."

"So if you'd like to talk, maybe it would be easier if you sat at the bar."

"No," she said, "I'll take that table by the bookshelf. It has better feng shui, and I do enjoy reading your selection of books."

"Right this way." I led her to the table, sat her down, took her order, and had a silent meltdown in the kitchen.

Hyperion poked his head through the doorway. "I don't see deep breathing."

I sucked in a long breath of air and exhaled.

More customers arrived for the afternoon seating. They kept me busy running between tables and kitchen. My mother kept me busy listening to her dissertation on how to improve my vibrational level. Finally, we closed the tearoom, I took a breath, and I started cleaning up.

I hadn't forgiven my mother, but I had managed to pretend I'd been happy to see her. At least I *think* I had. But it worried me that she was still nursing a cup of tea at her table.

"Abigail," she said.

I started, banging my head on the oven roof. Smothering a curse, I extracted myself and forced another smile. My cheeks were starting to ache from all the fakery.

She stood in the middle of the doorway, her hands folded in front of her. "Don't you think we'll be late for our meeting with Archer?"

"*Our* meeting?" I bleated.

"And his noise committee."

"You heard about that?"

She nodded. "Hyperion should spend more money on his office door. I assume his readings are meant to be private. On the drive there, I can tell you all about that lovely French restaurant. Who knew San Borromeo would become such a cultural mecca?"

"Oh, good. Good, good, good." *This was a disaster.* I swallowed. "I'm just about finished here. And I've got some extra scones. Maybe you can take them back to Gramps's house. He loves them."

She wafted deeper into my kitchen. "Oh, no," she said. "Dad couldn't possibly eat anything with so much sugar. It's terrible for his *chi.* You really should be more careful with what you give him."

My jaw tightened. Gramps wasn't a pet on a special diet. He was an adult man who chose what he wanted to eat.

...And who frequently made poor choices. I gnawed my bottom lip. But every time I'd tried to healthy up the lasagna or other meals I brought him, he'd smile wanly and say it "tasted healthy." So I settled for sneaking in extra veggies.

Hyperion bustled into the kitchen. "Excellent, your mother's told you she's coming along," he said in a strained voice. "Are you ladies ready? I have a new rental, and it's got room for eight."

My mother frowned. "Sounds like a gas guzzler."

"Like you wouldn't *believe.*"

I finished up in the kitchen. My mother returned to the tearoom to collect her purse.

I met Hyperion's gaze. "I'm sorry about this," I said.

"Six of Swords," he said. "I just keep thinking of the Six of Swords."

And my mother would be leaving soon.

The three of us strolled to Hyperion's latest rental—a black Dodge Durango.

"Nice racing stripe," I said, pointing. "That won't attract traffic cops at all."

"Do you really need something so big?" my mother asked.

"It came with the stripe, and no, I don't need something this big. But my insurance company is paying for the car. The guy on the phone insisted on making up for the last car I got stuck with."

"See Abigail?" my mother said. "Hyperion knows the power of positive thinking."

I glanced skyward, at the deepening dusk. I was willing to believe in Tarot if it meant the Six of Swords coming true.

We drove to Archer's house, and he let us inside. "They're both here, Cosmo and Pepper. Cosmo's feeling terrible. He blames himself."

I followed the elderly man down the wide hallway. "He does? Why?"

"For telling everyone Vanella was going to keep renting the house," Archer said. "Someone must have gone straight there from the HOA meeting and killed her."

In the sleek living area, a slender blond bent close to Cosmo, and I started, then realized it was Pepper. From the back, she'd looked like Vanella.

Hyperion cleared his throat, and she and Cosmo turned toward us.

Cosmo's face creased. "I never should have shot off my mouth at that meeting."

"They would have found out as soon as the next party happened," Pepper said. "You only delayed the inevitable."

"Then you think it *is* my fault?"

"It's the fault of whoever killed her," Hyperion said. "No one else's."

Pepper smoothed her long, blond hair. "Vanella knew why her husband was killed. She was foolish to continue in his footsteps."

"There is such a thing as Karma," my mother agreed.

"Is that what you were talking about Tuesday night?" I asked.

Pepper's eyes widened. "Karma?"

"We saw you and Pepper on the pier Tuesday night," I said.

"Did you? Oh. I think we did run into each other."

"What were you two talking about?" I pressed.

"I'm not sure I can remember," Pepper said.

I smiled. "Try."

"Oh. Let's see. I ran into her, and—"

The doorbell rang.

"Who can that be?" Archer bustled from the room.

"Did you invite the HOA president?" Cosmo asked.

"No," I said. "Just your noise committee."

"Should we have invited her?" Hyperion said.

"I doubt she would have come." Cosmo shrugged, his muscles bunching. "She *says* it's important to keep separation between official HOA activities and our committee."

"And you doubt her?" my mother asked.

"For more reasons than that. She was furious about *So Long, Farewell*."

Pepper's gaze flicked toward the globe ceiling light. "All because her daughter was playing Maria."

"It *is* a starring role," Hyperion said.

I shook my head. We were getting off track. "The HOA president has an alibi. Pepper, what were you and Vanella talking about Tuesday?"

"It was a little awkward at first." Pepper colored. "After our spat, I mean."

I rubbed my jaw. "Spat. Yeah."

"I apologized, and we made up."

Cosmo's eyes widened. "You apologized?"

I pursed my lips. *Apologized for having an affair with her murdered husband?*

"I didn't know she was thinking of going on with renting the house," Pepper said. "But I should have. Vanella was always the power behind the throne. She told me that Tom didn't have a penny when they met," she said, lowering her voice.

Hyperion reared backward. "No."

"Yes," Pepper said.

"He was a musician, right?" I said.

"He was?" Pepper blinked rapidly. "I mean, yes. The money was all hers. She felt guilty he died, because she'd been wanting to divorce him."

"Why didn't she?" I asked.

"She knew the California courts would insist she pay him alimony so he could live in the manner he was accustomed. Vanella was actually happy we were… *you* know. She thought Tom might leave *her*. And since he was cheating..."

"She wanted him dead," Cosmo said.

"She wanted him gone," Pepper said, "and without taking half her money with him. But I wasn't sure if she felt guilty because she wanted him dead and then he died, or because she killed him. We made up, but we weren't that close."

Archer's voice floated down the hall. "Detective Chase, I'd really rather you didn't."

Horrified, Hyperion and I looked at each other.

"We're in for a quavering, poisonous death if he catches us," my partner whispered.

I darted toward the wide, glass doors and yanked a handle. The door didn't budge.

"The lock," Hyperion hissed. "Undo the lock."

I flipped the switch and tugged again, to no avail.

"Let me do it." Hyperion nudged me away with his hip. He tugged frantically at the door.

I scanned the room. The only other exit was through the hallway, where the rapping of Detective Chase's boots was growing louder.

"What are you two doing?" Pepper asked.

"Leaving," Hyperion said.

I studied the doors. "There." I knelt and pulled out a locking bolt. "Thank you for your time. And we were never here."

The sliding door scraped open. We raced onto the patio and past the lit pool.

Halfway down the lawn, I realized my mother wasn't with us. I ducked behind a banana plant and scanned Archer's floor-to-ceiling windows. My mother stood in the living room and gestured at Detective Chase.

"We can't help her now," Hyperion said, tugging me behind a banana plant. "Come on."

"We can't abandon my mother."

"She left you at an airport."

"It's not the same."

"And at a pier."

"So did you," I pointed out.

Hyperion groaned. "You don't think your mother's going to tell Tony we left her at Archer's?"

"She might. We've got to get her back."

"How? I suppose we could ring the bell and pretend we just arrived. But you know one of them is going to act surprised and give away the game."

"I'm calling my grandfather," I said.

"Why?"

"So *he* can ring the bell and pretend he just arrived."

"Oh, that's good."

I called Gramps.

"Abigail, I was just about to call. I took that chicken parmesan out of the freezer tonight. I'm following your instructions, but your handwriting is terrible. It does bake at three-fifty, right?"

"Yes, but forget the chicken." I told him everything.

"You left her with a detective?" Gramps yelped.

"Yes, but—"

"No buts. I'm coming to get your mother."

CHAPTER 17

My grandfather's Lincoln crested Archer's street. His car's headlights swept eucalyptus trees and high stone walls. He cruised to a halt beside us and unlocked the car's doors.

"Thanks for coming," I said and got inside. Hyperion clambered in behind me.

"What else could I do?" Gramps started the car, and it glided forward. "Your mother's not going to protect you. She's too self-centered." His head lowered slightly. "She'll tell that detective whatever will make her look good, even if that means you wind up in jail. We've got to get her away from him before she talks."

The duck hopped into my lap.

"You brought Peking?" I asked.

"I couldn't leave him alone," Gramps said. "He's been frazzled since your mother arrived. It's given him separation anxiety."

The duck did look a little wan. I stroked his silky plumage.

"Has he lost some of his feathers?" Hyperion asked.

Gramps nodded shortly. "Like I said, stress."

"Stress will do that," my partner agreed.

We pulled into Archer's driveway. It was empty except for Hyperion's rental.

"Chase must have left." I unbuckled my seatbelt and stepped from the car.

Gramps grunted as he heaved himself from the Lincoln's plush leather seat. "Then where's your mother?"

I handed my grandfather the duck, and Peking perched on the shoulder of his tweed blazer.

We hurried to the front door and rang the bell.

Archer opened the door. "I was wondering when you'd return." He turned and trudged into the house.

We looked at each other, then followed.

"What happened?" I asked. "Where's my mother?"

"Oh, your mother! No, I won't say anymore. I have a strict policy of not criticizing any of my friends' relatives."

"We know what Lisa's like," Gramps said. "What happened?"

"It was a disaster. That detective seems to think I'm somehow responsible for all the deaths. Just because I had means, motive and opportunity! Can you imagine?"

"So Vanella *was* murdered?" I asked.

"I don't know, and honestly, I don't think that detective does either. But what are the odds she wasn't?"

"We'll figure this out, Archer," Gramps said. "Don't you worry. We've got your back."

Archer ran a hand over his silver hair. "You're a good man, Beanblossom. Why is there a duck on your shoulder?"

"But where is everybody?" Hyperion asked.

"They all left," Archer said.

"How?" I asked. "My mother didn't have a car."

"Oh." Archer motioned toward the glass doors. "She went with the detective. And seriously, what's with the duck?"

I gaped. "She was arrested?"

"No, they went for drinks."

My grandfather groaned.

Hyperion gaped. "With Tony?" He clutched my arm. "We have to find them. Did they say where they were going?"

"Why would they tell me?" Archer asked. "Are you planning on eating that duck?"

"He's a pet," Gramps said. "Abigail, you've been spending time with your mother. Where would she go?"

"To the most expensive place she thought she could get Chase to buy her drinks," I said promptly.

My grandfather frowned. "Abigail, that's... probably right."

"There's Elegy," Hyperion said.

"My mother said she thought it was tacky."

"Sure." Hyperion folded his arms. "Like she'd pass up riding a gondola with someone like Detective Chase."

He had a point. "Elegy it is."

I returned with Gramps to his car. Hyperion followed us in his rental, and we roared down the hill and through town toward Elegy.

"I've been thinking about what you told me over the phone," Gramps said. "It doesn't seem likely two women fighting over the same murdered man made up that quickly."

"If Vanella really was looking for a way out of her marriage," I said, "she might."

"But if Pepper was having an affair with this Henderson fellow, would she kill them both?" Gramps asked.

"I don't know. If Pepper wanted to kill Vanella because she thought she'd killed her husband... But we don't know if Vanella or someone else killed Thomas Henderson. And keep in mind, we have no evidence yet if Vanella was murdered or killed herself."

"Murder-suicides do happen," Gramps said.

"Vanella did mention she was heavily medicated," I said. "I assumed she was trying to dampen her grief for her husband, but it could have been about guilt. There's so much we don't know."

"Then we need to find out."

"Do you know any realtors I can ask about the situation with the party house?"

"What do you want to know?" Gramps asked.

"How it's affecting home values, info on any mortgages outstanding, that sort of thing?"

"I don't know any realtors who might be able to help, but Tomas will." He pulled his flip-phone from the pockets of his khakis and handed it to me. I dialed and put it on speaker.

"Beanblossom," Tomas bellowed. "What do you want now?"

"I'm with Abigail, and you're on speaker," Gramps said. "You know any realtors Abigail can talk to?"

"Is she thinking about buying? If she wants to move out of the bungalow—"

"No, I'm not thinking of moving out," I said. "How can I, when you just installed that answering machine? It's about murder."

"The Hendersons?"

"Yeah, those." Gramps pulled into the parking lot at the base of a thickly wooded, steep hill. "She needs a property information search for the Hendersons and their immediate neighbors. Mortgage info, that sort of thing, if you can get it."

"Maybe," Tomas said. "I know a guy. I'll call you."

"Thanks," I said. "Bye."

We hung up.

"Um," I said, "speaking of murder, did you know about all the odd deaths at my mother's retreats?"

"You saw the postcards she sent. They never mentioned any deaths.

Where *is* your mother?" Gramps looked around the half-empty lot.

In the seventies, Elegy was San Borromeo's version of high-class. Perched at the top of a steep hill, it had amazing views. But you needed to take a gondola attached to a high cable to reach it. Now the gondola waited at the bottom of the hill, its small windows gleaming with light.

Hyperion pulled beside my grandfather's Lincoln. The three of us walked across the lot. I'm sure it was a coincidence we moved from lamppost to lamppost, keeping to the well-lit areas.

The three of us stepped into the gondola, and Gramps pushed the button. The gondola lurched forward. We sailed upward, rocking high above the eucalyptus trees scenting the air.

The back of my neck prickled. I turned, bracing my hands on the railing and staring down at the swiftly receding parking lot.

A figure shifted in the darkness between the lights.

I blinked, and it was gone.

I shivered, rubbing my arms.

"Need a jacket?" Gramps asked.

Peking quacked.

"No thanks," I said. "And I don't think they'll let a duck in the restaurant."

"Then I'll wait at the gondola."

"You could always say he's a comfort animal," Hyperion said.

Gramps drew himself up. "I'll do no such thing. I have no respect for people who lie about their animals to get them into places where they're not wanted."

"Neither do I," Hyperion said meekly. "I just thought as an emergency measure..."

Gramps harrumphed. "I know *you* wouldn't. I've never seen you try to pull those shenanigans."

We soared higher, the lights of San Borromeo twinkling off the Pacific. A waning moon hung above the ocean and left a faint, mercury trail on the dark water.

The gondola vibrated on the cable, and my grip tightened on the railing. Not that hanging on tight would help if we plummeted fifty feet to the steep hill below.

Finally, the gondola shuddered to a halt, and we stepped out.

The hostess eyed us and pointed at Peking with her pen. "Is that a—"

"I'm not going in the restaurant," Gramps said.

"We're looking for some friends," I said. "A tall man in a cowboy hat and an older woman in a caftan."

The hostess motioned toward a path between flowering bushes. "They're on the patio. And animals are allowed there. It's not like we can keep the birds off it anyway."

"Thanks," Hyperion said.

We made our way to the flagstone patio overlooking the ocean. Gas heating lamps warmed the tables, covered in white cloths. My mother sat across a small, square table from Detective Chase.

"Lisa," Gramps hurried to my mother.

Her face pinched. "Leaf. You know I changed my name to Leaf."

"What are you doing here?" I asked.

Detective Chase smiled. "Leaf and I were just having a friendly chat. She's been telling me all sorts of interesting things about her investigation."

She beamed at him, and cold terror slithered into my gut.

Hyperion's face turned a sickening shade of gray.

"Why don't you join us?" my mother asked.

"Can't," Gramps said. "Got chicken parmesan in the oven courtesy of Abigail."

"That doesn't sound safe," my mother said.

"No," Detective Chase said. "It doesn't. Leaving something baking while you're not home?" He shook his head.

"The oven's on a timer," Gramps said.

I had to get her away from the detective. "Mo—Leaf." I grimaced. "I really need to have a mother-daughter talk. It won't take long."

"I'm a little busy now. Unless you'd like to join us for a drink?"

My jaw tightened. "But… I have questions about… improving my Karma. And you know so much after all your years of study."

"Not so many years." Her brow puckered with annoyance. She pursed her lips. "But it's true, you clearly do need spiritual guidance, and I am an advanced practitioner."

The detective grinned. "I can take a hint." He grabbed his hat off an empty chair, clapped it on his head, and winked. "Folks. I'm sure I'll be seeing you later." He strode from the patio.

Hyperion pulled out the chair for my grandfather. He grabbed two more from a nearby table and collapsed into one. "Now I really do need a drink." He motioned to a waitress. "Tequila. Straight."

"As a Tarot reader," my mother said, "you of all people should know how alcohol dulls the third eye."

"I'm a spiritual being in the material world," Hyperion said, "and I'm going to enjoy it."

"That is one way of looking at it," she said.

"What did you tell that detective?" I hissed.

She stretched out her legs, circling her feet. "We were only chatting."

"What did you tell him about us?" I asked.

"I'm not sure you came up."

Gramps blew out his breath and sagged in his chair.

The waitress brought Hyperion his drink.

My partner shot it back. "Are we done here? Because I have places to be."

"But the night is young," my mother said.

"And Gramps is your ride," I said.

She shrugged. "Very well. If you insist on ruining the moment."

We paid and loaded her into the gondola. Gramps drove her home. Hyperion and I followed the Lincoln into my grandfather's driveway.

I got out of Hyperion's rental and met them beside the front step. "The chicken—"

My grandfather squeezed my hand. "I can manage the chicken. Your handwriting's not that bad. You go home and have a rest."

"I hope the chicken is plant based." My mother sniffed and marched inside the house.

"It's not vegan," I told Gramps. "It's real chicken."

"Thank you," he whispered fervently and shut the door.

Feeling guilty for reasons I didn't want to explore, I stood for a moment on the stoop. A creeping feeling chilled the back of my neck.

Hyperion straightened off his rental. "What a night. I know she's family, but she's putting the brakes on our madcap adventures. How are we supposed to detect when we have to keep running interference for her?"

"I'd apologize, but I have a strict policy of only apologizing for things I'm actually responsible for. And I can't control my mother." I sighed. "But I'll try harder." She really was complicating our investigation.

Something rustled in the thick foliage that framed my grandfather's lawn.

I shrank closer to the front door.

A raccoon waddled onto the neatly clipped grass, and I relaxed. My paranoia was getting out of control.

My phone rang, and I checked the number. *Tomas.*

"Hi, Tomas. Thanks for getting back to me so fast."

"No problem. My friend can meet us for lunch at noon tomorrow at the Yacht Club."

"I'll be there."

He chuckled. "So will I. See you."

We hung up. A light went on in the turret, my old bedroom. My mother had taken that over too.

I returned to the SUV. "Well, tonight we did learn that Vanella had two strong motives for killing her husband. He was having an affair, and she wanted out of the marriage without having to pay alimony."

"Where does that get us? She's dead." Hyperion reached for the car door.

There was a whirring sound, like a hummingbird zipping past my cheek, and a thunk.

I gaped.

"What was that?" he said. "The car shook. The car definitely shook. What did you do?"

I leapt to the front bumper and ducked. "Get down!"

Hyperion blinked and crouched. He duck-walked to me. "What is it?"

I gulped and pointed to the spear sticking from the side of the SUV. "Someone's trying to kill us."

CHAPTER 18

Hyperion hunched against the SUV's front bumper. "What does this guy have against my cars?"

I scanned the bushes. My grandfather had planted them for privacy. We'd never expected someone would use them to launch an attack.

Heart thumping, I pressed my elbows into my sides and tried to make myself as small a target as I could. At least spears were single-use weapons. Unless… "Do you think he's got more than one spear?"

"What kind of person even has *one* spear?" Hyperion whispered.

"Beatrice might."

We sat, pondering that. I bent my head. Something rustled in the bushes, and my pulse rocketed.

"We could use a rescue right about now." Hyperion fumbled his phone out of his rear pocket.

My legs trembled. Not because I was terrified. I just hadn't been practicing my squats much lately. "I think we're on our own. Did you hear that?"

"Hear what?"

"That rustling in the bushes. What if he's repositioning for a better angle?"

Hyperion made a call. "Tony? You won't *believe* what's happening."

I lightly punched my partner's shoulder. "Get to the point."

"Ow." Hyperion rubbed his arm. "Someone tried to spear me. Us... No, that isn't a double entendre. There's a killer lurking in Mr. Beanblossom's bushes... He's fine... I'm fine... She's fine... Okay." He hung up. "He says we should wait somewhere safe."

"Good advice." My voice cracked, and I cleared my throat. "Where?"

And how? My grandfather's front door was a short fifteen feet away. But I'd definitely heard him lock it. It might take him several aching minutes to open the door. And the light on the stoop would make us an easy target while we waited.

"Don't you have a key?" Hyperion asked.

"I gave it back to Gramps so he could give it to my mother." She ruined everything.

"Maybe we should stay here. Here seems safe."

"Right," I said. "No one's tried to kill us lately. Here's fine."

A growl raised the hair on my arms.

Slowly, I turned.

Two red eyes glowed from beneath the SUV.

I gasped, shuffled backward an inch on my hands, then realized I might have just exposed myself to the spear thrower. Sweat stinging my eyes, I glanced toward the thick foliage at the edge of the lawn.

"Holy crap," Hyperion breathed. "What *is* that?"

The shadows beneath the SUV shifted, and the eyes grew larger. An animal hissed, its bandit-face coming into view.

So here's the thing about raccoons. Yes, they're adorable and smart, and once I caught one trying to ride my tricycle. (That was a long time ago). They're also wild animals and mean as hell, with sharp teeth and claws.

I don't like them.

The raccoon snarled and bounded toward us.

We shrieked—okay, I shrieked—and ran.

Hyperion, having longer legs, made it to the corner of the house first and bolted around it. Shoulders tight, I followed, expecting something sharp to strike my back at any moment.

"The shed," I shouted. Gramps usually left that unlocked.

Hyperion bounded across the lawn to a heavy-duty plastic garden shed and yanked on the door. He swung on the handle. "It's not opening."

"Hold it," a gruff voice said. A light blinded me.

A duck quacked.

The light lowered, and I blinked black dots from my eyes.

Gramps aimed a shotgun with a flashlight on the barrel toward the ground. "Abigail?"

"Gramps, we've got to get inside. Someone threw a spear at Hyperion's..."

But Hyperion was already streaking past me toward the open glass door. "Hurry."

Gramps shuffled me inside and shut the door, swiftly pulled the curtains.

My mother strolled into the room. "Good heavens, what are you doing with that gun?"

"The police are on their way," Hyperion said. "And thanks for not shooting us."

"Give me some credit," Gramps said. "I never put my finger on the trigger unless I'm ready to shoot. It's basic firearm safety."

"If I'd known you kept a gun in the house," my mother said, "I wouldn't have come to stay."

Gramps ignored her. "What's going on?"

"There's a spear sticking out of Hyperion's car," I said. "Someone threw it at us. Hyperion called the police, and they told us to shelter in a safe place. We didn't know how quickly you could make it to the front door—"

"So you went around the back," he said. "Good thinking."

Hyperion yanked more curtains shut. "You were pretty quick with that shotgun, Mr. Beanblossom."

"I thought you were burglars, and I told you to call me Frank."

A siren sounded, faint and far away.

"You could kill someone with that gun," my mother said.

My grandfather's nostrils pinched. "That is the point. Did you see who threw the spear?"

"No," I said. "It came out of nowhere."

He raised a snowy brow.

"Okay," I said, "not nowhere. But it seemed that way."

"And you say it's sticking out of the car?"

I nodded.

Gramps shook his head. "They don't make cars like they used to. It's all plastic these days. If you get in an accident, you're done. You need to be more careful, Abigail."

"*Abigail* needs to be careful?" my mother asked. "You need to be more careful with that gun. I can't believe—"

Gripping the shotgun, barrel aimed toward the floor, my grandfather stomped from the room.

Someone had tried to kill us. Again. I tamped down my rising fear and anger. This wasn't the time for a freak out. It was time for a talk. "Hyperion—"

"No," he said. "I'm not quitting."

"Good for you," my mother said.

"I'm mad too," I said. "I want to take down whoever did this. But you could have been killed."

"That javelin thrower was aiming for you," he said.

"Well," my mother said, "that's just rude."

"Do you really want to stop now?" he asked.

No. I wanted to punch whoever had done it in the face.

"I don't either," he continued. "And I'm not going to. Someone tried to kill my partner. This means war."

I tried again for a modicum of rationality. "But—"

"You're afraid you'll do something that will get me killed," he said. "And I'm afraid I'll do something that will get you killed. But we're both adults, and we both make our own decisions, and we both want to finish this. Right?"

I hesitated. "Right."

"That's very mature of you, Hyperion," my mother said.

"Oh, for God's sake..." I stormed into the kitchen.

Detective Chase arrived five minutes later with a horde of men and women in blue. They searched the bushes and took the spear as evidence, but not before I'd taken photos of it, sticking from the SUV.

While Hyperion gave his statement, I sat on my grandfather's concrete step and studied my photo. The spear was painted yellow and looked like it had been made out of wood. In short, it looked a lot like what Beatrice had thrown in her office.

When I got home, I searched for javelins online, but I couldn't find the exact style of javelin I was looking for. Which seemed weird. I mean, javelins aren't running shoes. How many different kinds could there be?

The next day, a hostess escorted me through a dark-wood room and to a window table at the Yacht Club. Tomas half-rose. He motioned me into the chair beside him. A buxom, sixty-something brunette sat opposite him in a pale blue linen suit.

"Abigail, this is Sam. Sam, Abigail."

The woman grinned. "I bet you were expecting a man."

"Tomas sort of led me to think that." I sat. Outside the window, sailboats bobbed in the harbor.

She laughed. "It's our little joke. We met... How long ago is it now?"

"Forty years, at least," Tomas said.

"When I was young and hungry." Sam's eyes seemed to glow.

The waiter came and took our drink orders, and I arranged a cloth napkin in my lap.

"I got the message you sent through Tomas," Sam said. "What a crazy case. What do you know about the murder?"

"Only that pretty much the entire neighborhood is glad they're both dead," I said.

She shifted in her chair. "I just read about the wife's death. The newspaper was rather coy about what happened. But I understand the police are treating it as something worth investigating?"

I nodded. "It's a little coincidental—first the husband, then the wife dying under suspicious circumstances."

"Unless the wife did it and killed herself out of guilt," Sam said.

"Maybe." But as Hyperion had said, what were the odds?

"How did you get involved in this?" she asked.

"Abigail's naturally nosy," Tomas said, and she laughed again.

"What can you tell me about the property values in that neighborhood?" I asked.

"They've dropped twenty percent since the parties began," Sam said. "But people are still buying."

"And now that the parties have stopped?" I asked.

She shrugged. "All things being equal, I'd guess they'd go up again. On the California coast, there's still a lot of money chasing a limited supply of housing. It's simple supply and demand."

"Did you have any success with the property info search?" I didn't know if that sort of information was public knowledge, but Tomas assured me Sam had her ways.

She nodded. "Archer—"

The waiter appeared at her elbow with a breadbasket and our drinks—sangria for Tomas, a vodka tonic for Sam, and iced tea for me. "Here you go." He took our orders and bustled away.

Sam sipped her drink and briefly closed her eyes. "This bartender knows his stuff."

"He knows how to make real sangria," Tomas agreed. "But let's stop torturing Abigail. What did you find?"

"Ah." She set her glass on the white tablecloth. "Archer refinanced his house for a hundred-k four years ago. Pepper had no mortgage. Cosmo inherited his parents' mortgage, which is twenty-nine years old. Considering how low property values were thirty years ago, he can't have much left on it."

"So none of them are horribly underwater on mortgages if their property values fell."

"Most likely not," she said.

I tore apart a warm, sourdough roll. "So much for that as a motive for Pepper and Cosmo," I grumbled.

"It's a motive if one of them wanted to sell the house," Tomas said.

"A twenty-percent drop is nothing to sneeze at when you're talking about multi-million-dollar homes."

"Says San Borromeo's secret property mogul," Sam said. "Did you know I sold him the bungalow you're living in? And let me tell you, it was a real dump. But it had good bones, and I knew Tomas could turn it around."

He winked at her. "It pays to have friends in real estate."

The two clinked glasses.

It sure did. I doubted I could have found out that mortgage information on my own. And since it hadn't seemed to go anywhere, I felt guilty about putting Tomas and Sam on the case. "Thank you for all the research. I hope you'll both let me buy lunch."

She waved the offer away. "It was my pleasure. And it was easy for an old hand like me."

"And you're not buying," Tomas said. "For the pleasure of dining with two beautiful young ladies, lunch is on me."

Sam colored and glanced at the white tablecloth.

Before the afternoon seating at the tearoom, I walked to Hyperion's twinkle-light door. It was cracked open.

"No," he said to someone, "I'm not drunk… No, I'm not eating funny mushrooms... *Yes*, I'm still a Tarot reader…" He sighed. "I just wanted to say thank you. You were always there for me. I didn't appreciate it at the time, but I do now… No, I'm not dating any nice young men. Well, maybe. I mean—Augh, we'll talk later, Mom. Byeeee."

I bent my head, my eyes burning. Waited a beat. Knocked.

"Come in," he said in a distracted voice.

I opened the door and stepped inside his Bohemian office. "How did it go with the car rental company?"

"They've banned me," he said, not looking up from his laptop. "I had to walk here this morning. If I wanted more exercise," he griped, "I'd get a gym membership."

On the altar table, Bastet rumbled an agreement, his striped tail lashing.

I winced. It's not like Hyperion was out of shape, though the tabby could stand to lose a pound or two. But Hyperion without wheels was just wrong.

"So… what are you working on?" I asked.

"I'm researching suspects. I'm sick and tired of people attacking innocent cars. I want to end this, Abigail."

I scootched a high-backed chair around the table and sat beside him. "Find anything?"

"Photos of Maylene at kung fu championships posing with half a dozen different weapons."

"Including spears?"

He nodded.

"We knew she was a champion."

"Did you know she used to be a web marketer?" he asked. "She had her own business."

"I didn't know. What happened to it?"

He shrugged. "No idea. She had good reviews, but then she shut it down and after about a year, she switched to bridal expos."

"That's a big switch. What about Pepper?"

"Are you kidding me? There are thousands of selfies of her online. I started going blind looking at them all. Screen glare is a real problem."

I sighed. "Give me her social media account addresses. I'll go through them tonight."

"Thank you," he grumped. "If I had to look at one more product placement shot, I might vomit."

"And Cosmo?"

"Surprisingly interesting. Did you know he was once a Peace Corps volunteer in Tanzania?"

That was unexpected. "No."

"It was decades ago, when he got out of college. He still blathers about the glory days with other ex-volunteers online. You'd think they hadn't done anything interesting since living overseas."

"Joining the Peace Corps is a pretty big deal," I said. "Can you blame them?"

He sat back in his throne-like chair. "No. I just want to *keep* doing interesting things, you know?"

"Yeah. I know." And that desire had gotten us both into worlds of trouble. I checked my watch. "I keep thinking we know one person who used to be a pro javelin thrower."

"Beatrice."

"And it's Friday. Her office will be closed over the weekend. So if we want to catch her—"

He stood. "Say no more." He grabbed his blazer off the back of his chair. "Can you get away from the tearoom? Because I'm not driving."

It turned out, I *could* get away. But I didn't drive. Beatrice's office was only a few blocks away, and it was another gorgeous, sunny day.

Ignoring Hyperion's lamentations, I hustled him past ice cream parlors and art galleries, t-shirt shops and snow cone stands. We walked into the air-conditioned splendor of Beatrice's multi-story office building and rode the elevator to her office.

Hyperion and I stepped into the reception area, in its mid-century modern orange, blue and gray.

A blond woman looked up from behind the glass-topped desk. "Hi. Can I help you?"

"Yes," Hyperion said. "We have an appointment with Beatrice."

The blonde frowned and adjusted her glasses. "You must be mistaken."

"Nope." Hyperion leaned against the green-edged glass. "We're in the book."

"I'm quite sure you're not."

"Are too," Hyperion said mulishly.

The woman sighed and pulled a red-leather book from a desk drawer. She opened it and shook her head. "What did you say your names are?"

"Hyperion Night and Abigail Beanblossom," I said.

"Ms. Carson has no appointments this afternoon."

"We must have mixed the days," I said to Hyperion. "Is there any chance we can meet with her now?"

She tucked the appointment book beneath her arm. "Please wait here." She marched to a set of double doors, knocked, and walked in.

"I'm not leaving here without answers," Hyperion said in a low voice. "This is a small town. How many people in it know how to throw a javelin?"

"Agreed," I said, grim.

The receptionist strode into the blue-carpeted waiting area. "Ms. Carson is busy at present."

"That's okay." Hyperion took a seat and crossed his arms. "We'll wait."

"It may be a long wait," she warned.

"It's critical we speak with her." I sat beside Hyperion.

We waited. Fifteen minutes. Thirty. I bounced my foot. True, we'd come without an appointment. And true, Beatrice had no reason to talk to us at all. But was she really going to do this?

An hour passed.

It looked like she was. I checked my watch. I'd been away from the tearoom a lot longer than I'd intended.

"Follow my lead," Hyperion said out of the corner of his mouth. He stood. "I'm going to go push the elevator buttons."

Follow his lead? There was only one elevator with buttons to push.

The receptionist looked up, alarmed. "You can't do that."

"I'm pretty sure I can." Hyperion strode to the elevator, and the doors slid open for him. He stepped inside. The doors stayed open.

"There's only one elevator." The receptionist bustled to the elevator and leaned in. "You're going to make it impossible for other people to use it."

"Not impossible," he said. "Difficult."

"Get out of there," she squawked.

"There's no law against pushing buttons."

I stood and sidled to the reception desk. Flipping open the calendar, I took photos of last week's and this week's pages.

I glanced toward the elevator.

"What does the alarm button do?" Hyperion asked.

Yeah, they'd be a while. I strode to Beatrice's office doors, knocked once, and went inside.

Beatrice looked up from her desk and frowned.

Maylene Soon twisted in her chair to face me and smiled.

CHAPTER 19

Breathing hard, Hyperion gusted into the office, the receptionist hot on his heels.

"Come back here," she said. "I'm sorry Ms. Carson. I couldn't stop him."

Beatrice glanced toward the ceiling. "It's not your fault. They're an unnatural disaster." She flicked a speck of dust from the wide, white cuff of her forties-era jacket. Behind her, dark clouds gloomed above the Pacific.

Hyperion pointed at Maylene. "You killed my Jeep."

"What?" Maylene tucked her chin.

"A dumpster crushed my Jeep outside your office, and you didn't come out to look. All your neighbors did, but you pretended you didn't care."

"I *didn't* care. I was busy." Maylene smoothed the front of her slim-fitting gray pantsuit.

"Who can resist near death by dumpster fire?" he asked.

"He's got a point," I said.

"I watched out the window," Maylene muttered. She snatched a pen off Beatrice's desk.

"Wait," Beatrice said. "A dumpster really destroyed your Jeep? Outside Maylene's office?"

"Would we make something like that up?" I asked.

"No," the PR consultant said. "There's no way to spin that and look good. It'd be an intriguing challenge though," she added thoughtfully.

"And you had the skills to toss Tom Henderson over a balcony," Hyperion said.

Maylene gaped and clicked the pen. "You think I killed the Hendersons?"

"You wanted him dead," I hazarded. Everyone else seemed to. Why not Maylene?

"He ruined my business," she said. The pen clicked frantically. "All he had to do was pay my bill. But he kept stringing me along..." She blew out a long breath. "But there were other problems," she said more steadily. "I can't blame it all on him."

"Your bridal business? But wouldn't you be paying *him* to rent the mansion?"

"Before that. My other business building websites."

Huh. She really did have a motive. "So that's why you were arguing with him."

"I shouted at him when he wouldn't pay. But that was ages ago." The pen gave a final, mournful click.

"You were heard more recently."

She colored. "Oh."

"Because his refusal to pay your bill put your web business under?" I asked.

Her fingers dug into the leather arms of the chair. "Do you have any idea what it's like working with brides? They're crazy. But I'm not the only one who got into it with him recently. He owed money to some contractor."

"A contractor?" Hyperion asked. "Did you get a name?"

"It was something about construction. I thought it was funny at the time."

I swayed, sickened. *No.* It couldn't be.

"Brik?" Hyperion asked.

"Yeah," she said. "That was it, Brik. He'd been stiffed, and Tom laughed in his face. I thought the guy was going to snap him in two, but he just said he'd see him in court and stalked off."

This didn't make sense. If Tom had stiffed him, then why had Brik gone to work for Vanella? He must have been paid. Right?

"So when I learned Tom was renting out his house for big events, I decided to rent it out and stick *him* with the bill. He died before I could do it." Maylene set the pen on the desk and folded her hands.

Beatrice raised her finger. "Ah, Tricia. Would you please tell these maniacs where I was on Wednesday night? It's why they came, I'm certain. Wednesday *is* when Vanella was killed, wasn't it?"

Hyperion nodded.

I stood dumbly. *Brik? A suspect?* My brain batted against the idea like a moth against a closed screen door.

"We were in San Francisco," the receptionist said, "at a charity event."

"All night?" Hyperion asked.

"We left here at four—you know what traffic's like," Tricia said. "And we got home around midnight. There are photos of us on the event website. I'll send you the link if you like."

"I don't think that will be necessary," Beatrice said. "Why take away their fun investigating?"

My brain took another hapless run at the screen door. *Brik?*

"What about that spear?" Hyperion blustered. "Someone tried to kill us with one, and you're a javelin thrower."

Beatrice raised a brow. "When was this so-called attack?"

"Last night," Hyperion said. "Around nine."

"Beatrice was with the mayor then," the receptionist said. "They had dinner together at Sea Raven between seven and ten."

"Oooh," Hyperion said. "That place is nice. I've been trying to get reservations for ages."

"Is the mayor an adequate alibi?" Beatrice asked.

"I guess so," Hyperion said grudgingly.

"Then get out," Beatrice said, "before I call the police."

Hyperion bustled me from the office and into the elevator. "What happened in there?" he asked when the doors closed. "You went practically catatonic."

"Didn't you hear? Brik's a suspect." I studied my partner, and an unpleasant sensation wriggled in my stomach. Why didn't he seem shocked?

The doors opened, and Hyperion strode into the sunshine.

A lump hardened my throat. "It can't be Brik." I trotted after my partner. "Think of all the other suspects. Maylene didn't exactly give us an alibi. And, okay, Beatrice gave us two great alibis, but there's still Pepper. Why was she so buddy-buddy with Vanella before she died? It makes no sense. They tried to kill each other at Vanella's house. And then there's Cosmo. I don't trust him. We need to find out when *exactly* Vanella was killed. Cosmo and Pepper don't really have alibis for Tom's death, do they? And—"

"Abigail." On the brick sidewalk, Hyperion turned to face me.

Cars crept past, looking for parking.

"It's not Archer," I said. "It can't be Archer. True, he had means, motive, and opportunity, but he's *nice*. And he hired us, even if he's not paying us."

"Abigail, there's something I need to tell you."

I rubbed the back of my neck. "And who did put those snakes in the

Hendersons' yard? Who super-glued the locks? Those are real escalations, and Archer didn't do it."

He laid his hands on my shoulders. "Abigail. We may need to face the fact that Brik is a suspect."

"No. No way. He's my neighbor."

"What do you know about his life before he came to San Borromeo?" he asked gently.

"Before? He doesn't really talk about it."

"And don't you think that's a bit strange?"

"No. There's plenty of stuff I don't talk about."

"He used to live in Eureka," he said.

"Lots of people lived in Eureka."

"Where his girlfriend was murdered."

I blanked. "What?"

"Abigail, he was a suspect in her death."

CHAPTER 20

I came home to silence.

It was a Friday night, and Brik wasn't having a party. No booming music, no shrieks of feminine laughter, no crash of beer glasses from next door. The silence was empty. Hollow.

I collapsed on my blue couch, picked up my headset, and logged into a video game about zombie Nazis. But shooting them didn't bring me the unholy joy it usually did. Maybe that was why I accidentally trapped myself in a drainage tunnel. My head wasn't in the game.

Brik's girlfriend had been murdered. I couldn't imagine what that must have been like, because I didn't *want* to imagine it. I didn't want to think of someone I loved being taken from this earth by a nameless, faceless someone.

But that's what had happened to Vanella. So I guess I was a hypocrite, because I hadn't been particularly empathetic with her.

Zombies poured in from both sides of the tunnel. I listlessly exploded undead heads.

Brik… a suspect. And that was even more unimaginable—the fury and frustration of being accused, when you knew someone else had killed the person you loved. No wonder he'd moved.

Was that why he'd pulled away after our kiss? Fear of another loss?

I was about to go down in a sea of grasping arms and snapping teeth, when a familiar figure clambered through the rubble partially blocking the end of the tunnel.

"Grenade," my friend, Razzzor, bellowed in my headset.

I ducked, sending cushions flying, and the screen went white. When I lifted my virtual head, Razzzor was clearing the remaining evil undead.

"Yo," he said. "Long time, no see."

"It's been a crazy week."

"You sound depressed. What's up?"

Not so long ago, Razzzor and I had done our own amateur detecting.

His contribution had been mainly online and terrifyingly effective. So I told him everything.

"And you've met Brik," I concluded. "He's no killer."

Razzzor was silent for a long moment.

"What?" I said.

"I guess I don't know what a killer looks like anymore."

I slouched lower on the couch. "Not Brik."

"Any other suspects?"

"Yeah." And there was one I should have thought to have asked Razzzor about earlier. "What do you know about Cosmo Terzian?"

"The VR guy? I know he's looking for additional investment in his company. I don't think he's going to get it though."

"Why not?" I picked up a fallen cushion.

"He has a great product—the best on the market. But best doesn't beat market power. There are other virtual reality firms out there that dominate the gaming scene. He's a small fish in a very big pond. Hey, you should get a VR set-up."

Like I could afford virtual reality. I could barely afford actual reality. "Maybe later."

"I'll send you one."

"No thanks." Razzzor was generous to a fault, and he had money to burn. But I wasn't about to take advantage of either. "Tell me more about Cosmo."

"I don't know much. Want me to see what I can learn?"

"That would be great. Thanks."

"No problem. But seriously, I've got an extra VR set-up. I'd bought one, and then the company sent me one as a gift. I think they think I'm some sort of influencer. Or something."

I rolled my eyes. Razzzor *was* an influencer. In the business pages and the computer gaming community, he'd become an urban legend. But he was too geeky to know it. It was one of the reasons I liked him so much.

"Anyway," he continued, "let me send you my extra."

"I don't suppose they have any zombie Nazis in VR?"

He was silent again, but I could hear the wheels in his head clicking along. "You know," he finally said. "I don't think they do yet. Could be an interesting project. But there's a decent VR first-person shooter game with aliens."

"I'll take aliens. Send me the set." Because if he had a free one lying around... What the heck? "Um, there is something I should probably tell you though."

"Uh, oh. You sound guilty. I hate it when you sound guilty."

"Your PR consultant, Beatrice, might be tangled up in all this."

Razzzor was silent.

I winced. "You still there?"

"That's... interesting."

"It is?"

"Tom Henderson was on the board of Clean Bay, that environmental non-profit. You heard of it?"

"Yeah," I said. "They're involved in water issues."

"So, Beatrice was angling for her firm to do their work. It would have been big. They're going global."

"Was angling?"

"Whoa. Watch your six," he shouted.

I spun and blasted a zombie emerging from a pile of rotting body parts.

"Was angling?" I repeated.

"Tom killed her chances. He made sure another firm won the bid."

"How do you know this?"

"I was in her office when she got the bad news," he said. "She was really mad."

"And she knew Tom Henderson was responsible?"

"Not then," Razzzor said, "but she found out later."

"How did *you* find out?"

"I, uh, was sort of dating her receptionist."

"Sort of?" I teased.

"She's really smart," he said defensively.

"She'd have to be smart to work for Beatrice." I didn't know the woman well, but I didn't figure her for putting up with stupidity.

We played for another hour, but my heart wasn't in the game. I signed off, and the house was silent.

I pulled out my laptop and found Pepper's social media feed. If the posting times were anything to go by (and they weren't), she had alibis for both Tom and Vanella Henderson's murders.

I studied the photos I'd taken of Beatrice's date book. Her alibis seemed to check out too.

I wandered onto my front stoop. Lights glowed from Brik's modernized bungalow. I checked my watch.

"The heck with it." I walked down my steps, down the sidewalk, and up the wide concrete steps to Brik's house. I knocked.

A minute later, the door opened.

Brik's face brightened. "Hey. What's going on?"

"I saw your lights on, and..." I tugged down the hem of my blouse. "Mind if I come in?"

He stepped back, opening the door wider. "Sure. Come on in."

Insides knotting, I followed him inside. The house seemed smaller when it wasn't jammed with people, though it should have been just the opposite.

"Want a drink?" Brik asked.

"Sure. I'll have a beer."

Brik grabbed two from the fridge and handed me one. He ambled to the back of the house, where one of the massive sliding glass doors stood open.

I followed him onto the porch and down the concrete steps to his backyard.

We sat in wooden lawn chairs beneath the pergola and drank beer without speaking.

"What's happening with your investigation?" he finally asked.

"Lots of questions, few answers."

He snorted a laugh.

I sucked in my cheeks. "It's always confused at this point in an investigation."

"You have no idea how disturbing it is that you have a timeline."

I hesitated. "Did you ever…?"

"Did I what?"

"Build anything for Tom Henderson?"

A breeze rustled the dogwood leaves in my garden next door.

"Yeah," he said. "I installed that closet that tried to swallow you."

"I won't hold it against you." But I was surprised he'd work such a small project. "How did it go?"

"It took me a day. A gig between real work."

Which wasn't the answer I was looking for. "Did he pay you?" I blurted.

"No, he didn't."

"So why work for his wife?" I asked quietly.

He shrugged. "It wasn't her fault I got stiffed. And I told her I was billing her extra to make up for it. She was good with it, and she paid me."

I scraped at the bottle's label with my thumb. "Someone we spoke with heard you arguing with Tom about the bill."

"Yeah. I wanted to knock him into his pool, but I managed to restrain myself. He's not the first deadbeat I've encountered. He won't be the last."

"I'm worried the police might think there was more to it."

Brik's mouth quirked. "The police? So you're here to give me a heads up? That's nice of you, but I can manage."

"Yeah, I guess you could."

"What's that supposed to mean?" His brow puckered.

"I mean after what happened in Eureka," I said, stomach roiling.

The bottle paused halfway to Brik's lips. "Eureka."

"I heard the police gave you a rough time," I said, not meeting his gaze.

He didn't respond.

An owl hooted in the darkness.

I looked up. "What happened?"

"It sounds like you already know." He sat rigid in his chair.

My grip tightened on the bottle, cool and slippery in my hand. "Only that you were a suspect after your girlfriend... died."

His laugh was bitter. "Was murdered, you mean."

"Was murdered." I lowered my head again. Then it was true. Hyperion had been right, and for a moment, I hated him for it. But only a moment. And then sadness and resignation took anger's place.

"And you think I'm a suspect now?" he said.

"No. Of course not. You're no killer. But if I found out about Eureka and the argument, the police won't be far behind."

A muscle in his jaw pulsed.

Tell me what you're thinking. Tell me you forgive me for this intrusion. "If you want to talk," I said, "I'll listen."

He didn't speak. I sat there a long minute, waiting.

"I don't," he said.

I gulped the rest of my beer and tasted dust. "I'm sorry, Brik. You know where to find me."

Feet leaden, I walked home.

CHAPTER 21

"I can't take it anymore." I burst into Hyperion's office. "I need to investigate something."

"Take what anymore?" Hyperion said. "Is your mother here?"

For once, my mother *wasn't* haunting the tearoom. This was a good thing, because Saturday was one of our busiest days, and I didn't need the distraction.

Or maybe I did need one. Because what I couldn't take was thinking about the Brik situation. And it was pretty much *all* I could think about.

"I think we should check out the Henderson's other neighbors," I said. "Check their property, I mean. Archer said the gate was closed and locked when Vanella was killed. But the closed gate could have been a red herring."

"Red herring?"

"To make it look like an outsider did it. How hard was it to get onto the property without using the front gate or Archer's gate?"

"You mean could Cosmo or Pepper have accessed the property easily?" Hyperion asked. "Probably. They were neighbors. But how are we going to get permission to make sure?"

"I already called Cosmo and got it," I said, smug.

"When are we going?"

"Now?"

He checked his computer. "I can manage it. But I have to be back by six for a class."

"Deal."

"And I'm driving."

"You got a car?" I asked, surprised.

"Of course I rented another car. I had to pay for it myself, but I'm sure I can get the insurance company to reimburse me."

"What did you get?"

"Come and see for yourself." He led me into the parking lot and to a sporty red convertible.

"Nice."

"Want to go for a ride?"

Thirty minutes later, Hyperion's convertible was parked in Cosmo's driveway and we stood gawping on the flagstone path to his front door.

I gazed up at the massive house. It was mid-century modern, like Archer's, but two-stories. The front garden was a bit overgrown. Its weathered concrete had a sinister, decaying look.

"Look at this place," Hyperion said. "I should have gone into tech, but I don't have the engineering mindset. Do you ever regret leaving that world?"

"It was never my world. I was just a tourist." And I'd only been an executive assistant. A well-paid executive assistant, thanks to my friend and old boss, Razzzor. But I much preferred being in charge to taking orders.

"I'll bet he has an ocean view from the second floor," Hyperion said.

"And we can look at the beach any day of the week. All we have to do is walk down the street."

"It's not the same." My partner rang the bell, and a gong echoed inside the house. "Admit it, that's just cool."

"Cosmo has style. I'll give him that."

The door opened, and Cosmo smiled out at us. "Come in, come in. You said you have more questions?"

"Actually," I said, "we were hoping to tour your yard."

"Especially the part where it connects to the Hendersons'," Hyperion said.

Cosmo's muscular neck reddened. "You think I snuck through my yard to kill that bastard?"

"No, but someone else might have," I said. "Have you got security cameras?"

"No." He rubbed his cheek with his broad hand. "The police asked me the same thing. About the cameras, I mean. I know I should get them, but I haven't had the time. And this is a good neighborhood. Or it has been, up until now. Well, come on then."

He led us around the corner of the house and into a dense eucalyptus grove.

"Have you turned up anything new?" Cosmo asked.

"The security system was off when Tom Henderson was killed." Hyperion grimaced apologetically at me.

I nodded. It couldn't hurt to give Cosmo *something*.

"Off?" Cosmo asked. "Who turned it off?"

"Vanella," Hyperion said.

"She must have killed him," Cosmo said. "It's almost always the spouse, isn't it?"

I stepped over a fallen branch, its bark a dull, pinkish red. "That's what they say." I shot Cosmo a sideways glance. But who had killed Vanella?

We stopped in front of a high chain link fence topped with coils of wicked looking razor wire. A row of cypress trees lined the other side, but we could see the Hendersons' chateau in the distance.

Hyperion grasped the fence and rattled it. "This looks new."

"It is," Cosmo said. "Drunken partiers kept wandering onto my property. I had to do something. The razor wire might have been a little unnecessary, but it made me feel better."

I studied the high fence. It wouldn't be impossible to climb, but I wouldn't want to deal with that razor wire. "Does this go all the way along the property?"

"All the way to Pepper's."

"May we see?" I asked.

Cosmo shrugged. "Why not?"

We walked along the wire fence until we reached a stone wall.

Cosmo jammed his hand between the fence post and the wall. It stuck midway. "You'd have to be a pixie to get through that."

Hyperion motioned toward the wall. "Pepper's property?"

"Yes, it—" Cosmo's pocket buzzed. He frowned and pulled out his phone. "I've got to take this call. Excuse me. The cell service here isn't very good." He hurried away.

"What do you think?" Hyperion asked. "I snoop on Cosmo and you check out Pepper's?"

"Deal."

Hyperion prowled in the direction Cosmo had taken, and soon disappeared in the eucalyptus trees.

I walked along the stone wall and tried not to think about Brik.

A crow cawed above me, and I suppressed a shiver. The tangled branches, the brush clawing at my slacks… it was all a little *too* haunted-forest. I reached an arched, fairytale gate in the wall and tried the latch.

The gate creaked open.

I peeked through. Blue hydrangeas bordered the other side of the wall. Steppingstones led through a path of foxglove and purple salvia to a lawn and a set of garden chairs.

The path seemed an invitation, but my scalp prickled. I'd be trespassing if I continued.

Listening for footsteps, I stepped through. But instead of taking the path, I walked down the tanbark trail bordering the stone wall.

The hydrangeas gave way to bushes of purple echium. The latter were so thick I had to push their wide leaves aside every fifteen feet to make sure there was still a wall behind them.

And suddenly, there wasn't.

I squeezed between two large bushes and stared at the back of the Hendersons' ginormous French chateau.

"Abigail?" Hyperion hallooed. "Where art thou, Abigail?"

Leaves whacking my face, I returned to Pepper's yard and trotted back to the gate.

Hyperion and Cosmo stood just inside it.

Cosmo glowered at me. "That's Pepper's house."

"Is it?" I asked, my face heating. "I mean, I guessed as much. The path was irresistible."

"It's private property," Cosmo said sharply.

"Shame on you, Abigail," my partner said. "Trespassing again." He turned to Cosmo. "It's the curse of being a snoop. She can't turn it off."

"We should go back." Cosmo turned on his heel and marched into the eucalyptus trees.

Meekly, we followed.

Hyperion cleared his throat. "Cosmo was just telling me about those rubber snakes and glued gate locks."

"Oh?" I said.

"I assumed Archer had done all that," Cosmo said, gruff.

"Not Pepper?" I asked.

The corded muscles in Cosmo's neck relaxed. "She told me she thought Archer had done it too. We knew *we* hadn't. Who else could have?"

"No other neighbors?" Hyperion asked.

"We lived closest to the party house," Cosmo said. "The other neighbors were upset by the noise and the cars, but they weren't as affected by it as we were. And Archer…"

"Archer?" I prompted.

Cosmo walked another ten paces before answering. "He's old. Things affect him more. I guess I feel a little protective of him. There's something fragile beneath the surface."

"You're saying the parties bothered him more than most?" I asked.

"He told me his final days were being ruined." Cosmo shook his head. "But I'm sure Archer didn't kill anyone."

Cosmo saw us to Hyperion's rented convertible. He watched as we drove through his gate.

Hyperion's grip on the wheel didn't relax until we'd rounded a bend and put the house out of sight.

"Find anything?" he asked.

I shook my head. "There's a gap where you can walk from Pepper's to the rear of the Hendersons' house."

"So, Pepper could have snuck through."

"Cosmo could have too, if he knew about it. Did you learn anything?"

"Tragically, Cosmo decided to have his conversation in an open clearing."

"Bummer. You couldn't get close?"

"There was nothing for me to hide behind. But it seemed like he was talking about a loan."

"A loan?"

"And he didn't seem happy."

"And he's sure Archer didn't kill anyone," I said.

Hyperion adjusted his hold on the wheel. "A less than enthusiastic endorsement."

I shifted in the bucket seat. Archer had hired us. He wasn't a killer.

Was he?

CHAPTER 22

I couldn't win.

I'd hurt Brik, and I felt like dirt because of it. And he didn't trust me enough to talk about what had happened. Okay, sure, he didn't *owe* me an explanation. I just thought we were better friends than that.

Or that we were something more?

I fiddled with my skirt. It had gotten static-y and clung to my apron. I couldn't fool myself any longer. I wanted that something more. Now I just hoped I could make things right.

Sunday trudged along. I gazed at Beanblossom's full tables and wished Hyperion were here. He always knew what to say to take my mind off things.

At least Mrs. Bicklesworth had kept her promise and returned. She sat at a table near the brick wall and sipped Empress Tea, a soothing blend of lavender, chamomile, and lemon thyme. The white-haired lady seemed content in her solitude, so I wouldn't bother her. But I wanted to bother *somebody*.

"Just a little distraction," I muttered. I edged toward Mrs. Bicklesworth, my teapot at the ready. "That's all I ask for."

A hip-hop beat roared through the tearoom. I looked around, confused.

A tall, good-looking man leapt to his feet, knocking back his chair. He rapped out lyrics that were familiar but not… quite… right.

Was that *Sixteen Going on Seventeen?*

A woman at a nearby table jumped up. She whipped off her long, kimono-style jacket revealing a dirndl and rapped back at him.

I set down the teapot.

Three more people sprang up. They ripped off their jackets, exposing black uniforms. Roughly yanking away chairs, they launched themselves at the rappers.

"Dance off!" one shouted.

Customers yelped. Half-a-dozen gray-haired women scuttled from their tables. A teacup crashed to the floor. They pressed their backs against the brick wall.

This was so wrong. "Um," I said. "What's—"

A Nazi who most definitely was not a zombie whirled past me.

Mrs. Bicklesworth set down her teacup. "Oh, my."

I gaped, aghast. There were Nazis in my tearoom.

True, they were getting their butts handed to them by the first two rappers, who'd apparently become martial arts experts in this version of the musical. But this was not elegant and genteel. This was… bad. Very bad.

"What's—?" I said more loudly.

Someone turned up the music, drowning out the rest of my words. Teacups rattled in their saucers to the beat. A horde of nuns swarmed through the front door.

In less time than it took to drop a sugar cube into a teacup, half the restaurant was dance fighting. A deck of Tarot cards skidded across the floor. Mrs. Bicklesworth sat frozen and wide eyed.

"Stop!" I gestured widely.

Two Nazis grabbed my upper arms and half-lifted me backwards. They released me and my calf struck a crouching Nazi. I tumbled backward, ass over teakettle. Before my head could hit the floor, hands grasped me again and lifted me to standing.

I stood, panting, and yanked down my skirt.

I was unhurt, so that was good. But I was pretty sure I'd flashed my panties to half my customers.

I *really* hate Nazis.

A nun raised a gun toward the ceiling.

"Not my ceiling!" I shouted at the exact moment the music ended.

There was a bang, and confetti burst from the gun barrel and into the air.

The two leads struck a triumphant pose.

Heads swiveled between the actors and me.

"No Nazis allowed," I said faintly.

"*So Long, Farewell*, flash mob," the first man bellowed and took a bow. "Courtesy of Beatrice Carson PR. Tickets available online."

Beatrice. My hands fisted in my apron pockets.

The remaining patrons applauded politely. The flash mob filtered out the door leaving a crumb-strewn mess at half the tables.

Maricel, eyes wide, joined me beside the hostess stand. "Did you know about this?"

"No," I said. *Good Lord, no.*

"Um, are they coming back?" Maricel said.

I shuddered. "I hope not." I could just see the headlines now. *Nazis invade local tearoom.* I groaned. We were supposed to be genteel.

"Because none of the dancers paid," Maricel said.

I stared in horror at the three-tiered plates on the empty tables. Those were only used for the Royal Tea, our most expensive menu item. "Beatrice," I ground out.

"Who's Beatrice?"

"Someone who'd tell you that no publicity is bad publicity," I said. "And she'd be lying. Extra tea and scones for everyone. I mean, anything they want. No charge." I bustled between the tables assuring the confused guests I was as surprised by the flash mob as they were.

I *think* Mrs. Bicklesworth believed me.

The next morning, I dropped heavily onto my couch and logged onto my game. After yesterday's tearoom disaster, I was more ready than ever to kill zombie Nazis. I just hoped this was the last of Beatrice's revenge.

"Hey," Razzzor said in my ear. "I was wondering where you were."

I adjusted my headset. "You could have picked up the phone and called."

"That's so twentieth century. I got that intel you wanted on Cosmo Terzian."

I scanned the Italian mountain village with my scope. Broken windows. Empty streets. No shambling undead. "What did you find?"

"Turns out his company's in real trouble. They've had a series of big losses. He's looking for a cash infusion."

"Venture capital?"

"The VC firms won't touch him. He's too small and too shaky. He's looking for smaller investors."

"How much does he need?"

"Only a million or so."

I rolled my eyes. *Only.*

A zombie shuffled from behind a sausage shop, and I blasted its head off.

"Does any of that help?" Razzzor asked.

I frowned. "I don't know," I said slowly. "Cosmo has an alibi for Tom Henderson's murder."

"Who?"

"His neighbor, Pepper. And she has an alibi for the second murder. But it's another piece of the puzzle." Now I needed to figure out where it belonged.

We killed undead monsters for an hour or so, and then my stomach started rumbling, and I logged off.

I know food isn't love, and one shouldn't comfort-eat. But trying out new recipes just made sense. So, I experimented with a blackberry scone that used Earl Grey tea crushed fine as a seasoning.

I nibbled a corner of the scone. Good, but not quite there…

I whipped up a lemon glaze and slathered it on top.

Perfect. It's hard to go wrong with blackberries and lemon, but using tea as a seasoning gave it a delicious twist.

And since I also had frozen raspberries, I baked raspberry and coconut scones too. The leftover lemon glaze from the Earl Grey batch improved the latter as well.

I spread more clotted cream on a scone. It's a rough life, being a test baker. But I'd soldier on.

The only thing lacking was someone to share my baked goods with, and a needle lanced my heart. Bracing my hands on the counter, I looked through the kitchen window at the high redwood fence separating my property from Brik's.

A fat bumblebee sampled the climbing jasmine then buzzed away.

My doorbell rang.

Wiping my hands on a dish towel, I hurried to the front door. I almost threw it open, but then I remembered that javelin.

"Hello?" I called.

"It's Hyperion. I'm alone. And I'm absolutely not being forced at gunpoint to knock on your door."

I opened the door, and he strode inside. "Do I smell scones?" he asked. Though it was our day off, he was dressed for success in a forest-green blazer, white button-up shirt, and khakis.

"You do," I said.

But my partner was already making his way to the kitchen. He stopped short in the doorway and pointed. "What is that?"

I looked past him. "An answering machine."

"Those still exist?" He strolled to the counter and took a scone. "I'm loving its retro look though," he mumbled through a mouthful of blackberry scone. "What's that spice?"

"Earl Grey."

He gave me a thumbs up. "I knew you'd be baking. You always bake when you're depressed. And when you're happy."

"So the odds were good."

"You're also always baking on Mondays. Are those scones different?" He pointed.

"Raspberry coconut."

He polished off the first and grabbed a raspberry scone. "What's with your coconut obsession? Not everyone likes coconut you know."

"*I* like coconut."

"Mmphl-mmph."

"What?"

He swallowed. "You could call these The Lovers scones—for the Tarot card."

"I'm all for brand marketing," I said, dreading having to tell him about the flash mob. "But are raspberries connected to the card?"

"No, but remember that magical herbalism course I took? I seem to remember raspberries are often used on love spells."

"Tarot scones. Why not? We've already got Tarot tea."

"So." Hyperion picked at a fleck of coconut. "Let's talk singing Nazis."

I groaned.

"It's not what I would have gone for as a tearoom promo," he continued, "but that *is* your side of the business."

"Beatrice sent the flash mob." And the Royal Teas they'd scarfed down hadn't been cheap.

"I figured as much," he said.

"Have any of the Tarot readers complained?"

"They were oddly charmed by the ninja nuns. But confess—the flash mob's not what's got you down. You talked to Brik, didn't you?"

My breath hitched. "And he wouldn't tell me anything."

"Hm."

"Yeah."

"I think you misunderstand my *hm*."

I crossed my arms. "And it's so easy to interpret."

"Brik is resisting opening up to you."

"Yes," I said. "I got that."

"But what are *you* resisting?"

"Beating down his door and making him talk?"

"Eh…"

"Okay," I said. "I'll bite. What am I resisting?"

"You've been doing it all week," he said. "Your mother."

"She's very resistable. And what does she have to do with Brik?"

"It's not about Brik. You can't control that situation, so let it go and focus on what you can."

"Which is?"

He brushed a crumb off his blazer. "I get that it's hard to forgive someone when they refuse to acknowledge they've done anything wrong. But—"

"Forgiveness isn't for them, it's for me." I slouched against my counter. "Yeah. You've told me that already, and I don't disagree. I'm only saying… I'm not sure it's possible." My throat hardened. "Anger's always been easier when it came to my mother. It doesn't feel as… bad."

"I know."

"But I know it's not right."

"No." He paused. "And let's be real. Throw in some self-righteous victimhood, and it feels weirdly good."

One corner of my mouth lifted. "Oh, I've got plenty of that, don't you worry."

He took a thoughtful bite of the scone, swallowed. "Have you told your mother how you really feel?"

"I think I've been pretty clear, but my words bounce right off her."

"You sure about that?"

"About me being clear or her being resistant?"

"Both. Either," he said. "All I know is, you can't change other people, as much as you may want to."

"I guess… I could try harder." I stared out the window at the redwood fence. A breeze tossed the climbing jasmine.

I *should* try harder, and that meant I couldn't give up on Brik either. Not like my mother had given up on me. "We've got to help Brik."

"Okay, I don't think you *quite* got my point."

"And I know just who we need to talk to."

"There's no way she's going to talk to us again," Hyperion said. "Not after the last time."

The elevator doors slid open.

Beatrice leaned across the glass-topped receptionist desk. She looked up and groaned. Her head dropped forward. "What now? I thought we'd agreed I hadn't killed anyone."

I strode into the reception area. "Thanks for the flash mob."

Beatrice smiled, a crocodile in a vintage green suit. "You're *so* welcome. The actors gratefully accepted your contribution of tea and scones, since I wasn't paying them."

My jaw hardened. "You told them to order the Royal Tea, didn't you?"

"It seemed only fair," she said.

My nostrils steamed. "Fair!"

"Truce?" Hyperion's gaze ping-ponged between Beatrice and me. "Are we even?"

"Maybe," she said, her gaze boring into mine.

"Okay." I shuffled my feet. "We might have deserved the flash mob." As revenge went, it *had* been fairly creative.

"Is that why you're here?" she asked. "To apologize?"

My eyes bulged. "*Us* apologize?"

"We're here because we need your expertise," Hyperion said hastily. He nudged me.

I set my phone on the desk and slid it across to her. "What can you tell us about this javelin?"

She picked up the phone and raised a brow. "Whose car?"

"Mine," Hyperion said.

"Nice aim," she said.

"I'm pretty sure they were aiming at one of us," I said.

"So, not such good aim." She smoothed her pencil skirt. "What do you want to know?"

"Anything you can tell us," I said. "I've tried to find this javelin online, but haven't had any luck."

"You wouldn't," she said. "They haven't made these since I was in high school."

"Did you use one?" Hyperion asked.

Her lip curled. "I'd never use anything so cheap. Seriously, this is high school gym level."

"But you *were* a high school track and field star," I said. "And you did have reason to want Tom Henderson dead."

She crossed her arms. "I thought we'd finished with that."

"You didn't mention Tom had killed your chance of a big contract with Clean Bay," I said.

"I win and lose lots of contracts. And when it came to track and field, I used my own equipment. I was fortunate. My parents had money. They got me extra training."

"In other words," Hyperion said, "the javelin could have come from someone's garage and is, therefore, impossible to trace."

"Yes," she said. "Essentially."

But I wasn't so sure that was true. A strange idea had begun to form in my mind. It didn't make sense—not yet.

But maybe...

Other ideas blundered through my brain too.

And one of those ideas grew into dread certainty.

Hyperion had lied to me.

CHAPTER 23

"You have a source." I stepped onto the brick sidewalk beside Hyperion and squinted in the California sunshine.

My partner's eyes widened. He splayed one hand against his blazer. "What?" It was a terrible impression of an innocent man.

"And now you're acting innocent," I said to Hyperion. "That means you're totally up to something."

A man carrying a surfboard on his shoulder sauntered past. We both edged out of his way.

"I have no idea what you're talking about," he said.

"You didn't dig that stuff up on Brik on your own. You like him too much to snoop. You got the Eureka story from someone. Who was it? Detective Chase?"

A flush stained Hyperion's cheeks.

"Oh. My. God." I pointed. "You're blushing."

"Am not."

"Are too. It *was* Detective Chase. Why is he...?" *Oh.*

"We're dating, okay?"

"Well, okay," I said. Chase was a great guy. And Hyperion was a great guy. I was happy for my partner. But I was also worried that Chase considered Brik a suspect. "Cool."

"But you have to keep it on the DL."

"Detective Chase doesn't seem like the sort of guy who hides."

"He's not, but he's private. And you and I *are* sort of interfering in his investigation. And Vanella died before the HOA meeting, not after." He sagged against an iron lamp post. "Whew. I've been dying to get that out. But I couldn't figure out how to tell you without revealing my source. You're not mad, are you?"

"No. He told you that?"

Hyperion glanced around the street. A woman walked into a flower shop across the road. "I might have accidentally looked at his murder board," he whispered.

"You saw a murder board?" Now I really *was* jealous.

"It was amazing."

"I totally want to date a cop."

Hyperion gave me a shrewd look. "Do you?"

No. I didn't. Absently, I rubbed my lips. Brik and I had both pretended nothing had happened after our kiss. But for me, something *had* happened.

"I might have also accidentally seen the autopsy report," he said.

"Accidentally?"

"Vanella didn't die in that car. She was unconscious when she was put inside it."

"Put into it?"

"There was bruising to indicate she'd been carried, probably over a shoulder. And there were particles from the garage floor caught up in her clothes."

"Like at some point she'd been set down?"

"Can you see her sitting on the garage floor voluntarily?"

"No, I can't." Vanella's death definitely hadn't been a suicide. "But she'd swallowed pills?"

He shrugged. "She may not have known what she was swallowing. The pills could have been ground up as part of a spiked drink."

We walked to my car. Hyperion fell silent.

"He thinks you should be careful with Brik," he said.

Nausea swam in my gut. "Then he really does consider Brik a suspect."

"I don't know."

But I knew. My partner was lying again. And I let him.

Because it was almost lunchtime, we walked to a little Mexican restaurant. It perched on a low cliff overlooking the bay and its rows of pastel color houses.

Hyperion sweet-talked the hostess into giving us the last window seat—a two-top beside a brightly tiled arch. I ordered iced tea, and Hyperion ordered tequila.

I perused my menu, though I knew I'd get the vegetarian burrito and Hyperion would get fish tacos. When it came to Mexican food, we were creatures of habit.

"Abigail?" a woman said behind me.

I flinched, shoulders to my ears.

My mother smiled down at me. "How marvelous to find you here. I'll join you." She grabbed a chair from a neighboring table, startling the couple dining there. My mother set it at the end of our table, fluffed out her caftan, and sat.

"This is a surprise," I choked out.

"Isn't it?" she said. "I just felt drawn to the place. Now I know why. The universe was bringing us together again."

The universe clearly had something against me.

She took the menu from my hands. "What's good here?"

"Everything," Hyperion said.

The waitress appeared with our drinks and set them on the table. "And can I get anything for you, ma'am?" she asked my mother.

"Is that iced tea?" My mother took the glass in front of me and sipped it. "I'll have this. And we're not quite ready to order yet."

"I'll have a margarita," I said.

My mother tsked. "How many times must I tell you? It dims your third eye."

"Make it a double," I said.

The waitress smiled and bustled off.

"Really, Abigail," she said, "I think you ordered that drink just because I suggested it was bad for you. That's inauthentic behavior."

"Oh, that's totally Abigail," Hyperion said.

I glared at him.

"She's had a shock," Hyperion amended and sank lower in his chair.

"A shock?" my mother asked. "What's happened?"

"Not a shock," I said. "An idea. We're about to go on a stakeout. We're fortifying ourselves."

"With alcohol? Who are you staking out?"

Which of my suspects could I throw to the wolves today? "Maylene Soon."

"But you need to be alert when you're watching someone," she said. "A double margarita does not make one alert."

"I suppose..." I pretended to think. "Would you like to stake her out instead?" We'd diverted her once that way. It had cost me a French dinner, but it had been totally worth it.

"Well of course I'll go with you. We haven't spent nearly enough time together. Your aura needs smoothing, and I suspect at least three of your chakras are blocked."

Hyperion tossed back his shot and glowered at me.

Now I really needed that drink.

The three of us ate lunch. My mother stuck me with her share of the bill. We collected Hyperion's newest rental and drove toward the wedding expo office.

"We could have a long wait," I warned my mother as we crested the hill. "Stakeouts can get pretty boring."

At the bottom of the cul-de-sac, the front door to the squat, cinderblock building opened. Maylene, in bicycle shorts and a tank top, stepped from it. She turned, talking to someone inside.

Hyperion pulled to the side of the steep road.

"Changing cars like this is brilliant," my mother said. "No one will know you're following them when you have a different car every day."

"Let's hope this one survives," Hyperion muttered.

Maylene nodded to the person inside the tiny office building and stepped into her SUV. After a moment, her car pulled from the curb.

She drove past us, and we ducked. Hyperion made a U-turn and followed her onto the freeway.

"There," my mother said. "We didn't have to wait long at all for something interesting to happen. I've always been lucky that way. I think it's due to my positive mental attitude."

Maylene drove north to Santa Cruz. Hyperion kept us a cautious two car lengths behind her SUV. We slowed on the main street, crowded with cars.

"Santa Cruz didn't used to be this crowded when I grew up here." My mother sighed. "But condensed populations *are* more environmentally friendly."

Maylene's SUV turned left.

"Is she going to the Boardwalk?" my mother asked. "I haven't been there for ages. So why do you think Maylene may be a killer?"

"She had means, motive, and possibly opportunity," I said.

"Possibly?"

"I didn't get a chance to ask her where she was when Tom and Vanella were killed," I admitted. Maylene had distracted me with her revelation about Brik.

"Not getting her alibi sounds sloppy," she said.

"I know," I said, voice sharp.

"Really, Abigail. There's no need to get so defensive. If you stayed in the present, like I do, you'd be much happier and more effective."

"Your mother isn't wrong," Hyperion chimed in.

I closed my eyes and took a slow, calming breath. "No doubt."

"You were distracted, thinking about something else when you were interrogating Maylene," she said. "Weren't you?"

"Okay, okay. I may have had something on my mind."

Maylene parked in front of a chic burger joint.

Since it was a Monday, and tourists were scarce, we managed to find a spot only a block away. While Hyperion loaded the meter with quarters, I walked closer to her SUV.

Maylene stepped into a purple tutu, slapped on a set of black studded shoulder pads, and shrugged into a pair of fairy wings. Slinging a backpack over her shoulder, she marched toward the beach.

I watched her departing back. Her outfit *would* be unusual, except this was California.

"What's happening?" Breathless, Hyperion jogged up to me.

I pointed at Maylene, trotting down a set of cement steps. "I'm guessing she isn't here to commit murder. She's not exactly going for the inconspicuous look." But her outfit would make it easier to tail her.

Hyperion's brows rose. He rubbed his hands together. "Wings? Best. Stakeout. Ever." He strode after her.

"Now your partner has the right attitude." My mother walked after him. "Be in the moment."

I trailed after them both and reminded myself that sulking was unattractive. I'd only suggested the stakeout to get rid of my mother. But the tutu, wings, and shoulder pads had me intrigued. Was Maylene in a roller derby?

The scent of burgers, baking ice cream cones, and suntan oil floated on the breeze. I paused on the embankment overlooking the beach. The boardwalk's colorful Ferris wheel was unmoving. A rollercoaster arched above fluttering banners. At the south end of the boardwalk, a set of bleachers had been set up.

Maylene trudged across the sand toward the bleachers.

I trotted after Hyperion and my mother. When I reached the beach, I pulled off my sandals. It was easier walking barefoot, and I love the feel of sand between my toes.

Maylene stopped at a gate in a chain link fence that blocked off the bleachers. She showed something to the guard, and he let her inside.

We strolled to the gate.

"Hey," Hyperion said to the guard. "What's going on here?"

The beefy guard crossed his arms over his golf shirt. "Finals for *Global Gladiators for Guts and Glory*."

Hyperion gaped. "What? Are you meaning to tell me it's here? Today? Now?"

The guard nodded.

"Can we go in?" Hyperion asked excitedly.

"Not through this gate. This isn't for the public. You'll have to go around to the other side. But only if you've got tickets, and we're sold out."

Hyperion whirled and grabbed my shoulders. "We have to get in. This is hands down the best gladiator show on TV." He jogged along the wire fence and up the embankment.

"Global Guts and Glory?" My mother wrinkled her nose.

"We go where the stakeout takes us," I said. "If you want, I can call you a rideshare to take you home?"

She sighed. "No. I never say *no* to new experiences." She wafted up the hill after Hyperion.

Dammit.

By the time I made my way up the sandy slope, Hyperion had vanished into the churning crowd at the front gate.

I waited in the shade of a cotton candy stand while Hyperion tried to wheedle tickets from people in line. My mother drifted into the crowd.

Thirty minutes later, my partner trudged to my side. "There's not a single scalper here. Can you believe it?"

"What are the odds?"

He clawed his hands through his thick hair. "I can't believe I'm going to miss this. I can't believe I didn't know *Global Guts* was here. I've gotten too focused on murder and mayhem."

"You think?"

"Have you seen the guys on this show?" he asked. "They're practically superhuman."

"Which doesn't interest you at all because you're seeing someone."

"I can still look," he said defensively. "I'm not dead."

The crowd roared behind the fence.

Hyperion hung his head. "They're starting. I'll keep looking. Maybe there's *someone* who'll sell us their tickets."

My mother materialized beside him. "Let's go in."

"We couldn't get tickets," I said.

"Oh, you don't need tickets," she said. "You're with me." She turned and drifted to the gate.

My jaw slackened. What was she up to now?

The ticket taker stepped aside. My mother sashayed through the turnstile, her caftan fluttering. She turned and motioned toward us. "Aren't you coming?"

Hyperion and I swapped confused glances and followed.

The ticket taker smiled and let us walk on through.

"Um, did you buy tickets?" I asked my mother.

"No. I just asked for Xavier."

Hyperion stopped short. "Xavier... Ultra?" he sputtered.

"Who's he?" I asked.

"He's the *Global Guts* CEO," my partner said. "He used to be a fighter before he blew out his knee. He drove race cars. He set a cliff diving record."

"Delightful man," my mother agreed, "if a bit intense. We spent a memorable weekend together at a spiritual retreat in Iceland." She clapped her hands together. "There is nothing more mind expanding than meditating in a hot spring beneath the northern lights."

"You *know* Xavier Ultra?" Hyperion squeaked.

"Yes, that's what I said."

He grabbed my arm and shook me lightly. "Your mother knows Xavier Ultra. Why didn't you tell me?"

"I can't imagine how it slipped my mind, since I had no idea about it." And I tried not to be irritated by the fact my mother was actually being useful. But even a stopped clock is right twice a day, etc., etc.

Instead of walking toward the stands, she took us to a VIP room overlooking the arena. My mother led Hyperion to a tanned, balding, muscular man. By the look of awestruck glee on Hyperion's face, I assumed the man was Xavier Ultra.

Abandoned and flummoxed by our sudden good fortune, I sat at a table and studied the arena.

Contestants climbed, swung, and jumped across a series of tortuous devices above greenish pools. Most of the contestants failed at a section where they had to traverse an uneven wall while clinging to a narrow ledge by their fingertips.

I scanned the crowd for fairy wings.

"Ever thought of being a gladiator?" Xavier asked me.

I swiveled in my chair. "Not in my wildest nightmares."

He laughed. "Smart girl. Those athletes had to train like Olympians just to get this far."

"How *did* they get this far?" I asked. "What's the process?"

"Tryouts." He nodded to a clipboard on the wall.

I stood and studied the clipboard. There had been tryouts last Tuesday, from four to eight p.m.. And Maylene was in costume and a martial artist...

I mentally slapped my head. She wasn't here as a fan. Maylene was a combatant.

I pointed at the board. "Everyone who's here today, were they at Tuesday's tryouts?"

He nodded. "Yep."

My pulse quickened. "Do you have any photos or video of the tryouts?"

He raised a brow. "Yes. Why?"

"I'm looking for a particular competitor, Maylene Soon."

"Anything to help out Leaf's daughter." He crooked a finger at a scrawny man with a clipboard and a *Guts and Glory* lanyard around his neck. The man trotted to us.

"Maylene Soon," Xavier said. "What was her tryout schedule on Tuesday?"

My heart beat more quickly. She really was a gladiator?

The man flipped through the pages. "She was one of the last, scheduled for six o'clock. We were running late though, so she actually had her tryout around seven."

"I don't suppose you know what time she arrived at the tryouts?" I asked.

"All the competitors were required to be here by four o'clock or be disqualified."

So Maylene had an alibi. And why was that disappointing? At least we could cross her off the suspect list.

Xavier nudged me. "There she is now."

I moved to the window.

A woman in fierce black and white face paint, a tutu, and fairy wings emerged from beneath the stands. The crowd cheered.

Maylene made it about halfway through the course, getting stuck at the wall traverse. She fell, plummeting into the green pool, and I sucked in a breath. That was a long fall.

I leaned forward, watching.

A hand reached from the pool. Dripping slime, Maylene pulled herself out and clambered to her feet. She raised both fists in the air. The crowd roared. She strode off the field.

Hyperion clapped me on the shoulder, and I started.

"Come on," he said. "Xavier said we can meet Maylene."

"We don't need to meet Maylene. We know Maylene." But I followed Hyperion and my mother from the VIP room and to a sort of holding area beside a slime pool.

Maylene stood signing forms held by the man with the clipboard.

"Maylene?" I asked.

She pivoted, hung her head. "You."

"That was amazing," Hyperion said. "You're a gladiator."

Maylene chewed her lip. "But I didn't make it through the finals." She brushed slime off her wings, and it dripped to the slick concrete. "So I'm not a gladiator after all." She shook her head. "This is so embarrassing. How did you even recognize me?"

"We saw you walk in," I said, "before you put the makeup on."

She blew out her breath.

"Do the police know you were here Tuesday night and couldn't have killed Vanella?" Hyperion asked. "Because they should."

Maylene shrugged. "I *could* have killed Vanella."

I started.

"All I needed was an accomplice," she continued.

Hyperion and I edged backward. My heel struck the edge of the pool.

Maylene laughed. "You two are such suckers. I'm kidding. Of course I didn't kill anyone." She turned and strode into a changing room.

My mother touched my arm. "I didn't think it was funny."

Neither had I, but it had given me an idea. We needed to talk to Archer.

I swiveled toward my partner. "Hyp—" My foot stepped in something slick. It skidded out from beneath me at the same time my mom stepped backward, laughing at something Xavier had said.

We collided. I gasped and pitched backward. Xavier grabbed my arm and yanked me forward before I could fall into the slime pool.

"Whoa," he said, releasing me. "Careful."

"Thanks," I said.

My mother shook her head. "Yes, Abigail, be careful." She leaned closer and whispered. "Honestly, this attention seeking is very unattractive. Throwing yourself into the ocean and now a pool? Do you think Xavier can't see right through it? He's got women throwing themselves at him daily."

My face tightened. Ignoring her, I strode away and called Archer.

"Abigail," he said. "I have good news. I'm quitting the paper."

"Congratulations." *I guess.*

"The corporate media isn't the free press anymore. They don't have any incentive to search for facts—facts don't sell. Opinion does. The free press now are citizen journalists online."

"You're becoming a citizen journalist?" I shook my head and slime splattered the pavement. This wasn't why I'd called, but… Archer had seemed more down than usual, even for someone suspected of murder.

"Pepper and Cosmo gave me the idea. If they can make videos, so can I," he said. "I've decided to make viral videos."

"I'm not sure it works that—"

"Now, tell me *you* have some good news."

"Not yet," I said. "But I have a question. That story about the Maasai you told us, where did you hear it?"

Archer confirmed what I'd suspected, and I swayed, realization striking hard.

"Are you sure?" I asked.

"Of course I'm sure. Why?"

Because I had a bad idea whodunnit.

CHAPTER 24

I braced my hand on the white stone counter and reviewed my lack of evidence. My theory about the murder was a little complicated, but I was growing more and more certain I was right.

"That little French restaurant is divine," my mother boomed to a Tarot reader. "We should go. My treat."

My shoulders hunched. By "my treat," she meant Gramps or I'd be paying. And better me than him. He'd suffered enough.

My mother had taken up her usual post at the best table in the tearoom, overlooking the street. Afternoon sunlight made her brightly colored caftan glow.

I thought of that Six of Swords. It had to come true sooner or later. Eventually, she'd move on to her next spiritual retreat, and my life would get back to normal.

Whatever *that* was.

Tarot readers drifted between the tables. Diners feasted on our Tuesday tea special of blackberry scones and Temperance Tea.

As several Tarot readers had pointed out, the Tower card is associated with Tuesdays, not Temperance. But the Tower is about chaos, upsets and destruction. No one likes it. So, I'd gone with the Tuesday Temperance alliteration instead. We'd had enough chaos lately. Not that I was superstitious or anything.

"Though I must say," my mother continued, "it doesn't attract the best element."

An elderly woman swiveled in her chair. "Not the best element? Who else could afford that place?"

"Well," my mother said, "not everyone with money is at their personal best, if you know what I mean. Why I saw Pepper Schripsema and Cosmo Terzian together there, and—"

I hurried to the table. "Would anyone like refills of tea?"

The whitehaired lady smiled. "Why yes. I'd love more of your

Temperance Tea."

"Mother?" I asked.

"The same," she said.

I bent and whispered in her ear. "Please don't gossip about murder suspects. It brings down the vibration."

My mother straightened in her seat. "I was *not* gossiping. And you shouldn't assume the worst in people. You'll only get what you expect."

Biting back a smile, I bustled into the kitchen. Hyperion lounged in a corner eating a scone.

"Archer called," he said.

I rocked backward, my stomach pitching. "Has something happened?"

"No, and I told him we're getting close to solving this thing." He set down his plate and arched a brow. "We are, aren't we?"

I shifted, uncomfortable. "I think so, but I don't *know*. I have no proof, so I could be wrong."

"You're not the only one who pinged to it when we were talking to Maylene yesterday, you know." He walked to the kitchen's central worktable and braced his elbows on it.

I nodded and wiped my dry hands on my apron. "If they were lovers, it's strange Pepper didn't know Tom Henderson was an ex-musician. And it's strange that the home's video cameras were off when Tom Henderson and Vanella were killed."

"Vanella admitted she'd turned them off."

"Yes, she did. There are a lot of things about these murders that don't add up–like Pepper trying to knock Vanella's head off one day and being buddies with her the next."

"It's almost as if everybody's been lying to us," he said dryly.

"Imagine that." I rolled my neck. "The thing is, I've been looking at the individuals involved. Maybe we should be looking at the relationships."

"I agree. Now what are we going to *do* about it?"

"More internet research to look for connections between our suspects?"

Hyperion sighed and straightened off the metal table. "Boring, but sound. I'll get started."

And I'd sneak into his office to pester him about what he'd found in between serving customers. I brewed pots of Temperance Tea and returned to the tearoom.

Thirty minutes later, I slipped into Hyperion's gypsy-caravan of an office. He hunched over his table. Bastet sat beside the laptop, his tail lashing.

Absently, Hyperion shoved the striped tail off the keyboard.

"Find anything?" I asked.

"Pepper and Vanella took a spin class together."

"That's online?"

"Pepper puts everything online. But I don't think she intended to include Vanella in this shot." He pointed to the screen.

I squinted at the photo. Pepper had taken a selfie, capturing herself at a flattering angle. Vanella was on the machine behind her and to the left, face red and mid-huff. "Or maybe it wasn't an accident." It was the ideal snap to embarrass a frenemy.

"Meow," my partner said. "But no, it's not the best shot."

"See if you can go back farther. Most of these people grew up here. Maybe you can find something in the local papers. Beatrice on the track team, that sort of thing."

"I thought we'd ruled Beatrice out."

"You know what I mean."

"I think I do," he said.

I returned to the tearoom. A seating ended and customers trickled out the door. We cleared and reset the tables, gave the room a quick sweep, and the next wave of customers rolled in.

When I got my next break, I stuck my head in Hyperion's office. He was chuckling over his computer.

"Find anything?" I asked.

"Get this. Pepper and Cosmo went to high school together. They were prom king and queen. Did you go to your prom?"

"Junior prom." Remembered embarrassment flushed my cheeks. "It was a total disaster. You?"

"Nope. I was just coming to accept I played for the other team. I decided it was all too awkward."

"I hated high school."

"Me too. I *knew* there was a reason we'd be great partners."

"All right. I'll get back to work."

I popped back into his office a few more times, but Hyperion didn't find much. There were a few articles about Cosmo's VR firm, all glowing.

Maylene was mentioned in a martial arts tournament or two, boosting my desire not to mess with her. Since she was off my suspect list though, I shouldn't have to.

Finally, I closed up the tearoom. My mother lingered at her window seat.

"Do you need a ride home?" I asked her.

She set her teacup on the white tablecloth and looked up. "Why haven't you invited me to your home?"

"Uh..." *Uh, oh.* I looked away. Outside the window, a retriever sat tied to an iron lamppost, a hopeless expression on his face.

Hyperion strolled into the tearoom.

"It strikes me as rather selfish," she said, "leaving me with your grandfather. He's an old man."

Fuming and guilty, because I *had* stuck her with Gramps, I clamped my mouth shut. But how could she not see what a pest she'd made of herself? How she took advantage, how she just expected everyone else to take care of her and clean up after her? "You—"

"Six of Swords," Hyperion hummed from behind me. "She's leaving soon."

Heat flushed my face. "You—"

Hyperion clapped me on the shoulder. "Why don't we talk homicide?" He dropped his voice. "And how you're *not* going to commit one."

"No." I turned to my mother. "Leaf, we need to talk."

CHAPTER 25

"Talk about what?" My mother examined her French manicure. "Your inability to connect on a real level?"

My head pounded. When had she gotten a manicure, and who had paid for that? *No.* I needed to focus on what mattered. I needed to get this off my chest, to make her hear me. But my throat was suddenly so tight I wasn't sure I could speak.

"Abigail," Hyperion murmured.

I stuffed my hands into my apron pockets. "If you want to be a part of my life," I said evenly, "you need to act like it. That doesn't mean mooching off my tearoom, and my Tarot readers, and my grandfather—"

"My *father.*"

"Who was more of a parent to me than you and Parker ever were." My neck corded. "If you're only here because you need a place to stay, or because it's entertaining, I'm not interested in that kind of relationship."

She steepled her fingers and smiled. "I hear you. I feel you. And I accept you as you are. But I also feel you're getting a little caught up in the doingness of your own mind."

My nails bit into my palms. "I really don't think you did hear me."

"That's because you're not present with what *is.* Have you checked your pineal gland? It may be calcified."

I covered my face. If I got any more present, I'd lose my mind, pineal gland and all.

"I can see you're not in a place of awareness," my mother said. "I'll come back later." She drifted out the front door.

On the brick sidewalk, a middle-aged couple collected the retriever. He thumped his tail gratefully. The three walked away.

I locked the blue door on the scene, turned to Hyperion, and leaned against the solid blue wood.

Hyperion's brow wrinkled. "Are you all right?" He steered me to a table and pulled out a chair. I sat.

My pulse was slowing. I felt a little shaky. I'd had decades of practice telling her off in my head. Now that I really had, now that I'd set some boundaries, I should feel relieved or unburdened.

Instead, I just felt small.

"I don't know what I want," I said slowly, throat aching. "I thought I wanted… I don't regret what I said. It was all true, and I needed to say it, even if she didn't listen to a word of it."

"You sound like you're trying to convince yourself."

I stared at a pack of Tarot cards, abandoned on the table.

I wanted things to be different, and wanting others to change was a fool's game. I could only control my own behavior. But maybe for tonight, standing my ground was the best I could do.

None of that made me feel better.

"Abigail?" Hyperion removed his blazer, draped it over the back of a chair, and sat across from me.

My eyes burned. "She's my mother, even if she hasn't been around much."

He rested his hand on mine. "For what it's worth," he said in a low voice, "I think you did pretty good."

"Thanks." I smiled briefly. "But I didn't take your advice. That wasn't exactly forgiving." I picked up the Tarot deck. Idly, I pulled out the cards and drew one.

The eight of cups, a cloaked man walking away from eight golden cups. He wasn't looking back.

"That card's not your mother walking away," Hyperion said. "That's you, moving on."

"You can't be sure of that." Tarot meanings changed with the reader and the circumstances. "Tarot can be tricky."

"I *am* sure. You're going to get through this and come out stronger. And that isn't a Tarot reading. It's what I know about *you.*"

"You're a good friend." I returned the card to the deck, shuffled it, and put it in its box. "Sorry you had to hear that."

He shrugged. "That was nothing. Try working a Ren Faire sometime. High drama like you wouldn't believe." He paused. "I've been, um, reading up on narcissists. Not that your mother—"

"Oh, she is."

"Well, neither of us are clinical psychologists, but…"

"What did you find out?"

"You're not supposed to let them drag you into their crazy," he said. "Instead, you're supposed to be calm but firm. And you did that." But an expression of unease crossed his face.

"What didn't I do right?" I smoothed the white tablecloth.

"Nothing. It's only… when you confront them, there's a chance the narcissist might escalate."

"Escalate? What's she going to do? Demand I pay for another French meal?" I blew out my breath. "Sorry. I guess I haven't calmed down yet. Forget my mother. Let's talk about something else."

"Murder?"

"That'll work. The stuff you found online supports our case. I mean, it doesn't prove it, but it supports it. Maybe it's time you told Detective Chase."

He tipped his head. "Tell him exactly what?"

"Who killed the Hendersons."

"And you believe that to be...?"

I shifted in my chair and crossed my arms. "Are you trying to get me to say who because you don't believe I know? Or because *you* don't know?"

"Oh, I know. I just want to know if you know."

I told him my theory.

He goggled at me. "What? No way."

"Fine. Who do *you* think did it?"

My partner told me what he'd put together.

I shook my head. "Someone had to put Vanella, unconscious, in that car. Can you see Pepper carrying Vanella over her shoulder?"

"No," he admitted. "That would be a fluctuating, anomalous distortion."

"What?" Lovecraft couldn't have said that.

"You must be right. But I was *half* right."

"I wonder if a part of Archer suspected all along?"

"He *is* a keen observer of the human condition." Hyperion pushed back his chair and stood. "Fine. I'll go and let Tony know."

"Will he be angry with you?"

"Because I'm a crime-solving genius? Tony's a bigger man than that."

I yawned and stretched, suddenly tired.

"Are you going to be okay?" he asked, peering at me with concern.

"I will be after I get some sleep."

"It's only seven o'clock."

"After I eat, read a book, and get some sleep," I amended. I felt drained.

"That's not much of an improvement. But I suppose finally letting your mother know how you really feel must have been exhausting."

I winced. "Was it that bad?"

"No. You were firm but friendly." He patted the top of my head. "Things will work out. You'll see." Hyperion swaggered out the door.

But *how* would things work out? I locked the door again behind him and made myself a cup of Earl Grey. Sitting at the table with the discarded Tarot deck, I shuffled the cards and drew one.

The Tower.

I sat unmoving, a shiver touching my spine. Thanks to my mother, I knew a lot about Tarot. And the Tower was rarely good, representing sudden disasters and upsets. But it was also a card about breakthroughs. Maybe I'd just made one.

I returned the card to its deck and finished my tea. Then I locked up and drove home.

Brik's house was silent, but it was Tuesday—not one of his bigger party nights. At least I hoped that was why it was so quiet, and not because of what I'd said to him.

Though I appreciated the peace, I owed him an apology. But instead of knocking on his door, I unlocked my own and went inside, toeing off my sneakers.

I warmed up a leftover burrito in the microwave and carried it out to my redwood deck.

Solar lights glowed along the garden paths. The night was still warm enough to enjoy without a jacket. But a breeze rustled the dogwood tree, and I thought I scented ocean fog in the air. The coast would turn chilly soon, and my part of the world would slowly turn to autumn and endings.

I set the burrito on the table and sat.

A gate opened and clanged shut. Footsteps padded up the path alongside my house. I stiffened, gripping the tines of the fork between my fingers like a gouging weapon.

Brik emerged from the side of my bungalow. He looked up at me on the deck.

"Hey," he said.

"Hey."

"Can we talk?"

CHAPTER 26

"You're a good person." Brik slowly climbed the steps to my deck.

"Sometimes." I set my fork down beside my half-eaten burrito. A night bird flapped above us.

He shook his head. "No, at your core. You're patient, and kind, and you care about doing the right thing."

"Okay," I said, wary. Those all sounded like good things, but his expression was grim.

"Lyssa and I hadn't been dating long, but she was a good person too. And she'd attracted a stalker."

My muscles tensed. Years ago, a similar thing had happened to me. The police hadn't been able to do much, but they'd tried.

"She was sure it was her ex," he said. "He hadn't wanted the breakup. She told me he was controlling, and she'd split up with him when she'd seen his violent side."

I nodded.

He exhaled slowly. "She reported her stalker to the police. They never caught the guy."

"And then Lyssa was killed," I guessed, sickened.

He nodded, blinked, and looked away, toward the redwood fence that separated our properties. A whiff of jasmine, from the flowers climbing the six-foot fence, carried to the deck.

"I'm sorry," I said.

"She was a good person," he repeated. He met my gaze. "And she was tough, and funny, and she didn't take any crap from anyone, including me. She was a lot like you."

I shifted in my wicker chair.

"But someone killed her," he said. "They never caught the guy, and I became a suspect."

"Not her ex?"

"He had an alibi. A good one, I guess. I didn't."

My heart pinched. Was that why Brik didn't like being alone? So he'd always have an alibi? So he wouldn't be accused again?

"The police finally wrote it off as a random shooting," he continued, "a gang drive-by."

"And you moved to San Borromeo."

"All of Eureka seemed to know I'd been a suspect, that Lyssa and I had been seeing each other. And there were the memories." He looked at his heavy boots.

I swallowed. My hands tightened on the arms of my chair. "I'm sorry," I said again.

"I like you a lot, Abigail." His eyes seemed to darken. "A lot. But you're reckless."

"No, I'm not."

"And yet you keep getting involved in murders. Last month I nearly saw you get killed." Absently, he rubbed his shoulder.

My throat thickened. *Brik* had nearly been killed.

"I can't blame you for it," he said. "I know better than most that the police do their best. But they're human. They don't always get things right, and you have to protect the people you love. But I can't go through that again."

Brik walked down the deck steps. "Whatever's between us has to end." He disappeared around the corner of my house. The gate clicked open and clanged shut.

I slumped in the deck chair. *Well.* The lump in my throat hardened. *Damn.*

The backs of my eyes warmed. I replayed the conversation in my mind. I replayed other conversations we'd had. I replayed the kiss.

None of that was super helpful.

I understood more now. I understood why he'd backed off after that kiss, why he'd pretended nothing had happened, why he'd kept me at arm's length. I understood why he was so standoffish with Detective Chase. And I thought I understood all his parties, and that look of panic when he considered not having them quite so often.

A part of me wanted to run after Brik and tell him I wasn't reckless. I'd told the police everything I knew about the Henderson murders, and I'd done the same before. I wanted the police to catch the bad guys. I had no illusions Hyperion and I could do it on our own.

But there was no point. He was right. Last month a man had pointed a gun at me and shot Brik instead. It had only happened because I'd been helping a friend.

A certain degree of nosiness can't be denied either.

And I'd do it again. I wanted my mother to change, but it seemed change wasn't so easy.

Suddenly it seemed a little hard to breathe, the lump in my throat expanding into my chest. I took my uneaten burrito into the kitchen and rewrapped it. I was no longer hungry.

My doorbell rang, and I glanced at the clock on my stove. It was after eight. Too late for a casual caller. My pulse jumped. Had Brik returned?

I hurried to the front door and looked through the peephole.

My mother waved.

I hung my head. *Not now.*

Forcing a smile, I opened the door. "Hello mother. What brings you here?" Because I was pretty sure she hadn't had a good think about what I'd said and come to apologize.

"I never got to see your house." My mother bustled past me in a cloud of patchouli. She scanned the open space—the gaming area with its blue couch and console, the dining table where I'd left my laptop open, the French doors beyond.

Numbness flowed through my muscles. I wondered if she was getting tired of staying with Gramps and had decided to seek different pastures. If she had, she was out of luck. The bungalow only had one bedroom, and I didn't think she'd settle for a couch.

"You've created quite an oasis here." She wandered toward the French doors at the back of the house and stared into the dimly lit garden. "Is this where you get the herbs for your tearoom?"

"No." California has all sorts of rules about growing and preserving food stuffs, and I didn't grow the quantity here I needed for Beanblossom's. "I use these for myself and my friends."

"I've been thinking about what you said." She turned and scanned me, her brow pinching.

My heartbeat quickened. "Oh?"

"I've been listening, and I've finally figured us out."

I blinked, the ache in my chest releasing. Had I been wrong all this time? *Had* she listened?

"You have several entities attached to you," she said. "Obviously, it was them speaking this evening and not you."

"Entities." My heart dipped. This was my mother. She wouldn't change.

And suddenly, that was okay. I'd said my piece and knew where I stood, even if my mother refused to acknowledge it.

"Now don't freak out," she said. "I know people hate that word. *Entity* sounds so scary. But cutting the cords isn't difficult at all. You just have to consciously commit to the change."

Uh, huh. "And you can cut those cords?" I waited for the other shoe to drop.

She adjusted her silky caftan. "Oh, no. It's really not healthy for me to come in contact with such dark beings. But your friend Hyperion told me he knows a woman." Her eyes widened. "Why don't we both see her? I strive to keep my aura clear, but a cleaning from a professional can only be to the good."

An odd sound bubbled from my chest and emerged from my throat.

"What's wrong?" she asked.

I laughed, bending forward and pressing my hands to my heaving sides. The rush of lightness inside me couldn't be contained. With a jolt, I realized I had forgiven her. My mother could only be who she was.

"You shouldn't laugh at something just because you don't understand it," she said stiffly.

I laughed harder, then wiped my eyes and straightened. "Oh, I understand it just fine," I gasped. "You don't have the money to see this woman, do you?"

"Money is only a construct. And you should apologize."

"Why?"

"I don't like the way you made me feel."

"I'm not responsible for the way you feel." And in fairness, she wasn't responsible for my feelings—my feelings were on me and only me. God, I'd wasted so much time being hurt and angry.

"That doesn't matter. It's how I *feel. I* feel you should apologize."

"I only apologize for things I'm actually sorry for." Why was I arguing about this? There was no point to arguing about *anything* with a narcissist.

"The point is," I continued, "no. I'm not taking you to the aura woman, because I'm not your sugar daddy. I'm guessing Gramps refused to give you the money as well?"

"He said I have food and clothing and a roof over my head, and I should be grateful and get a job," she said, indignant. "He wouldn't apologize either."

I smiled. *Good for him.* "You're my mother, and you're a part of my life. But in case I wasn't clear earlier, unless things change, our relationship going forward will be on my terms."

"Your terms?" She huffed. "It takes two people to make a relationship."

"Yes, and if one person is only taking and the other is feeling resentful about it, it won't work."

"I can't believe how ungrateful you are."

"Ungrateful? For you abandoning me as a child and leaving Gramps and Gran to raise me?" I asked without rancor, and cocked my head. "You're right. I should get on my knees with thanks every day. They were wonderful parents. The best. Thank you." Warmth expanded in my chest, and I bowed slightly. "I mean it. Thank you."

She gave herself a shake. "We've left the now. We both need to return to the present."

"Okay," I said. "Want a cup of tea? Or I've got water and juice in the fridge."

"Tea would be lovely." She trailed after me into the kitchen and watched me boil water, measure tea into strainers.

"Why do you have this old-fashioned answering machine?" she asked.

"It was a gift." From someone who really did care about me. From family.

I poured water from the kettle into a ceramic teapot. Hyperion had been right. Ultimately, the forgiveness had been for me. I looked around my small kitchen. It seemed brighter, the glass-fronted cupboards gleaming.

"Anyway," my mother said, "I called Cosmo."

My hand froze, teapot poised above a mug. For a moment, I couldn't speak. "Cosmo? Why did you call Cosmo?"

"I told him if he didn't pay me a half million dollars, I'd go to the police with what I knew."

I set down the teapot so hard, a chip flew off the base and scratched my other hand, clutching the gray counter. "You what? That's... that's..."

"Blackmail, I know. Oh, I didn't mean it. I had to force his hand. I could see you and your friend weren't getting anywhere proving your case—"

"Hyperion went to tell his friend in the police tonight."

"He did?" She examined her manicure. "Anyway, I told Cosmo to bring the money here, so—"

I swayed, the blood draining from my head. "Oh my God."

I needed to call the cops. I strode toward the kitchen door.

The lights went out, plunging the house into darkness.

"Oh, look. It seems like my ploy worked," my mother said.

Dread spiraled in my gut. My mother had escalated. The killers were here.

CHAPTER 27

One arm extended, I groped my way through the kitchen door.

A strong hand grabbed my wrist, squeezing painfully. I flinched and pulled back, but my attacker yanked me forward.

Pulse rabbiting, I shrieked and hurled myself to the floor, hoping my body weight would break the iron grip that held me. My wrist slid a fraction. I spun on my back and kicked out with my heel, connecting with something hard and bony.

"Oof."

Cosmo released me then. I scrabbled to my feet, launched myself toward the French doors.

The lights flashed on.

"Stop," a woman said.

I kept moving, my breath coming in noisy rasps.

"Abigail," my mother said, "I really think you should stop."

I skidded to a halt inches short of the white-painted doors, turned.

My mother stood stiffly outside the kitchen door, a knife at her throat. Pepper, looking sharp in a white designer romper, held the blade.

For a shameful instant, I had the furious urge to keep running. But I didn't move.

Cosmo glared, rubbing his knee. "It's swelling," he said, accusing.

"Do you expect me to apologize?" I snapped.

My kitchen phone rang.

"Get over here." Cosmo tilted his head toward the two women.

Pepper held the kitchen knife at an awkward angle, but I knew she could still do deadly damage. My throat closed. My mother had no idea what she'd done.

"I said, get over here," he repeated.

"Or what?" My voice trembled. "Pepper isn't going to hurt her. She hasn't done any of your dirty work in the past. Do you really think she's going to start now?"

The phone kept ringing.

Wait. What *had* my mother done? Escalated, sure. But she had a strong sense of self-preservation. And I was willing to bet Cosmo's wasn't the only call she had made.

I needed to stall.

The phone rang again. Who was calling my landline? No one called my landline. *Let the caller be the police or Hyperion. Let the caller be someone who'll figure out something's horribly wrong. Let the caller be armed and dangerous.*

Cosmo strode toward Pepper and my mother. He grabbed the knife and my mother and pulled both in front of him.

His face crimsoned. "I won't be pushed around anymore. I won't be blackmailed. You can't push me. You can't. You can't."

"It was Abigail's idea," my mother squeaked.

I gaped. "What?"

"Tom pushed me," Cosmo said. "He didn't care what his parties did to anyone as long as he was making money. The bank pushed me. The investors pushed me. And after I killed him, Henderson's wife pushed me—"

"It's all right," Pepper said, stepping backward and into the shadow of the kitchen door. "Let's just get this over with and go."

"Now." Cosmo met my gaze. "Get over here." His knife hand trembled. "I won't be pushed."

Mouth dry, I edged closer. There was no sense denying I'd tried to blackmail him. In the end, it didn't matter. I was here and he was here and the knife was here.

"Having to deal with two of us must complicate things," I said. "I suppose you were planning on making it look like a murder-suicide, like Vanella? Of course, Vanella's was supposed to look like a delayed murder-suicide. You'd framed her as her husband's killer. But you should know, my mother's too narcissistic to kill herself."

"What do you know about Vanella?" Pepper asked.

The phone trilled.

"It doesn't matter," Cosmo said shrilly. "And will somebody unplug that phone?"

There was a beep. A woman's voice floated through the room. "Uh, is this Abigail? It's Wanda. From jail." She paused. "I'm not sure if you remember me, but I was calling about that Tarot reading. And we can steal a car too if you want. Anyway, I'll call back later." She hung up.

The three of them stared at me.

"It's not what it sounds like," I said.

"It sounds like you're stealing cars," my mother said. "Does your grandfather know?"

"I'm not. It's only, I met this stripper in jail—"

"A stripper?" my mother asked.

I sucked in my cheeks. "She's an environmentalist. And… never mind."

"Stop talking and get over here," Cosmo said.

Legs shaking, I sidled between my gaming couch and dining table. "You won't get away with this."

"That's a little cliched, Abigail," my mother said.

"But it's true," I said. "You two made a lot of mistakes. If I could figure it out, the police can't be far behind. Have you thought about fleeing the country? Mexico is only nine hours away by car."

"I don't know about *lots* of mistakes," my mother said. "But they really shouldn't have talked about the murder at that French restaurant."

I blinked. *Seriously*? My mother had overheard them blabbing about the murders? And she hadn't mentioned it? I shook myself. *Not a priority now.*

"Of course," my mother continued, "I didn't understand it at the time. You were annoyingly oblique. I do wish people would say what they mean. It would make life so much easier."

"The police don't know anything," Pepper said. "Your mother just admitted she overheard us."

"Pepper obviously hadn't had an affair with Tom," I said. "You didn't know he'd been a musician. How could you not know about that part of his past? But Pepper was having an affair with you, Cosmo."

"We've always been close," Pepper said.

Hands quivering at my sides, I paused beside my laptop, on the dining table. "What confused me was Pepper was obviously somehow colluding with Vanella."

"We followed you to the pier," my mother said.

"Someone had turned off the video cameras," I said, "making it easy for them to kill Tom without being seen. And then Vanella was killed. At first, I thought Pepper and Vanella had conspired to kill her husband. Their argument in Vanella's bedroom made no sense. Vanella had seemed genuinely surprised when Pepper had stormed in and accused her of murder. But Pepper and Vanella were thick as thieves later."

"She liked me," Pepper said. "She wanted to be more visible on social media and thought I could help her."

But you killed her instead. "But you couldn't have thrown Tom off a balcony, Pepper. You didn't have the mass or the martial skills. You needed an accomplice."

"And you thought of me?" Cosmo asked.

"Not right away," I said. "I wondered if two women—Pepper and Vanella—could have killed Tom? They probably could have managed it. But then Vanella was killed. I figured Pepper had killed Vanella to tie up a loose end. But there was too much physicality to that murder as well. Someone carried Vanella over their shoulder. She wasn't that big, but it still indicated someone with strength."

"Not inner strength, I'm sorry to say," my mother said.

"The spear throwing pointed straight at Cosmo," I said, knees shaking. "You must have learned to throw a spear when you were a volunteer in an African village. That's where Archer got his story about the Maasai."

"I remember a retreat in Kenya—" my mother began.

Cosmo shook her by the arm. "Shut it. Just shut up. Shut up."

I stared hard at Pepper. "Here's what I think. You both wanted the parties to end, and that meant getting rid of Tom Henderson. Vanella did want out of her marriage, and she had an infidelity clause. So, you talked Vanella into letting you pretend you and Thomas were having an affair. This gave you access to their house. Did you tell Vanella you were coming over the night Tom died?"

She shrugged. "The police won't think that. They'll think if Vanella wanted evidence for her divorce, she'd have turned the security cameras on."

"Vanella thought she *was* turning them on. But she was terrible with technology. You made sure the security cameras were already on when you came over that night. All one of you had to do was check the security camera at the gate while staying out of sight. There's a blinking red light when it's on. I'm guessing one of you made sure it was on and then Pepper called her. Pepper told her to turn the cameras on so she could catch Tom cheating. You convinced her that would get her the proof to get out of the pre-nup. But Vanella unknowingly turned the security system *off.* This gave Cosmo the chance to sneak in undetected where your two yards connect. And then when Tom was killed, you convinced her she was an accomplice to murder. Vanella had to stay quiet about you coming over that night."

"She hated Tom and wasn't very smart," Pepper said. "I hoped she'd stop the parties, but she was making too much money off them. She had no intention of shutting them down."

"Shut up," Cosmo said to her.

"So Vanella had to go," I continued. "And besides, you couldn't trust her to keep her mouth shut about her part in this. But the great thing about the fake affair is it also gave Vanella a motive for murder. Not that it matters. All the police have to do is check your phone records. They'll see a call from you to Vanella before you walked in, telling her to turn on the cameras."

"I never called her," she said. "We arranged everything at our spin class."

Well, damn. I met Cosmo's gaze. "Vanella turned off the cameras for real the night you came over to kill her. She thought she was meeting Pepper, but Pepper was busy giving herself an alibi. You came instead, Cosmo. She mustn't have thought there was any danger though. Because somehow, you got her to drink something with drugs in it. You knocked her out, carried her to the car, and killed her."

I was all stalled out. I couldn't think of anything more to say. I grabbed the laptop and threw it at Cosmo.

His knife arm whipped upward. The computer struck it and clattered harmlessly to the floor.

I stared, horrified. He hadn't even blinked.

"Is that it?" Cosmo lowered the knife. "Are you done?"

I swallowed. "No," I said. "You needed to sell your house so you could use the money to save your business. But the parties were driving down values and making sales more difficult. And you opened the front gate the night Tom died to distract from the fact that you'd snuck in from Pepper's yard," I added.

"Yes," he said. "*Now* are you done?"

"You can't kill my mother," I said, desperate. "Think of all the trace evidence. There'll be spatter patterns." I swayed, thinking about spatter patterns.

"Also," Detective Chase said from the kitchen door. "I'll shoot you in the head before you make a move. Now drop that knife." He cocked his head. "And I heard everything, so there's no sense adding a third murder to this mess. It only means more jail time for you and more paperwork for me."

Hyperion eased inside through the French door, his phone raised. "I got the whole thing on video."

"You're done, Cosmo," the detective said in a casual tone. "Put down the knife."

Cosmo's shoulders sagged forward. He dropped the knife.

CHAPTER 28

"And why the hell didn't you tell the police what you overheard at that restaurant?" I whisper shouted at my mother.

Police bustled around my living room, taking pictures and looking official.

She adjusted her filmy caftan. "I tried to tell you, over and over, but you wouldn't listen, you never listen."

"Never—"

"I told Mrs. Bicklesworth—"

"What?"

"She thought it was fascinating. And so did that Tarot reader, Sierra."

I clapped my hands to my forehead. "Oh my God." She'd told everyone but me?

"And of course I told the police. I called them before I came over here."

"I figured as much." At least, I'd hoped as much. When it came to my mother, I didn't count on anything.

"At last you understand," she said. "I wouldn't put you in danger. I want to be the most conscious parent I can be."

The adrenaline that had kept me going collapsed. My knees buckled. I dropped onto my gaming couch, and the controls on the cushions bounced to the throw rug.

"Why didn't you tell the police *before* someone tried to kill you both," my grandfather thundered. He strode past the uniformed men at my front door.

My mother smiled faintly. "Dad, if you were a little more spiritually evolved, you'd understand how things unfold. Have you read the book—?"

"No," he said. "And I'm not going to. I love you. You'll always be my daughter. But I am not going to continue to support this. It's not helping. I guess I've never helped, and that's on me. But I can't ignore the facts any longer. What I'm doing is more harm than good."

Her eyes widened. "What are you saying?"

"I'm saying you'll have to leave and find your own way."

I flushed, unaccountably guilty. "Gramps—"

"No, Abigail," he said gently. "There comes a time when we have to recognize the role we've played in a person's life. And then we have to decide whether to continue or change course. I'm changing course. This is my decision."

"It's all right, Abigail," my mother said. "I'm leaving for Portugal next week anyway. There's an amazing retreat I've been hearing a lot about. They focus on the chakras. I hear it takes one to an entirely new vibrational level." She wafted out the front door.

Gramps sat beside me and pulled me into a hug. "I'm sorry. I never should have let things get this far. I never should have— This is my fault," he repeated.

I shook my head. "This wasn't your fault. I'm the one who let her stick her nose into a murder investigation." Which I'd been sticking *my* nose into. My insides curdled. Did my mother and I at last have something in common?

We sat in silence for a long moment.

Gramps heaved a sigh. "So Archer tells me he's going to be an internet star reporter or some such."

"I'm sure he will be."

"Yes, Archer always lands on his feet. He's like a cat. But are you really all right?" Gramps asked. "Because you don't look so good. Did they hurt you?"

"No. I'm fine."

"Of course she is." Hyperion dropped onto the couch on my other side. "Abigail can take care of herself."

"But I've never been so glad to see you," I said.

My partner scowled. "Your mother might be in some legal trouble. Tony was muttering about interfering in an investigation and endangerment all the way here."

Gramps sighed. "I'll call Tomas." He shuffled to the open French doors and walked out onto my deck.

"Hey," Hyperion said. "You really don't look so good. Are you in shock or something?"

"Or something." I blinked rapidly. My own mother had nearly killed us. Fury, disappointment, and leftover fear spiraled through me in a toxic stew. But I remembered that feeling of lightness after I'd forgiven my mother, and I wanted it back. I might not be feeling forgiveness now, but I was going to have it again, no matter how much alternate-nostril breathing it took.

Plus, I wasn't going to cry in front of Hyperion and a roomful of cops.

So I changed the subject. "Do you, ah, remember all those mysterious deaths at my mother's retreats?"

"You don't think she's a murderess, do you?"

"No. I mean. No. But what if they were murders and... she just didn't notice?"

He snorted. "That's not hard to imagine."

"But... all those deaths. And we've been involved in, well, more than the normal amount, don't you think? Could murder somehow be attracted to us both?"

He cocked his head. "You think we're murder magnets?"

"Is that a thing?"

His mouth pursed. "Nah."

Whew. I sagged lower, relieved.

"Okay, fine," he said rapidly. "It could be a thing."

"What do you mean it could be a thing? You just said it wasn't."

"I was trying to make you feel better. Then I thought honesty was the best policy."

"Since when?"

He widened his eyes and angled his head at Tony, talking to Gramps.

"But if that's true, I've got some of my mother in me," I hissed.

"Only the murdery parts."

"That's not helping."

Hyperion slung an arm over my shoulders. "Relax and stop worrying about things you've got no control over. What will be will be and all that jazz."

"Bah humbug."

Hyperion shook me lightly. "Tony let me do a ride along."

There were all sorts of witty things I could say about that. But I leaned my head against the back of my blue couch instead.

"And, um, you and Brik?" he asked.

My chest tightened. I had to wait a moment for the lump in my throat to shrink enough for me to speak. "That ship has sailed."

Brik had revealed something big, bringing us both closer and pushing us apart. But if friendship was all that was on offer, I'd take it. I didn't have many friends, but the ones I did have counted.

Brik counted.

"I told Tony I might have seen that autopsy report," Hyperion said. "And the murder board."

"Good for you." I didn't know much about Hyperion's relationships, aside from the fact that he had lots of them. But this new philosophy of honesty made me wonder if this thing with Detective Chase might be a little different.

My partner sighed. "He's not the kind of person you keep things from."

"No, I'd guess not." I grinned. Hyperion dating a detective? Life was going to get interesting. Very interesting indeed.

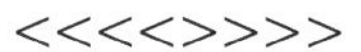

Note from Kirsten:

Archer was a character from *Hostage to Fortune* who really came to life for me. I hadn't originally planned to write him into *Oolong, Farewell*, but he was so much fun, I couldn't resist.

Abigail's mother, however, was a character I knew I'd have to bring into these stories. In the end, Abigail may not have gotten the resolution she wanted from her, but real life is complicated, and people don't always behave the way we'd like. At least Abigail reached a sort of closure.

And yes, Earl Grey tea as a scone seasoning is really delicious. I've included that recipe below.

Want more complicated heroines and relationships? Meet Maddie Kosloski from *The Perfectly Proper Paranormal Museum!*

A Perfectly Proper Murder

When Maddie Kosloski's career flatlines, she retreats to her wine country hometown for solace and cheap rent. Railroaded into managing the local paranormal museum, she's certain the rumors of its haunting are greatly exaggerated. But then a fresh corpse in the museum embroils Maddie in murders past and present, making her wonder if a ghost could really be on the loose.

With her high school bully as one of the detectives in charge of the investigation, Maddie doubts justice will be served. When one of her best friends is arrested, she knows it won't be. Maddie also grapples with ghost hunters, obsessed taxidermists, and the sexy motorcyclist next door as outside forces threaten. And as she juggles spectral shenanigans with the hunt for a killer, she discovers there truly is no place like home.

Praise:

"A delightful new series."—Library Journal (starred review)

"A quirky murder mystery with plenty of small town charm."—ForeWord Reviews

"A clever combination of characters."—Kirkus Reviews

"Humor, hints of romance, and twists and turns galore elevate this cozy."—Publishers Weekly

RECIPES

TURTLE SCONES

Ingredients:
Scones
3 ¾ C flour
¼ C sugar
3 T baking powder
¼ tsp salt
8 T cold unsalted butter
1 ¼ C cold milk
2 C chocolate chips
1 C chopped pecans

Turtle Topping
24 caramels, unwrapped
4 tablespoons milk
pinch of salt
½ teaspoon vanilla extract
½ cup pecans, for sprinkling on top of scones

Directions:
Heat oven to 375 degrees F.

Mix flour, sugar, baking powder, and salt in a medium-sized bowl. Cut butter into cubes and mix into the flour mixture with your fingers, crushing the butter, until the mix is coarse and sandy.

Add milk. Stir until almost combined. Add chocolate and chopped pecans and mix. You may need to add extra milk, a tablespoon at a time, until the mix is incorporated.

Knead dough in the bowl. Roll out to 1" thick. Cut circles 2 ½ inches in diameter, or cut into triangular wedges 2 ½ inches at the base. Bake on ungreased cookie sheet until light golden brown. Circles take approximately 15 minutes. Triangles will usually take 20-25 minutes.

To make the turtle topping, add caramels, milk, and salt to a small, heavy-bottomed saucepan. Cook over low heat, stirring occasionally, until caramels have melted (9-10 minutes). Bring the topping mixture to a gentle simmer and add the vanilla extract. Simmer for an additional minute, then spread over scones right away. Sprinkle the remaining chopped pecans on top.

Earl Grey Blackberry Scones with Lemon Glaze

Who knew Earl Grey tea made a delicious spice? These scones got raves from my foodie beta testers.

Ingredients:

3 ¾ C bread flour or all-purpose flour. (Bread flour will give you a lighter, more biscuit-like scone. All-purpose flour will give you a denser scone).

¼ C sugar

3 T baking powder

1.5 T Earl Grey tea, ground to a fine powder

¼ tsp salt

8 T cold unsalted butter

1 C frozen blackberries (frozen berries keep their shape better, so if you buy them fresh, freeze them before baking)

1 ¼ C cold milk

For the Lemon Glaze

2 cups powdered sugar

3 T lemon juice

2 tsp vanilla

Zest of 1 lemon

Directions:

Heat oven to 375 degrees F.

Mix bread flour, sugar, baking powder, ground tea, and salt in a medium-sized bowl. Cut butter into cubes and mix into the flour mixture with your fingers, crushing the butter, until the mix is coarse and sandy.

Add milk. Stir until almost combined. Add frozen blackberries and mix in. You may need to add extra milk, a tablespoon at a time, until the dried bits are incorporated.

Knead dough in the bowl. Roll out to 1" thick. Cut into squares or circles 2 ½ inches in diameter, or cut into triangular wedges 2 ½ inches at the base. Bake on ungreased cookie sheet until light golden brown. Circles and squares take approximately 15-20 minutes. Triangles will usually take 20-25 minutes.

Combine powdered sugar, lemon juice, lemon zest and vanilla in a medium bowl. Whisk until smooth and no lumps remain. Spoon desired amount of glaze over the scones. Let sit for 5 minutes and then enjoy!

The Lovers Raspberry Coconut Scones

Note: Raspberries are a traditional ingredient in many love spells. This is not *a love spell, but it was so delightfully pink, I immediately thought of Valentine's Day and The Lovers card.*

Ingredients:

3 ¾ C bread flour

¼ C sugar

3 T baking powder

¼ tsp salt

8 T cold unsalted butter

1 ¼ C cold milk

2 C shredded coconut

1 C frozen raspberries (frozen berries keep their shape better, so if you buy them fresh, freeze them before baking)

Glaze:

2 C confectioners' sugar

3 to 4 T fresh lemon juice

Directions:

Heat oven to 375 degrees F.

Mix bread flour, sugar, baking powder, and salt in a medium-sized bowl. Cut butter into cubes and mix into the flour mixture with your fingers, crushing the butter, until the mix is coarse and sandy.

Add milk. Stir until almost combined. Add shredded coconut and mix. Add frozen raspberries. You may need to add extra milk, a tablespoon at a time, until the mix is incorporated.

Knead dough in the bowl. Roll out to 1" thick. Cut circles 2 ½ inches in diameter, or cut into triangular wedges 2 ½ inches at the base. Bake on ungreased cookie sheet until light golden brown. Circles take approximately 15 minutes. Triangles will usually take 20-25 minutes.

Mix powdered sugar and lemon juice in a small bowl until the glaze is thick but pourable. Spread over scones.

BOOKS BY KIRSTEN WEISS

Wits' End Mystery Novels
At Wits' End | Planet of the Grapes | Close Encounters of the Curd Kind

Tea and Tarot Cozy Mysteries
Steeped in Murder | Fortune Favors the Grave | Hostage to Fortune

The Witches of Doyle Series
Bound | Ground | Down | Witch | Fey | Fate | Spirit on Fire | Shaman's Bane | Lone Wolf | Witch | Tales of the Rose Rabbit

Perfectly Proper Paranormal Museum Series
The Perfectly Proper Paranormal Museum | Pressed to Death | Deja Moo | Chocolate a'la Murder

The Riga Hayworth Paranormal Mystery Novels
The Metaphysical Detective | The Alchemical Detective | The Shamanic Detective | The Infernal Detective | The Elemental Detective | The Hoodoo Detective | The Hermetic Detective | The Gargoyle Chronicles

The Mannequin Offensive

The Pie Town Cozy Mystery Series
The Quiche and the Dead | Bleeding Tarts | Pie Hard

Sensibility Grey Steampunk Suspense
Steam and Sensibility | Of Mice and Mechanicals | A Midsummer Night's Mechanical

ABOUT THE AUTHOR

Kirsten Weiss has never met a dessert she didn't like, and her guilty pleasures are watching *Ghost Whisperer* re-runs and drinking red wine. The latter gives her heartburn, but she drinks it anyway.

Now based in Colorado Springs, CO, she writes genre-blending cozy mystery, supernatural and steampunk suspense, mixing her experiences and imagination to create vivid worlds of fun and enchantment.

If you like funny cozy mysteries, check out her *Pie Town, Tea and Tarot, Paranormal Museum* and *Wits' End* books. If you're looking for some magic with your mystery, give the *Witches of Doyle, Riga Hayworth* and *Rocky Bridges* books a try. And if you like steampunk, the *Sensibility Grey* series might be for you.

Kirsten sends out original short stories of mystery and magic to her mailing list. If you'd like to get them delivered straight to your inbox, make sure to sign up for her newsletter at kirstenweiss.com

Made in the USA
Las Vegas, NV
12 January 2022